Buddy

Encounters with the Holy Spirit

Arthur Perkins

SIGNALMAN PUBLISHING

Buddy
Encounters with the Holy Spirit
by Arthur Perkins

Signalman Publishing
www.signalmanpublishing.com
email: info@signalmanpublishing.com
Kissimmee, Florida

Scriptures are taken from the King James Version of the Bible

ISBN: 978-1-935991-65-6 (paperback)
978-1-935991-51-9 (ebook)

Cover design by Joel Ramnaraine

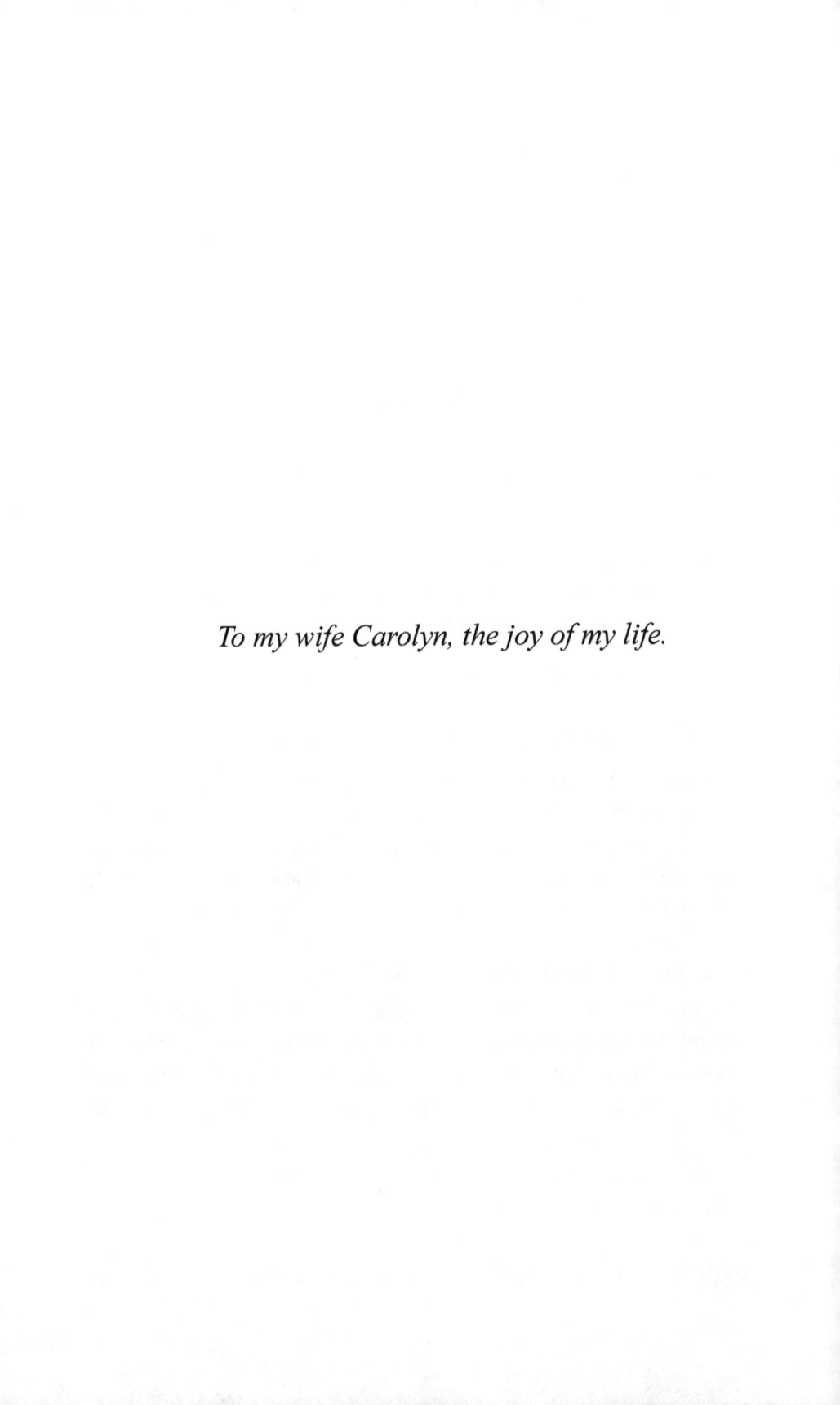

To my wife Carolyn, the joy of my life.

INTRODUCTION

In Deuteronomy Chapter 6 is found one of the most beautifully hope-filled passages in the entire Bible. Moses, being guided by the Holy Spirit, addresses the nation of Israel, saying,

Hear, O Israel: The Lord our God is one Lord: And thou shalt love the Lord thy God with all thine heart, and with all thy soul, and with all thy might.

The practical implications of this one sentence are immense. Jesus in Matthew 22 called it the great commandment, to be observed above all else, and by repeating it during His incarnation He extended its application beyond Israel to the Church as well. It tells us that we *can* love our God with all our hearts, which means that we were created to do just that. It also implies that God can love us back, for love is not unidirectional.

The theological implications of that commandment are no less profound. It means that Jesus' work on the cross was a demonstration of his love. Yet further, it says that our God is one, forming the basis of our monotheism, despite later passages that amply demonstrate His Trinitarian nature.

Therein lies a question of exceeding import to every person who wishes, in obedience to Jesus' words in Matthew 22, to love God: how can God be one while being several?

In the book of Ruth is found another beautiful passage that has tugged at the strings of countless hearts over the centuries since it was written. It has evoked tears and inspired poems and love stories and been held up as a golden example of devotion and loyalty.

> *And [Naomi] said, "Behold, thy sister in law is gone back unto her people, and unto her gods: return thou after thy sister in law."*

> *And Ruth said, "Entreat me not to leave thee, or to return from following after thee: for whither thou goest, I will go; and where thou lodgest, I will lodge: thy people shall be my people, and thy God my God: Where thou diest, will I die, and there will I be buried: the Lord do so to me, and more also, if ought but death part thee and me."*

These words of Ruth were originally directed to her mother-in-law Naomi, but, as in all Scripture, they were written under the direction of the Holy Spirit, who had in mind a much greater application, one in which both Ruth and Naomi were but types. There is much to say for considering Ruth to represent the Church and Naomi to be a type of Israel. But at a deeper level, Naomi gives us a different representation. Embedded in this song of Ruth, with this deeper representation, is an answer to the question of our monotheism toward a Trinitarian God. The answer itself is quite beautiful as well as being a wonderful promise to mankind.

Ruth, I would say, is a type of the Church; and Naomi of the Holy Spirit. Therein is the answer: the link between God as One and God as a Multiplicity is love within a perfect Family setting, as Paul declared in his letter to the Ephesians:

> *For this cause shall a man leave his father and his mother, and shall be joined unto his wife, and they two shall be one flesh. This is a great mystery, but I speak concerning Christ and his church.*

The connection between Naomi and the Holy Spirit suggests a love of God that is so beautifully magnificent as to dwarf His other attributes. It is a story that begs to be told, and I attempt to tell a part of it here. The medium that I use for this treasured task is a novel that chronicles the extraordinary love that God shows toward four severely handicapped individuals, two having an affliction of the body and the other two of the heart. Many of the events described in the novel are based on fact.

CHAPTER 1

He struggled to avoid the deepest ruts in the steep, winding logging road. The task was difficult, as his eyes kept watering with unbidden tears.

It really happened, he mumbled to himself, the thought infusing his body with another adrenalin overdose, one of a countless number. He'd known for years of Alicia's physical frailty, but he'd kept it subliminal until her fits of coughing had brought up blood, thrusting the issue out into the open. His first reaction to her final words had been a terrible empty loneliness, followed by an unquenchable physical need to be away from where he was the moment before. He had fled the hospital when the doctor, fingers on her pale wrist, had quietly shaken his head. He didn't remember arriving back at his house. *Their* house. In his bleak desolation of spirit the need to be away returned, sharper now. The heat of his emotion resolved into his nearly instinctive action of transferring his kite from the rafters of his garage to the top of his decrepit car and heading out to the nearest launch, a wooded mountain in the rural northwest.

It was late afternoon when he reached the peak. He left the car and walked to the launch that overlooked the steep slope down to the valley a few thousand feet below. The mountainside had been logged over once, many years ago. The forest had eventually returned, time having removed most of the traces of man's invasion. He stared down at the tree-carpeted gully, feeling the stiff breeze on his face. It would be a good flight; excellent, in fact, with plenty of ridge lift to keep him aloft as long as he wanted.

As long as I want. All the time in the world.

He wept briefly, then turned back to the car to get his glider and set it up. When the wire rigging was taut and the battens in, he climbed into his harness and hooked in, not waiting until he got to the edge. He hefted the downtubes and braced them against his shoulders, walking against increasing resistance as he left the meager shelter from the wind his setup site offered. Muscling the craft to the launch, he ran off without hesitating, pushing his harness prone as he became airborne.

He worked the front of the ridge line until he was a hundred feet or so over the top in smooth, stable air and reached into a pocket of his coat to turn on his iPod. The soft whisper of air was replaced by Emmylou Harris, her melodious lament blending in with the dark gray sky and the crystal purity of the almost uninhabited region.

The pristine beauty of the vast unobstructed view below took him outside of himself, as it always did. He became one with his rudimentary craft, dipping one wingtip and then the other in the pure existential joy of flight at the most basic, essential level by which man can experience it.

Something caught the edge of his eye. He turned his head to see a red-tailed hawk flying in echelon formation off his left wingtip. He marveled at the incongruity of life, so perfectly expressed by Charles Dickens in *A Tale of Two Cities*: "It was the best of times, it was the worst of times. . ."

Eventually the bird peeled off, signaling the decline of lift: the wind was easing up and he found himself below the launch. He reluctantly targeted a grassy field below and as he approached it he crossed the field diagonally to assess the ground-level wind. The picture having formed within his mind, he turned the craft into the headwind, went upright and made a good running landing.

After tearing down the kite, he looked up at the mountain and began the long trek to the car at its peak. He knew that it would be well after dark by the time he reached the top. But he had all the time in the world.

Later that night Earl parked his car in the driveway, took off the restraining bungee cords, and removed the glider from the roof. He re-hung the glider from a rafter and looked at it wistfully, knowing that today's flight may be the last that he'd be taking. He parked his car underneath the glider, sighed, and trudged over to the front door. He let himself in and went straight to his bedroom. It had been hours since he'd last eaten, but he wasn't the slightest bit hungry. He undressed and crawled into bed, but there he was confronted with the full force of his loss. Its bleak, uncompromising finality pressed in upon him and he cried out in pain. In near panic, he tossed off the covers and stood up. He paced the room for a while, then knelt down by the side of the bed.

"Dear God," he moaned, "why did this happen? Why did You let it? Answer me. Please," he begged.

Receiving no answer, he remained kneeling on the floor, weeping into the sheet. Hours later, he returned to the bed and dozed fitfully.

The next morning was a Sunday. He remained home, despite the special service at the nearby Lutheran Church in acknowledgment of his wife's death. He spent most of the day pacing the living room floor and sitting down on a kitchen stool, head in hand, weeping.

The funeral was held Wednesday. A drizzling rain fell out of the gray sky onto wet grass and leafless branches. Standing by the grave, he noticed neither the rain nor the guests, except for one friend, John, for whom the circumstances of their first meeting had been a bonding event. They shook hands with feeling and parted without exchanging words. Nothing could be said that would have any meaning, and they both knew it. He felt outside his tortured mind, aware of memories involving Alicia lurking behind his eyes and fighting to push them back. After the service he went home alone and stared out of a window onto the small back yard, attempting to come to terms with the finality of her absence.

He started to open a can of raviolis but the sight made him retch. He passed on dinner and trudged up the staircase to the bedroom for what he knew would be another sleepless night.

He felt a strange peace when he awoke in the morning. It lasted until Alicia flooded back inside and he grieved anew. But there was something else. Something he needed to do. After shaving he wandered into his den. His heart gave a flip of anticipation when he picked his Bible off a shelf. He brought it in with him to the kitchen and, after pouring himself a bowl of cereal, sat down with it in one hand, the page open to Genesis Chapter 1.

Earl Cook had owned the Bible for several years. As middle age had approached he had begun to go to church occasionally, especially when Alicia had insisted, but to him the Bible had been an icon of reverence, an object of worship of itself but its contents kept intact from digestion. Now he had an unexplainable eagerness to absorb the drama that lay between its covers, and he'd gotten past the Flood by the time he realized that he was going to be late for work.

It was the first day he'd come back to his job since Alicia had gone into the hospital. He walked head-down past Patty's reception desk, mumbling a quiet hello. He knew what he looked like and he knew as well that Patty would attempt to shower him with insincere so-sorries. He reached his cubicle and fell into his chair, grateful for the privacy.

"'Morning, Earl." Patty peeked above the cubicle, looking down at his desk. Barely out of her teens, Patty Blake had spent enough time before the mirror to know that she was a head-turner. She was also happily married, a fact that she never hesitated to disseminate to the community of her co-workers, especially the legion of her less happy associates. Her face was the last one in the world that he wanted to see. He looked up at her, awaiting the onslaught of her condescension.

"I'm so sorry, Earl. I think I know what you're feeling. Well, I guess I don't, I'm just thankful that my own life is so stable. I know that if something like that were to happen to Randy, well, gee, I'd go crazy. You need to watch your eyes. They look all red. Maybe you shouldn't have come in today. Is there anything I can bring you? Coffee?"

"Yeh. That'd be swell." Earl jumped at the chance to get her away. He quickly opened a file on the computer and got to work. Maybe if she saw that he was busy, she wouldn't stay to talk.

Earl was a software engineer with a hardware background. At the current state of the projects he was engaged in, he didn't need a lot of interaction with his peers. Outside of Patty, as a matter of fact, only his boss showed up to give him his condolences. Being well out of the boundaries of the supervisor-subordinate relationship that Walter had cultivated, the episode was embarrassing to them both and was quickly terminated. Patty must have forgotten about the coffee, for he didn't see her for the rest of the day.

His mind wandered throughout the workday, as he knew it would. All those neurons and synapses that were formed in his mind and heart in the sharing of his life with his other still remained connected. Their dissolution would only take place through the passage of much time.

Back home he retrieved the can of raviolis that he'd opened the evening before and ate them cold. Then he returned to his reading of the Bible, his anticipation picking up. *Go through the pain*, he told himself. The thought was strangely comforting.

He awoke again the next morning with that same ineffable feeling of peace, as if something wonderful had happened during the night, something that he couldn't recall. Alicia returned too, but it took just a tiny bit longer for her to make her entrance back into his heart. When she did, his melancholy was interrupted by the ringing of his telephone. "Hi, Earl, it's John," his friend said. "I'm not leaving you alone, man. I just thought you needed some time by yourself, is all. How are you getting along?"

"Thanks for your concern. It means a lot to me. I'm doing about as well as could be expected, I guess. Not so good, really. But I'll get by, I suppose."

"Hey, I'm here for you. Need anything?"

"Yeh. My wife back. Sorry, that wasn't fair. No, I just need time."

When the brief conversation ended, Earl thought about his friend and the circumstance of their first meeting two years ago. They had been neighbors for several years before that, but in the semi-rural suburb of a large and rapidly-growing city the enormous trees had helped to discourage neighbors from communicating with each other. Basic indifference had done the rest.

The couple who lived across the street from Earl and Alicia were both tenured professors at the university. That accomplishment separated them as well, for Earl, possessing but a Bachelor of Science degree, had not attained to that level of professional achievement. The husband had other achievements under his belt, one of which was his wartime service in Britain as a pilot of a Lancaster bomber. At any rate, more than a few years passed before Earl had realized that they had a son.

Busily pursuing his own interests, Earl basically ignored the boy's existence, although the boy knew of his and apparently respected his career, intermediate-level though it was. To him, Earl was known as Mr. Cook the engineer. More years passed before Earl was given to understand how high were the academic standards that his parents had set before him, and how desperately monstrous he perceived his own failures to be. His terrible depression had little to do with their characters, for they were warm and loving people. It was simply their example of achievement that did him in. He longed to satisfy his deep desire for the adventure he saw in his father's wartime experiences, but found no outlet in the stifling environment of the big-city school system. By the time he had reached his mid-teens, maintaining a surly distance from his frustrated and disappointed parents and unnoticed by indifferent neighbors, he quietly attempted to take his own life. He bungled that, too.

He eventually reached that point where he knew he could sink no lower, so he made up his mind to pursue that which he knew he would love. He had saved some money, and he spent it on a used hang glider and lessons on how to operate it. In secret, of course.

On the day that Earl really met this young man John was experiencing the most humiliating and discouraging time he'd ever experienced, worse even than the day he tried to take his life. His parents had discovered his secret pursuit and made him agonizingly aware of their disappointment in what they perceived was a frivolous waste of time. They had decided to ground him and threatened to divest him of the glider.

Upon Earl's first meeting with this unfortunate creature they were moving toward each other, John with his head facing the ground, shuffling disconsolately with his hands in his pockets and Earl behind the wheel of his slowly-moving car.

Hearing the approach of the car, John raised his head. In doing so, he underwent an amazing transformation. His eyes widened, attempting to assimilate what he saw. When recognition finally overcame disbelief his face broke out into the widest grin Earl had ever seen. An inner sun shone outward, completely dispelling his gloom.

What John saw, the thing that caused this abrupt change, was attached to the roof of Earl's vehicle with bungee cords. A few months back Earl had been reminiscing about a flying career that had never materialized. After acquiring several ratings as a pilot, he had been denied the ability to exploit his experience commercially by the onset of deafness. After having read an ad that offered inexpensive hang gliding lessons, Earl's brother Bob had decided to gift him with the offer as an outlet for the desire to fly that had remained with him. The surreal training experience involved much stumbling, headlong falling and raising of dust, furnishing an almost nonstop stimulus to Earl's sense of humor, and he was soon hooked. Upon his graduation flight off the big hill, he purchased his first hang glider which was atop the roof of his car on the day he met John.

Earl was thirty-seven at the time, John still in his teens. Despite the large difference in their ages they became fast and close friends. The friendship was symbiotic. John was quite gutsy, getting his older friend into flight situations that he never would have attempted on his own. He persisted without relent until Earl finally agreed to go night flying with him, each of them jumping off the big hill into the black sky at thirty-second intervals, their only source of visual reference being the occasional car that traveled along the edge of the landing field. Landing was accomplished by guess and feel, guessing when to go from prone to upright and feeling the approach of the ground with dragging foot. On the way down they'd communicate blind to keep out of each others' way. John livened the air with triumphant catcalls. If he'd known what a bat sounded like, his happiness would have been complete.

Infrequently the euphoria of flight was dampened at times for each of them. Accidents happened, sometimes approaching serious trouble. "Unplanned events" one might say if he was in a euphemistic frame of mind. "Overtaken by events" might be a better term, or even "overturned by events", to be more accurate. Actually, "squashed" would be the most appropriate word. To the ill-fated creatures involved in such things, they were humiliating or painful, or both. To the onlookers they were hilarious, providing that the pilot escaped death or serious injury. They were like a playback of the dawn of aviation, complete with all its mishaps and setbacks, most of which were of the kind experienced by the contestants on TV's Wipeout show. Most involved the unplanned aerial maneuver called the Auger.

An auger is an implement that takes a variety of forms and sizes depending on its intended use. A wood auger acts as a drill but is spiral-shaped with a hollow center to create the hole with a minimum of effort. A ground auger is larger, being used to bore holes in the soil. They have a common feature: the spiral shape of the bit. With regard to flying, mishaps in the air tend to assume this spiral-shaped 'twirl' as gravity flings the unfortunate craft groundward. But this isn't the main reason why the term 'auger' is used with respect to aircraft misfortunes. The word 'auger' is, instead, descriptive of the forceful manner in which gravity hurls the twisting man-machine system into the ground, thus boring an impressive hole. A more recent version involves the term 'crater', evoking the image of an asteroid impacting the earth at a speed many times that of a bullet.

When an event that elicits colorful descriptors turns out to be not so serious, the typical response is to laugh about the process. It's just a fact of life: it's comedic to see normally dignified humans exposed to runaway, out-of-control situations. As he reminisced, Earl thought upon the movie *The Blue Max*, with its leader that showed all those ill-conceived flying contraptions that beat themselves to death against the tarmac. When it first came out there wasn't a dry eye in the audience for the laughter. While it's a lot more up-front and personal, the laughter over a hang flight mishap usually awaits a fortunate outcome and then is good-natured, carrying absolutely no intimation of mockery or indifference to the unfortunate creature's suffering. To the contrary, those who laugh are usually recalling their own related misfortunes, so they are actually laughing at themselves as well.

John became the perfect example of the intrepid adventurer, a daring pilot who, through his own cutting-edge techniques and their attendant mishaps, advanced the art of flight. Before his parents had discovered this love of his, he had learned to perform strange and wonderful maneuvers that most pilots wouldn't dream of attempting. He still did these things after Earl had met him, walking around with a limp and with scrape marks all over his elbows and forearms. His flying friends suspected that his legs looked the same way.

He had a gimped-up lip too. He wasn't born that way, but acquired it a few months after he met Earl. It happened on the flight that killed him. He was night flying alone, that being another of his pioneering adventures, at least in the local area. The night was so dark that he didn't see the high-voltage lines into which he flew. It was the electricity that did him in, entering through his lip and exiting out his foot, the side of which blew out from the force. As he lay there dead as a doornail his kite, which was all tangled up in the wires, began to burn. Eventually the aluminum tubes melted to the point where they could no longer support him, and he fell forty feet to the ground. It was the impact with the ground that got him going again, kick-starting his heart and giving him a massive chest resuscitation.

After his revival he resumed his flying activities, his parents throwing up their hands in despair. Despite his numerous accidents he was respected within the small community of hang glider pilots, and greatly so. The big point of his revival after being fried, though, is that God simply wasn't through with him on earth. He had only one love that was greater than his love of flight, and that was his love for Jesus, which he had also acquired after meeting Earl. He was the most enthusiastic Christian that one might have the privilege of encountering. His open joy as a Christian was strongly connected to his exploits in flight.

Now Earl cherished their friendship. It was the only meaningful relationship that he had left.

Chapter 2

Time dawdled along, one eternity followed by the next. But days eventually passed, and then weeks. Knowing that time does heal, Earl prayed to be just three years into the future. *I'll be able to bear it then, Lord. I know I will.* But he wondered it he could ever be happy again. In the meantime the memory of Alicia gripped him with tight cords of pain.

There came a day, of course, when the pain began to ease. It happened about two months after Alicia's passing. He could feel periods of respite, for which he was very grateful. When the thought of Alicia did return, he could start to picture her outside of himself. In the meantime, he had pursued his reading of the Bible and was now into the Genesis story of Isaac, whom his father Abraham had come within a hairbreadth of sacrificing. The story bothered him: why did God so cruelly ask Abraham to sacrifice his beloved son? He closed the Bible, unsure of what to believe.

The following evening was one that he would remember forever, because when Alicia's face appeared before him the pain came crashing back with an overwhelming intensity, leaving him as bereft as he had been on the day she had died. He wasn't prepared for this sudden return of agony; it tore at him with the fierceness of a wild animal. He staggered into the bedroom and lay down sobbing uncontrollably, certain now that desolation would lay heavily upon him for the remainder of his life. Hours later he fell into a fitful sleep.

Something startled him and made him sit bolt upright. His room was suddenly bathed in light, its source indistinct. A face appeared in sharp clarity, commanding his complete attention. She was the most beautiful woman that he had ever seen. Her dark eyes gazed steadily into his with an earnest expression, her eyelids crinkling with warmth. She radiated intimacy and pure love. He sensed that she knew him well.

"Hello, Earl," she whispered. "I want to have a chat with you."

Astonished, he tried to speak, but words wouldn't come. "You don't need to talk," she said. "I know your every thought. I know your pain. I feel it too, right along with you. Alicia wants you to understand how much she loves you. She misses you but she knows that you'll be together again when the time is right. She's not sad, though. She's very happy where she is."

"B-but," he stammered in his head. "Who are you?"

"I'll let you know presently. For now let's just say that God sent me. Right now you need to know that He is in control of everything that happens to you. You're thinking how unfair it is that Alicia's gone, that God could have prevented it. Know for certain, my beloved Earl, that indeed He could have kept her alive. But that wouldn't have been the best for either of you. God has plans for you, wonderful ones, and for that Alicia needs to be where she is and you need to be right here."

"Does God enjoy seeing me suffer?" he thought, a tear dribbling down his cheek.

"No, of course not," she responded, a gentle finger brushing the tear away. "But suffering isn't always bad. Sometimes it's necessary to make you all that you can be – all that God wants you to be. You will continue to suffer, but through it you are going to grow into someone capable of responding to God's plan for you. It's an exciting plan, too."

"Will I always suffer? Will I always miss Alicia so terribly much?"

"No. I can promise you that. The pain will go away eventually. Time heals wounds, even this, and it will gradually fade. Some day you're even going to meet another woman, one that God is even now preparing especially for you."

"I'll never fall in love again!" Earl responded vehemently.

"Okay, Earl. Let's drop the subject for now. I'll be going soon. Like before, you won't remember me when you awaken. But there is something that you will remember . . . "

"Before?" he interrupted. "You've been here before?"

"Yes. I've been here every night as you slept. I've put my love into your heart. And where do you think you got your desire to read the Word? You got a little ticked at what you read last, as you recall. I'm going to help you find your answer to that, and you'll remember enough to get it done. First off, I'll quote you from the Gospel of Matthew, Chapter 27, verse 46:

And about the ninth hour Jesus cried with a loud voice,
saying, Eli, Eli, lama sabachthani? That is to say, My God,
my God, why hast thou forsaken me?

"Did God actually forsake Jesus?"

"He had to. Jesus became sin for your sakes. Father couldn't bear to look upon sin. He had to turn away from it. But when Jesus died on the cross, He threw all that filth into hell. When He was resurrected, he was clean and praiseworthy forever, and He sat on the right hand of Father in heaven. It was quite a reunion."

"Did Jesus know that this was going to happen? Did God know?"

"Oh, my," she laughed. "Of course. From the very foundation of the world. If you think about it, how else could God demonstrate the passion of his love toward mankind than by becoming one of you and dying on your behalf?"

"But then why didn't God let us know what was going to happen beforehand?"

"Do you actually think that He didn't? The times back then were much the same as they are now. Nobody bothers to read Scripture enough to understand it. Have you read about the Passover in

Exodus 12, or Psalm 22 of David?"

"Well, no, but . . ."

"See what I mean? There are a lot of people out there just like you. Some even go to church every Sunday. They get tips on how to get more out of life, to be healthy, wealthy and wise, but they're starving for the Word. Moses instituted the Passover ceremony the night before the Exodus from Egypt of the nation of Israel. It was a ceremony to be observed forever, and to this day it is indeed observed by a great many practicing Jews. But it's all about Jesus. Every family was to take a yearling lamb, one without spot or blemish, and keep it for four days, just long enough to get attached to it. Then they were to kill it and sprinkle its blood on the lintel and doorposts. For every house that did this, God passed over without harm on His way to kill the firstborn of every family. That's why John the Baptist called Jesus the Lamb of God. Jesus, by the way, was crucified on the day of the Passover. Psalm 22 begins with the words *'My God, My God, why have you forsaken me?'* and goes on to describe the agony of crucifixion, a form of punishment that wasn't known until several centuries after that Psalm was written. Then there's the matter of all the people in the Old Testament who were representing the Jesus to come in the flesh. The drama with Abraham over the sacrifice of Isaac was one of those many events. Abraham, of course, preenacted the pain the Father felt in giving up Jesus to the cross. Isaac, of course, represented Jesus who was obedient to His call. It was a great honor for Abraham and Isaac to make these representations, and they'll be everlastingly grateful for that opportunity. As I told you, I'll give you enough memory of this conversation to get you started on Exodus 12, Matthew 27 and Psalm 22. Do it. Goodbye for now, my beloved."

Earl drifted back into a dreamless sleep. When he awoke the next morning he had no awareness of the visitation the night before. But he was drawn back to the Bible. Before he went to work, he'd read three specific passages, and he no longer fretted over Abraham's attempted sacrifice of Isaac. As a matter of fact, in grasping the event's intended symbolism, he left for work with a new appreciation of the depth of Scripture and the love of God.

He was late to work that morning, because he made a detour to his church and looked up the pastor to tell him that he wanted the free gift of salvation offered by Jesus through His vicarious suffering, death and resurrection. He'd heard the offer enough times, he admitted, but today he wanted to receive it for his own. George the pastor responded with joy, and gave him a hearty welcome into the community of believing Christians. Before Earl left, George gave him a brochure outlining the Church's basic beliefs and extended to him an invitation to attend on a regular basis.

After work the next day Earl cooked for the first time without the microwave. He scrambled a few eggs, stuck bread into the toaster, and cut some lettuce into a salad. It wasn't much, but it was a start. When he sat down to eat he brought the Bible with him to the table. He continued reading where he'd left off, going into Chapter 23 of Genesis. In it was an account of the death of Sarah. The subject was too close to his loss of Alicia and he quickly put it down. But then he reconsidered. *Go through the pain,* he reminded himself. He read it with difficulty, tears streaming down his cheeks. But he persevered and read it through.

He went to bed early that night and cried himself to sleep. He was awakened again by the beautiful face bathed in light. Gentle fingers brushed away his tears as before. "Hello," she whispered. "That was a good move you made yesterday. Welcome aboard, my beloved."

"I sure picked a chapter this time. The death of Sarah."

"I know. But you got something else out of it."

"What? I wasn't concentrating."

"Sarah was buried in a place called Hebron. Hebron is very, very important to God, and it's full of meaning for today. I'll give you the details later. For now, when you read your Bible, I want you to think of the Book of Genesis as a Gospel of Jesus Christ."

"Gospel? There's not a word in it about Jesus. As a matter of fact, in church I've been given the impression that our focus should be on Jesus. Maybe I should have started in the New Testament rather than the Old."

"The choice wasn't yours to make. I directed you to the book of Genesis. And yes, it is a gospel of Jesus Christ, in many ways the most significant one. You'll appreciate that as you get deeper into it. I'll tell you now, though, that it speaks of Jesus on several levels. And as you get into it, your focus will be on Jesus indeed. But to have the kind of intimate relationship with Him that He wants, you'll have to know Him from the standpoint of the Old Testament. It's where you truly meet Him. I've given you enough to think about, so I'll leave. In the meantime, keep reading Genesis. When you get to Chapter 37, slow down and pay close attention. It's about a man named Joseph, and, except for the side account of Chapter 38, the story of Joseph runs all the way through Chapter 45. I'll come back again to explain it to you when you're finished with it."

At work the next day Earl's attention span had noticeably improved, to the great relief of his boss. Up to then he had begun to try and figure out how he could let the man go without bringing down the wrath of the rest of the workforce. Now he saw a ray of hope, and decided to shelve his machinations in that direction, at least for the time being.

By the time Earl had finished dinner that evening, he had read the account of Isaac's marriage to Rebekah in Genesis Chapter 24. He wondered if the story was significant.

He received no answer that night; he awoke once in the early hours of the morning, but when he opened his eyes his room remained cold, empty and dark.

CHAPTER 3

After a particularly troubling day at work, Earl dejectedly popped a frozen dinner into the microwave and sat down to eat. In reviewing the events of the day as he picked at the meal, he wondered whether his emotional frailty had convinced his boss that he wasn't pulling his own weight. He chastised himself, vowing to suck it in and focus more on work. It was no longer just a matter of survival. He appreciated that it was a responsibility of Christians to give a good representation of their faith to the world at large, and he'd made it plain to his associates that he was a Christian. As a matter of fact, Patty had been avoiding him since he'd told her.

His spirits picked up as he got out his Bible and began to read where he'd last left off. He was now on Chapter 37, the beginning of the account of Joseph. He quickly read Chapter 38, which was a digression from the story, and slowed down again at Chapter 39. The story captured his entire attention, and he didn't put it down until he'd read through to its end at Chapter 45. As moving as the tale was, he was unsure of its relevance to God. Yet he had a deep-seated feeling that it did. He fell asleep with that question on his mind.

He awoke again to the beautiful face before him. "Hi," she said. "Good story, wasn't it? Yes, Earl, it is indeed relevant to God, and particularly to Jesus. There are many such stories in the Old Testament like that, that point directly to Jesus. You might say, in fact, that these tales actually define the Jesus who will later come in the flesh. God's like that. He didn't need to do it that way, but he involved mankind in showing itself just how Jesus would appear when He came down to earth to live among you."

"Can you show me how Joseph fits into the picture?"

"I'll be most happy to. First, you had the same question about Isaac's marriage to Rebekah. That's very relevant to God. Remember that Abraham's attempt to sacrifice Isaac spoke of God's sacrifice of Jesus on the cross. In that way Isaac represented Jesus on the cross. In the marriage of Isaac and Rebekah, Isaac again represents Jesus, but under much happier circumstances. We'll talk about that later." She smiled enigmatically.

"Now, as to Joseph," She continued. "Of all the sons of Jacob, remember, Joseph was the most loved by him. That status of his didn't particularly sit well with the others, and his own actions only made things worse. He was given to telling his father of his brothers' evil deeds, and then when he told them of his dreams in which he was their leader, even over his own father and mother, they'd had it up to their eyeballs with him. They were in a remote field when he came upon them again to check up on them, and, unable to take his attitude any more, they rid themselves of him by selling him to a band of Ishmailites who were traveling with goods into Egypt. By doing so, they handed him a sentence of lifelong slavery. They covered his coat with the blood of a goat and told their father Jacob that Joseph had been killed by a beast.

"This was the beginning of a remarkable adventure of Joseph, one that spanned years of slavery and jail, times of distress in which the possibility of freedom, except for a miracle from God, was nonexistent. But that is just what happened. As he raised up the prophet Daniel many centuries later through the circumstance of dreams, he did the same with Joseph by giving Pharaoh of Egypt a dream of seven fat and seven lean animals. The dream troubled him greatly, but when he commanded his soothsayers to explain what it meant, they were unable to do so. But Joseph, still in jail, had already interpreted the dream of a fellow prisoner, Pharaoh's butler, who had been released and restored to his former position as Joseph had predicted would happen. When Pharaoh had heard of this ability of Joseph, he was released from jail to appear before the lord of Egypt and interpret the ruler's own dream. Joseph responded by explaining that the dream foretold of seven future years of plentiful harvest, to be followed by another seven years of drought and famine. He went on to recommend to Pharaoh that he appoint an overseer to supervise the storage of surplus food during the good years to offset starvation during the lean years to follow. Pharaoh, recognizing the hand of God in Joseph's talent, not only released him from jail, but appointed him to be that very supervisor. This commission came in Joseph's thirtieth year, as it was for Jesus when He was baptized for His mission. In a grand demonstration of God's power to raise up the humble, Joseph carried out his assigned duty, in the process becoming a mighty ruler, second in command to Pharaoh over all of Egypt.

"As years of plenty passed and were replaced by years of drought, the stores of grain laid up by Joseph began to be used. Now the supervision of Joseph turned to the distribution of food to the needy. Meanwhile, the widespread famine extended outside the borders of Egypt. Other people were beginning to starve, and among these were Joseph's Israelite brothers. Their father Jacob, seeing the plight of his people and the relative ease with which the Egyptians were weathering the drought, sent ten of his sons to Pharaoh to plead for food. Of all his sons, only the youngest, Benjamin, remained behind.

"In one of life's great ironies, they were granted an audience with the Egyptian potentate in charge of distribution, who, of course, was their brother whom they had abused so many long, eventful years ago. As so much time had passed during which they thought he was dead they failed to recognize him. As for Joseph, he knew immediately, but declined at that time to make the connection known.

"Can you imagine, Earl, how at this point Joseph must have struggled with feelings of hurt and anger? Put yourself in his place. He was obviously in control over their very lives. He was in the perfect payback position and he knew it. Can't you imagine that had you been in his position, over the years you would have dreamed of having just such an opportunity to exact revenge on them for their savage treatment of you? Now Joseph had the perfect chance to even the score and he began to cash in on the opportunity with harsh words and harsher terms. He did give them some food, but kept Simeon behind as a hostage, refusing to release him unless they brought Benjamin to him as surety that they were not spies. Eventually they were forced by the continuing famine to return for more food, bringing Benjamin with them to the terrible distress of their father Jacob. Joseph played a bit with their fear, framing Benjamin for theft and insisting that he stay behind as his slave. Faced with calamity, they spoke among themselves with shame and guilt of God's retribution for the evil manner in they had treated their brother so long ago. Finally, still not recognizing that it was his brother he was standing before, Judah repented of his evil deeds before Joseph, offering his substitutionary enslavement for the freedom of Benjamin.

"Throughout this drama Joseph was beset with mixed feelings of hatred and love. Now, in the wake of Judah's repentance the situation changed dramatically. In one of history's great defining moments, Wisdom was imparted to Joseph such that he understood the events shaping his life in the context of the magnificent loving hand of God. Casting away the temptation to indulge in his petty retribution, he decided to obey his God. I particularly like what Joseph said to his brothers in Genesis Chapter 45:

Then Joseph could not refrain himself before all them that stood by him; and he cried, Cause every man to go out from me. And there stood no man with him, while Joseph made himself known unto his brethren.

And he wept aloud: and the Egyptians and the house of Pharaoh heard. And Joseph said unto his brethren, I am Joseph; doth my father yet live? And his brethren could not answer him; for they were troubled at his presence.

And Joseph said unto his brethren, Come near to me, I pray you. And they came near. And he said, I am Joseph your brother, whom ye sold into Egypt. Now therefore be not grieved, nor angry with yourselves, that ye sold me hither: for God did send me before you to preserve life. For these two years hath the famine been in the land: and yet there are five years, in the which there shall neither be earing nor harvest.

And God sent me before you to preserve you a posterity in the earth, and to save your lives by a great deliverance. So now it was not you that sent me hither, but God: and he hath made me a father to Pharaoh, and lord of all his house, and a ruler throughout all the land of Egypt. Haste ye, and go up to my father, and say unto him, Thus saith thy son Joseph, God hath made me lord of all Egypt: come down unto me, tarry not. And thou shalt dwell in the land of Goshen, and thou shalt be near unto me, thou, and thy children, and thy children's children, and thy flocks, and thy herds, and all that thou hast: And there will I nourish thee; for yet there are five years of famine; lest thou, and thy household, and all that thou hast, come to poverty.

"So, Earl, what came of Joseph's obedience to God?"

"Well, he got to a pretty high position. Being second-in-command to the ruler of Egypt is miraculous in itself. I'll bet he was rich, too."

"Yes, he was, but that's such a tiny part of his blessing that it pretty much accounts for nothing. What was important is that Joseph was given the privilege of presenting a very important part of Jesus' character to the world at large. What Joseph did was to suffer on behalf of those who caused his suffering, who hated him. At the end he did it willingly, to save them from starvation and death. Jesus did that very thing – He suffered on behalf of those who, still being in their sins, hated and rejected Him. He did it willingly, out of love, for the salvation of their souls."

"Wow. That's deep. Are there any other people who represented Jesus?"

"Are there. The Old Testament is full of them. You've read about some of them already. How about Abraham coming so close to sacrificing Isaac? Isaac, of course, represented the Jesus who, being God, yet was obedient to the exceedingly painful disgrace of the cross. When you get to the New Testament Gospels, you'll appreciate more what I'm saying. I'll make sure that when you come to that point, you'll be able to put the pieces together. And remember the question you had about whether the marriage of Isaac and Rebekah was significant, and we left it up in the air about who Rebekah represented?

"Yes, now that you mention it."

"Yes, my beloved, the marriage is quite significant. It has a lot to do with you, as a matter of fact, and your own future. Oh, you're going to enjoy this. Let's start back in the Book of Genesis. Do you remember what Adam said when he was presented with Eve?"

"Something about leaving father and mother and . . ."

"Let me say it. *'And Adam said, This is now bone of my bones, and flesh of my flesh; she shall be called Woman, because she was taken out of Man. Therefore shall a man leave his father and his mother, and shall cleave unto his wife; and they shall be one flesh.'*"

"But why did he say that about leaving his father and his mother, when he had neither? Being the first human, he wouldn't have known anything about that."

She brought her hands up and clapped them. "Very perceptive, Earl. Actually he did have a Father and a Mother, although not of the human kind. But the main point is that he was delivering an extremely important prophecy. Jesus repeated it in Matthew Chapter 22. Having accepted the gift of salvation offered through Jesus, you're now a member of the Church, the body of believers. Adam's prophecy has to do with that same Church, so it applies to you as well. You know from Abraham's call to sacrifice Isaac that Isaac was a type of Jesus. What does that say about Rebekah?"

"Well... Jesus Himself never married. Not while He was in the flesh, anyway... Oh! Rebekah was a type of the Church! She'd have to be. Then does that mean that when I get to heaven I'll be a woman?"

"Not exactly. The woman is the entire Church. But you will be a part of that woman, a component. And a vital one, too. That's a big reason why you've been commanded to love your neighbor. You may just end up working together in a very intimate way."

Earl was astonished. "You're saying then that there's a romantic association between us believers and Jesus. I don't get that kind of understanding at all from the church I go to."

"How true. And how very sad. So many churches nowadays have twisted the Bible in their own mean-spiritedness to mean the opposite of what God intended. Yet we have a remnant who truly understand . . . well, back to the marriage business. In the Old Testament, many of the prophets foretold of that romance. Yes, it is a romance, indeed. Isaiah, for example, was clear enough about it that there should have been no question in anyone's mind. Let me quote you from his Chapter 54:

Sing, O barren, thou who didst not bear; break forth into singing, and cry aloud, thou who didst not travail with child; for more are the children of the desolate than the children of the married wife, saith the Lord. Enlarge the place of thy tent, and let them stretch forth the curtains of thine habitations; spare not, lengthen thy cords, and strengthen thy stakes; for thou shalt break forth on the right hand and on the left, and thy seed shall inherit the Gentiles, and make the desolate cities to be inhabited. Fear not; for thou shalt not be ashamed, neither be thou confounded; for thou shalt not be put to shame; for thou shalt forget the shame of thy youth, and shalt not remember the reproach of thy widowhood any more. For thy Maker is thine husband; the Lord of hosts is his name; and thy Redeemer, the Holy One of Israel; the God of the whole earth shall he be called. For the Lord hath called thee like a woman forsaken and grieved in spirit, and a wife of youth, when thou wast refused, saith thy God. For a small moment have I forsaken thee, but with great mercies will I gather thee.

"For a very long time mankind refused to understand this passage for what it was. Finally, well into the New Testament, the Apostle Paul had to spell it out for you in the fifth chapter of his letter to the Church at Ephesus:

Husbands, love your wives, even as Christ also loved the church, and gave himself for it, that he might sanctify and cleanse it with the washing of water by the word; that he might present it to himself a glorious church, not having spot, or wrinkle, or any such thing; but that it should be holy and without blemish. So ought men to love their wives as their own bodies. He that loveth his wife loveth himself. For no man ever yet hated his own flesh, but nourisheth and cherisheth it, even as the Lord the church; for we are members of his body, of his flesh, and of his bones.

For this cause shall a man leave his father and mother, and shall be joined unto his wife, and they two shall be one flesh. This is a great mystery, but I speak concerning Christ and the church.

"That blows my mind! It leaves no doubt whatsoever as to the Church's role with Jesus. What about Jesus' time here on earth? Was He involved with a woman like some books have suggested? But we know He wasn't married here on earth. It would seem very wrong to attribute an extramarital relation to Jesus."

"How right you are. There has been some speculation over the centuries as to whether Jesus may have had a hidden romance. His supposed celibacy somehow makes Him incomplete in many minds. But His celibacy did make Him incomplete! As the Son of God He was already betrothed to His Church. That is the mystery of which Paul spoke and His great promise of future joy to those who love Him, that without His Church He is indeed incomplete. That is the wedding for which He is yet waiting, and which He joyfully anticipated at the wedding in Cana. Just as He permitted the prophets to define Him before he came to earth, he permits his Church to complete His masculine function. In the fullness of God's time, mankind will yet serve again in the function of implementation, this time alongside the risen Jesus as His partner in marriage."

"So Jesus does partake of gender, even in His spiritual form. Which means that the entire Godhead also does"

"Yes. And congratulations. You're beginning to show some theological maturity. As you grow out of your spiritual childhood stage, you're starting to understand the significance of male and female as heavenly roles, the importance of 'complementary otherness' in God's economy. Jesus is going to have redeemed mankind at His side when he performs his new functional role as Divine Will on earth. Mankind will have a functional role to play also, that of Jesus' wife. Which, by the way, should confirm to you and everyone else who bothers to read that passage that God does indeed partake of gender. For why would one Member of the Godhead, namely Jesus, have a gender role in His spiritual form while the other Two don't?"

She gave him a loving gaze, as if she was memorizing his every feature. "Let this soak in. Have some fun for a change. Maybe you'll want to get your glider off the rafter in the garage and take a ride."

CHAPTER 4

Earl remained on the ground for several minutes, the first few of which were occupied with an assessment of his dismal condition. Alicia remained at the top of his list of woes. Three months had dragged by since her passing and he thought that he was beginning to recover some semblance of life. Now he was forced to reconsider.

The job had suffered too. He looked up at the sky, watching the clouds move past with force and dark purpose, and thought painfully about his job. He couldn't manage to focus at work in the wake of his loss. When the boss noticed his lack of concentration he had hinted broadly that a replacement was sure to be available, which only darkened Earl's outlook.

He turned to his side, his eyes focusing on a bug crawling by in front of his face. The creature turned his way, stopped for a second of indifferent observation, and then went about its business as if he didn't exist. *What was I thinking? I guess I wasn't.* He raised his head and surveyed his clothing. Old, hopelessly outdated, and now in shreds. He felt like a bum. His dismal gaffe as a member of this last society, his only remaining refuge, would now complete his rejection. It didn't help that this particular society was, itself, on the fringe of rejection by the rest of the human race.

The movement of his head brought on a severe headache and he returned to his supine position, his thoughts as bleak as the clouds that raced above. Now he suspected that he didn't even have his health. But the pain told him that at least his spine was intact.

Inability to focus was the root cause of his problem at work as well as his present distress. It was certainly a factor in why he was lying on his back looking up at the clouds. Despite the headache he raised his head and looked at the bare flesh, blood just beginning to ooze through the coating of dirt that poked out between shreds of torn cloth. His eyes moved past his feet to the colorful but completely nonfunctional object that represented the latest confirmation of his fleeing fortunes. It used to be graceful. Now it was a useless collection of ineffectively flapping cloth and bent tubing. He pictured his luck, the only part of him that could still fly, flapping away into the sky beyond.

"Earl!" a voice above him shouted., interrupting his unproductive self-evaluation. "Hey, man, are you okay?" A branch snapped above him and the voice, closer now, was accompanied by the noise of falling pebbles and sliding boots. "Say something, Earl." The voice was worried now. "Are you hurt?"

"I'm okay, I think," Earl replied as loudly as his damaged ribs would permit. He wanted to think that he was okay. It was to be preferred over being a legend.

"Aw, no!" Bill exclaimed, looking down at him. "Don't move. You may have broken your back."

"I'm okay, I said." Earl reassembled himself into a sitting position to prove his statement.

More pebbles rained down. Bill looked up. "Earl augured pretty hard, Ray," he said to his descending companion. "I think we're going to have to take him to the hospital."

"Looks like fresh roadkill," Ray confirmed, standing next to Bill and looking down at the abused flesh that peeked out from Earl's torn clothing. Earl knew Ray and Bill, but not well. The hang gliding community was good about helping their own out of tough spots. The help came with a price. Ray started to collect.

"Hey, Earl," he said, pointing outward with his hand and grinning. "Sky's that way, dude. Hey, wasn't it you that landed on the cow last month?" he asked brightly.

"That was Grant," Earl said. "He broke his leg. Do you see me with a broken leg?"

"Well, I . . . " Ray looked dubiously at Earl's shredded pants. "Could be. Doesn't look that great. Looks like plop as a matter of fact. Can you move it?" He turned to Bill, grinning widely. "You shoulda seen that cow, dude," he said. "Pissed off? Ain't the word for it, dude. Took off like a runaway freight train bucking and bellowing, tossed Earl here ass over elbow like a rodeo clown." He turned back to Earl. Hey dude," he said. "you got a real act going. You could hit the rodeo circuit."

Why did I go up today with such a lousy attitude? he asked himself in vain. *Why on earth did I go for it with the wind heading down the hill? That and my careless attitude just amplified my clumsy handling.*

When the direction of the wind is toward the face of the cliff, the pilot who wishes to jump off into it enjoys the benefits of updraft lift and the relative smoothness of laminar flow. Running directly into a headwind, he also attains velocities above the minimum stall speed of the frail craft with relative ease.

The pilot who jumps into a wind heading downslope enjoys none of these benefits. The dreaded rotor, in particular, rules the sky of the downslope wind. "Earl! Wake up, dude." Ray nudged him with a foot as if he was an interesting bug. "Is he lapsing, Bill? Going into shock?"

Earl looked up at the two hovering faces. "I'm all right, I told you," he replied irritably. "You're not going to have to take me to the hospital."

He imagined Ray's mind at work constructing the latest local hang gliding legend, a tale in which he would be the star character. The sight of the peering eyes took him back to his first lesson. The kid who gave it had spoken with a stern voice wholly out of sync with his pimply face. Furrowing his greasy adolescent brows, he had stated with the assertion of a saint on a mission, "Never, NEVER fly into a rotor. If you do, you will DIE." He had sealed the importance of his statement with a slash of his outstretched finger across the festering pimple that jutted out from his neck. The inadvertent contact of his finger with the pimple made his eyes water, but, somewhat subdued, he had bravely continued on with the lesson.

In the afternoon, not wanting to wimp out of the demo flight that would complete the day's lesson, the kid had jumped headlong into the rotor of a downslope wind, ending the lesson on a somewhat negative note. The class watched him hobble off the field dragging the asymmetrical remains of the one decent shop glider along with a semi-useless right foot. One of the students, his face ashen with disbelieving horror, had stood at the top of the hill gaping at the carnage below. "Screw this crap," he had said under his breath, and had hurried down the other side to his car. He'd left in a cloud of dust, his car fishtailing in its haste to depart the area.

Earl tried using one leg, flexing it at the knee surreptitiously while Ray wasn't watching. *Nothing broken, thank God.* He tried the other, and then his arms. Nothing but scrapes and bruises and a few radically stretched muscles.

"Just give me a second, will you?" Earl told the peering faces that had come down closer. From his perspective they took on the appearance of ostriches, inquisitive heads supported on stalks. The heads turned to each other and receded.

He watched them as Bill and Ray began to tear down the kite. Bill removed battens from their pockets while Ray unfastened the landing wires from the king post. When they undid the flying wires and started folding up the damaged craft, Earl picked himself up from the ground, standing painfully on a swelling ankle. "Here, let me handle that," he said, hobbling over to them.

They let him do the final bundling, turning their attention to the faces peering down at them from the top. "Says he's okay," Bill shouted up. "Looks like crap. Someone send down a rope."

Ray turned back to Earl. "That makes two broken legs in two months, doesn't it?" He accused brightly. The truth didn't matter, Earl realized. It would get in the way of the epic that Ray was fashioning in his mind.

Bill tied the rope around the glider and signaled to the top to start hauling. Ray scrambled up to the ledge above and held out a hand. Earl ignored it, climbing painfully on his side. "Let's go," he said grimly.

As they climbed, Ray started to whistle a tune. He broke off in the middle, turning his head toward Bill. "Hey, remember that time when Frank stalled on takeoff and twisted his neck, dude? He was in the hospital for two weeks. Walked around like a zombie for months." He looked back at Earl. "Whatever happened to him, anyway? I never see him around."

Bill was beginning to get the picture. He looked at Earl with a trace of compassion. "You only made an epic out of it, Ray. He probably got tired of hearing the story. The way you went on about it, people were thinking you were going to put in for the movie rights."

"Hey, that's not a bad idea," Ray said. "I oughta get a videocam. Stuff like this would be great on America's Funniest. Remember Charlie Daniels? How he went prone before he reached the edge of the cliff and scraped his 'chute off the harness? Funniest thing I ever saw. He looked just like the coyote in the Roadrunner cartoon. Flew straight out until the 'chute inflated. That one would have made 'Real TV,' the way the 'chute stopped him and he dropped like a rock. Ninety degrees, dude. He made a square-corner vertical turn."

"He didn't think it was funny," Bill said. "He got a broken leg. It's lucky he landed on the road. Otherwise, he would have gone down the cliff and killed himself."

"Yeah," Ray continued, amusing himself with the thought of the Daniels epic. "I have to get a videocam."

Twenty physically exhausting minutes later they made it back to the top. For Earl it had been an emotionally exhausting ordeal as well. He rested above the face of the cliff next to the remains of his hang glider, lying there in a heap. He felt the need to reassert his control. Over something. Over anything. He hobbled over to the offending craft and kicked it with his good foot. Ray stared, wishing he had a camcorder.

Sleeping on his bruises didn't improve them, nor did it help on the pain. It took him twice as long as usual to shave and dress. Even the drive to work was filled with pain. As he walked stiffly down the cold linoleum aisle toward his cubicle, Earl's thoughts returned again to Alicia. He wondered how he would have handled the complicating factor of children. On the other hand, there was nothing at all of importance that remained of their years together. That desolate thought occupied his mind until he sat down.

Patty caught a glance at Earl's back as he entered his cubicle. His failure to greet her signaled in her mind his discontent. She paused from her work, thinking about the implications. From the way his outlook had improved over the past month, she wondered if another woman had already entered his life. Jumping away from her desk, she hopped on the opportunity to acquire an answer. Earl was leaning over an open drawer as she entered his tiny office and sat down unbidden in the ergonomically correct but frightfully ugly desk chair that belonged to his absent cubicle-mate. "How's it going today?" she asked. She peered intently, her eyes widening in sudden shock. "Good grief! What happened to your face?"

"Just a little accident, that's all." He covered his bruised chin with his hand.

She inspected his face. "I washed something like you off my windshield this morning. What did you do, total your car?"

"No."

"Are you still jumping off cliffs?" she asked with suspicion.

"What's wrong with that?"

She broke into laughter. "You're a walking testimonial to what's wrong with that. Really, Earl, you're not going to replace Alicia that way. Who wants to date Wiley Coyote. . .? Your face would drive your own mother away."

He sighed in discontent. "Does everything have to center around my getting a replacement? It's Monday morning, Patty. I have another long week to look forward to. Can't you forget about the boy-girl thing for once?"

The denial didn't come. She could not forget about the boy-girl thing, not even once. "Did you call my friend Kathy yet?"

"No, I haven't," he replied laconically. *No wonder she likes to come to work. She's turned her job into a soap.*

"She brightened with a thought. "Why don't you call her now?"

"Patty... I have to get to work."

"Yes, you do. Both of you." The intrusive voice came from Walter Jergens, whose face was poking over Earl's cubicle wall. He peered significantly into Earl's face, eyebrows raised. "We need to talk," he said, maintaining an officious stare as he came around through the entrance. He bumped into Patty as she left, fending her off with a groping hand.

Walter sat down on the chair vacated by Patty. He studied Earl's face with a barely suppressed smile. Now that a decent interval had passed since Earl's misfortune, open season on him had returned. "You slip in the bathtub?"

"Something like that."

"Have you looked at your e-mail yet?" Walter asked pointedly.

"No, haven't had a chance yet."

"That's the first thing we do in the morning. Do I need to remind you of that? Maybe I do. Do I need to remind you of what you're doing here too?"

"Fine, Walter. I'm here to have lots of fun. What do you have in mind?" The little creep knew about Alicia. He was one of those sadistic people who liked to amplify the pain of others.

"What I need you to do is to fill me in on where you stand with the Integrated Communications Package. Last week at the status meeting you committed to having it completed by close-of-business today."

The commitment to today's completion had been entirely Walter's. He had set the date to impress his own boss, who was also at the meeting, and had nodded in Earl's direction for confirmation.

"I'm having a problem with the display routine," Earl said. "We're trying to accomplish it without a hardware driver, but the service interrupt takes so long it's visually noticeable. I think I have an answer, though."

"Spare me the details. If you can't take care of it today, I'll put Mike on to help out."

Mike was a year younger than Walter and a red-hot toady. He would take whatever credit was due and pass any blame on to Earl.

"Tell you what," he added, looking at his wristwatch. "It's eight-thirty now. Let's say we. . ." he consulted his watch carefully, adding the hours in his mind, ". . .meet here again at three-thirty. I'll bring Mike along and you can fill us both in on where you stand. Mike may have some input on where we go from there." He stood. "Fair enough?"

When Walter left, Earl breathed a sigh of relief and got up himself to get a cup of coffee. As he walked back to his cubicle, he looked down the long corridor toward the distant glass door. It was bright. The sun had come out. The cheerful thought collapsed as he sat down in his chair and hit the button to activate the screen. It stared malevolently at him, his discomfort amplified by the specter of Mike sharing the project.

The e-mail window continued to glare sternly with its accusation of unread messages. There were two, both from Walter Jergens. The first message was a tersely-written command to see him for a special status briefing. He deleted it from the file. The second e-mail reflected the same intent, but took more words to say the same thing. Below the usual date-time/to-from format it read:

Earl, It is past 7:45 and as of yet you have input no response to me. Having received no status information from you, I presume that you continue to be behind our previously-agreed-upon schedule. We must get this out as promised! I have asked Mike to get up to speed on the project. He has already briefed himself on it and is available for immediate support. I expect you to take willing and full advantage of his availability. See me ASAP when you (decide to) come in to work. -Walter

Earl deleted the odious message, turning back to his project. He struggled the rest of the morning on his solution. When lunchtime came, he continued without a break. By two forty-five he had completed an aesthetically awkward but practical software patch. He had run it with satisfactory results by three fifteen and left the display on his screen for Walter's inspection.

Walter arrived five minutes later, trailing Mike. He motioned Mike into the vacant chair and rested his seat against the desk, observing Earl with his arms folded on his chest.

"Hello, there, Earl," Mike said brightly. The offhand grin perfectly complemented the insincerity of his greeting.

"So..?" Walter asked.

"It's on the screen."

Walter leaned over to look. Mike got up and went to Walter's side. They peered together, Mike's gaze intent and clearly disappointed in the worth of its content. "Where's the code?" he asked.

Earl reluctantly worked the keyboard and clicked his mouse to print. They watched in silence as the printer responded. Mike went over immediately to grab the first sheet as it came out. He studied it for a moment, then frowned and picked up the second as it emerged from the printer. His frown deepened and he looked at Walter, avoiding eye contact with Earl. "This code is pretty disorganized," he remarked to Walter. "It needs to be neatened out and compacted."

Walter took the sheets and looked them over. Then he handed them back to Mike. "Tell you what. Take this code and massage it up to standard. When you're through we'll let Earl here test and debug it."

"You got it," Mike responded, continuing to avert his eyes from Earl's face as he left the office.

Earl watched Mike leave, mouth open in shock.

"What's the matter, Earl? Mind go blank?"

What an irritating little cretin! Earl thought. "That's why I'm here, Walter. "If I had a working brain, I'd be somewhere else doing a job I'd get the credit for."

"That was uncalled for," Walter said petulantly. "But I guess that I can't expect better from you."

"You yourself told your own boss that by today we'd have the project out in quick-and-dirty form. You said that we'd have it cleaned up in another week. I am perfectly capable of doing the cleanup myself. That's the easy part, now that the code is working properly. Why did you give it to Mike?"

"I've seen his code work. I like his style. I know it'll get done right. The project's still yours. I told him that you'd do the debugging, didn't I? Besides, it's always good policy to double-team any effort. In case something. . ." he left the obvious conclusion unsaid. "Besides, I have another project for you. Do you know anything about interfacing software with servomotor drive circuitry?"

"I, well, yes, on the basics. I'd have to do some review, but..." *He doesn't mind me doing the grunt work as long as his fast-track associate gets the credit. I wonder how he'll stick it to me on that one?*

Walter was four years younger than Earl and was himself riding squarely on the management fast-track. He had a mentor in middle management, a pompous individual about Earl's age who showed no signs whatsoever of mental slowdown because, as far as Earl could see, he had nothing going for him to begin with. Mental prowess was not what Walter was looking for in a mentor. To him, a mentor's one significant function was that of passing the reigns of leadership on to him.

"Come on, let's get back on track," Walter ordered. "You were saying..?"

"Yes, Walter, I can do it."

"Okay. Good. I'll come back tomorrow with spec details and a tentative schedule. You'll have to be quick on this one. They need it yesterday." He left the cubicle.

Earl shut off his computer and turned to his bookshelf, extracting a long-unused tome on control theory. Driven by his desire to keep

Mike at bay, he read this until eight, after which he shut it and went out of the plant.

CHAPTER 5

When She appeared again in front of his bed she was smiling. "I guess the flight didn't work out too well," she offered.

"You were the one who suggested it, if you'll remember."

"It worked out better than you think. You got rid of a lot of mental baggage when you cratered in. You have to admit, it got your mind on other things. I liked seeing you occupied away from your fixation. Maybe you'll keep your job."

"Ha ha."

"You've come a long way, Earl. You're on the mend. But think on this: you need to continue to grow. It's time that you exercised some compassion toward others. I'll be helping you with that behind the scenes. And I have a little surprise for you that will be coming up soon."

The next morning Earl could remember bits of last night's visit, but the pieces were dim and distorted. Yet he had a burning sense of mission that was both clear and persistent. He felt a need, almost urgent, to display compassion toward someone else, perhaps someone less fortunate than himself. The direction that this new drive would take was still a mystery, but as the workday drew to a close he knew what he would do.

Earl grabbed a burger at a fast-food drive-through and continued toward his new and strange destination. As he approached his objective his discomfort increased. Three times he came close to turning around and heading home. But he found himself at the parking lot. Breathing deeply, he reluctantly stepped out of his car and headed for the front foyer of the Midtown Nursing Home. As soon as he opened the door he was assaulted by the fetid odor of stale urine mixed with cleaning solution. The cheap linoleum floor was clean for the most part, but a worker was bent over a puddle with a mop in her hand. His next impression was of noise, an indistinct hum that came from a multitude of inmates, the closer of whom emitted random groans and wails. Then his eyesight took over from his nose and ears, framing hellish scenes of wheelchair-bound bodies whose limbs flailed uselessly and assumed grotesque and unnatural attitudes. The enormous head of one poor creature rested on an arm of a wheelchair, its unseeing eyes looking up to the ceiling.

"Yes? What do you want?" The voice behind him was almost hostile.

He turned, not knowing how to express himself without appearing frivolous or perverted. "I, uh, I'm here . . . I mean, I'm here to volunteer . . ."

"Here? *Why?*"

"I'm a Christian. I think it's my duty." His voice was firmer now.

"Oh." She pointed to the front desk. "Over there. Talk to Sue."

He approached Sue at the front desk. She was occupied on the phone. When she terminated the call and looked up at him, he repeated his business, adding that he felt that it was a calling. She looked at him strangely. Without a word to him, she picked up the phone again and spoke into it briefly. "Mary's the Activities Director," she told him. She'll be here in a minute." Dismissing him from her mind, she occupied herself with paperwork.

Mary was as sweet as the previous two were churlish. She shook his hand, asked his name, and led the way back to her office, where she presented him with a form to complete. Subject to the background check, she told him, he'd be more than welcome here. She had an individual in mind, as a matter of fact, whose parents could no longer handle the rigors of dealing with a severely handicapped individual and had placed him here just a few months ago. He was quite lonely and could use a companion. She'd call him when the background check was complete. She walked him back out the door and shook his hand warmly as they parted.

A euphoric joy embraced Earl as he drove home. *I wonder,* he thought, *if this boy was dropped off there about the same time as Alicia died.* By the time he hit the sack, however, the elation had all but dissipated. Recalling the three-front assault on his senses when he first went into the facility, he began to wonder if he'd be able to handle the dismal surroundings and the terrible afflictions of the home's inmates. He didn't even know what kind of problems the boy had or whether he could stomach them.

That night she was there, looking at him fondly when he awoke. "It's time we got into some serious theology," she remarked as he rubbed the sleep out of his eyes.

"Serious theology? What do you think you've been giving me?"

"Just the basics of Jesus in the Old Testament. Beyond that, you'll have to know how He came to be. You could get it yourself out of the Bible, but you don't have time for that. After all, the vast majority of Christians never do get it. Sadly, that's the situation out there, so that's one thing I'm going to take care of with you right now. Earl, you've been blessed. You have a special mission in this life, something to add a splash of color to God's grand tapestry. For that, you'll need to be familiar with Jesus' family roots. Then you'll really understand who you'll be in love with." She reached out to brush a wisp of hair from his forehead, but dallied with a lock, twirling it lovingly in her fingers.

"Earl," she continued presently, "Jesus and I were always part of the Father, but at the very beginning there was no separation. We existed together as One, and that One was the Father, the Divine Will. Being alone and in full command of Himself, He had the choice to remain in that state and retain within Himself absolute power and authority over everything that He would subsequently create." A tear leaked out from her eye. She dabbed at it with a finger.

"But then," she said, regaining control over her emotions, "the Father did something that was the essence of selflessness. It was of an order of nobility that transcends everything that came after."

"Even Jesus on the cross?" he asked in wonder. "That was pretty painful. And humbling."

"Yes. Even that. The Father was first to humble Himself. He set the standard. And yes, it was painful too. Remember that He possessed everything that was and ever will be. He chose to give that up."

"What did He do?"

"He chose to create an Other out of Himself, giving up part of Himself in the process and restricting His portion in everything that is or ever will be to that of one Member of a Partnership. He decided to share His exalted position with that Other. But here's the great beauty of what he did: in relinquishing His singleness He added love into the mix. And through this love He again became One with His Other."

"That makes two. I'd guess that the Other is the Holy Spirit. I thought the Godhead was a Trinity. Three, not two. Isn't Jesus truly God also?"

"For certain," she laughed. Remember that I said that the Father and the Other came back together in love? What does that make you think of?

Earl thought about that, searching for something in his mind. He found it. "Oh," he though abruptly. Is that what Adam meant when he said that he shall marry his wife and they two shall be one flesh?"

"Exactly," she said. "You're pretty smart to make that connection so quickly. Jesus said it Himself. Look it up. It's in Matthew 19."

"Yes, but then. . ." Earl searched for a tactful way to express his thought.

"But then," she finished for him, "that would mean that the Holy Spirit is female. Yes it does. At least functionally. Remember that the Father exercises the Divine Will. He kept that function when

He created the Holy Spirit. The Holy Spirit serves as the Divine Executive, implementing the Divine Will. That's a responsive role, Earl. A female one, wouldn't you agree?"

"Ah. I think I see. It's a Divine marriage. The Will in Union with the Executive, the Divine Means. Produces . . . what? What is the thing that it produces?"

"Why, it's plain as day. The love-child Jesus! Jesus represents the Divine Implementation, the actuality or the reality. Read John Chapter 1. 'In the beginning was the Word and the Word was with God, and the Word was God. All things were made by Him, and without Him was nothing made that was made. . .'"

"Oh! Wow! I get it! That's deep. But, simple at the same time. It seems so natural, I don't understand why the Church doesn't shout that insight from the housetops."

"Too many hang-ups. Very few people have the will to read the Bible to the depth that issues like that even come to mind. When they do, ever fewer have the guts to think of God as possessing gender, or to associate the Holy Spirit with Motherhood. Yet, shallow as their understanding is, they act if they know what they are talking about when confronted with a deeper truth."

"But what of all the times that the Bible refers to the Holy Spirit by the word 'He', or 'Him'? That comes from the Bible itself."

"Good point. The most basic reason is that the unity in love of the Father and Holy Spirit is so perfectly close that they are truly one. In that condition they both can rightly be considered a part of the Father. Then, too, the Holy Spirit, while functionally female, was taken from the Father, so that the Holy Spirit possesses the male substance of the Father. In that sense, too, both Father and Holy Spirit can be thought of as male."

"That makes sense, I guess. But still . . ."

"I'm not finished. There's another factor, which is actually my favorite explanation. It's actually a promise to mankind regarding his future spiritual participation in the Godhead as the Bride of Christ. You'll learn more of this Bridehood role as time goes by. Think of it this way: redeemed mankind in his spiritual form, and in the collective sense, will still be substantively characterized as male. Nevertheless, that same Body will, like the Holy Spirit in Her role, be female in the functional sense. But you have another problem with what I just told you. Spill it out."

"Yes, I do. I haven't been very good about attending church, but I have picked up some things, one of which is that the Trinity existed throughout eternity. Now you're trying to say that isn't the case."

"It is and it isn't. Since you don't have a true understanding of what eternity is all about, it's difficult to explain. That's not a put-down, it's just that humans are more dimensionally restricted than spiritual beings. As far as you're concerned, the Trinity did indeed exist from eternity past. But there's another issue at play here. What's involved is the kind of groveling worship that God hates, where people want to extol God in the most grandiose terms that they can dream up, kind of a catch-all that releases them from the obligation of truly thinking about God. Their use of eternity is of that kind. It reeks of self-service and a don't-care attitude toward the nature of the Godhead. Scripture is plain on this, but people don't bother to check it out. For instance, in Revelation 3:14, Jesus describes Himself as the beginning of the creation of God. Now think about that, Earl. What does that imply?"

"Well . . .yeh, it does suggest a beginning."

"Yes, and that contradicts the teaching that you brought up, doesn't it? Which really means that the teaching itself leaves something to be desired. I'll quote next from Genesis 1:

> *In the beginning God created the heaven and the earth. And the earth was without form and void; and darkness was upon the face of the deep. And the Spirit of God moved upon the face of the waters. And God said, Let there be light: and there was light. And God saw the light, that it was good: and God divided the light from the darkness. And God called the light Day, and the darkness he called Night. And the evening and the morning were the first day.*

"Earl, what was that light?"

"Well, it must have been the sun." She made it sound like a trick question. What else could it be?

"No no. You need to pay more attention to what you read. On what day was the sun made? Think, Earl."

"Oh. Yes. The sun and moon were made on the fourth day."

"That's better." She made a frown, and then softened it with the tiniest of winks. "That light, Earl, was the first Word that God spoke, Jesus Christ. If you read the first few verses of Genesis 1 very closely, you'll grasp that the Spirit of God, the Holy Spirit, was moving in response to the Father, the Divine Will. He first willed Light, and the Light was also the Word. Listen to the Gospel of John. In the very first chapter, he says that,

> *In the beginning was the Word, and the Word was with God, and the Word was God. The same was in the beginning with God. All things were made by him; and without him was not any think made that was made. In him was life; and the life was the light of men. And the light shineth in darkness; and the darkness comprehended it not.*

"You see? Jesus is the Word, the Light and the Life. Awesome, isn't it?"

"Yeh. That means that He existed before He came in the flesh, all right. But not necessarily forever."

"Careful. With your dimensional limitation you can't even perceive the meaning of eternity. You can simply say that He existed before time began, which is the meaning that Scripture intended to convey. In fact, there was a man by the name of Arius who was pretty popular around the fourth century. He started one train of thought by saying that there was a time when Jesus was not, and extended that to imply that Jesus was inferior to the Father. He equated that perceived inferiority with the notion that Jesus wasn't God, or at least God of the same order. That notion was immortalized as the famous 'Arian heresy'. Arius violated common sense. A human father naturally predates his son because both of them reside in the domain of time. But as Jesus as the preexistent Son of God represents all of creation, time itself began with Him. For that reason the question of whether Jesus sequentially followed the Father has no meaning. Even if the Son did follow the Father sequentially in time, it still wouldn't imply inferiority. The same can be said of the Holy Spirit, who also existed with the Father when time began. The word "eternity" references time, so it is logically accurate to agree with the Council of Nicaea which in 325 A.D. defined them to be coexistent with God for all eternity, although the council probably was being somewhat reactionary to Arius' belief. But at any rate, as far as you humans are concerned, Jesus existed from eternity as you can comprehend it."

She frowned, as if she had something unpleasant to say. "You can count on this, Earl: I'll be with you always, and I'll make myself apparent to you when you need me."

"You sound like I won't be seeing you. You're not going to see me every night?"

"No. Not on a regular basis. Trust me. I will be with you, but you won't always know it."

The desolation returned. "First my wife," he told her bitterly. Now you. I don't even know your name."

"Just call me Wisdom. That'll do for now. I'll also miss our talks, but the pain of loss isn't always bad. As you'll understand some day, all things work for good for those who love the Lord. And I will come back from time to time. I promise you. Let me leave you with his thought: remember the issue you brought up about the Holy Spirit being referred to in the masculine gender? What was really intended by that is to give a promise to those who loved God enough to pursue the apparent contradiction. It means that redeemed mankind, properly thought of in the masculine gender, will serve as the Wife of Christ in precisely the same manner as the Holy Spirit serves as the Wife of the Divine Will. The implication is that the Trinity as a divine Family will be extended to include and lovingly embrace the Church. You need time to digest that. Let it sink in. Goodbye for now, my dearest one."

CHAPTER 6

Sitting down in his cubicle, Earl saw that he had a message. It was from Mike, heralding an afternoon demo of the ice cream packaging system with upper management. *As if Mike hasn't reminded us about it a million times already*, he thought.

"I see that you're reading the e-mail I sent." Mike walked into his office and sat on the tiny table. "It's all set up for one o'clock. The management staff will go to Dairy D-lite directly after lunch. "I'll give a short presentation while you warm up the system. Then I'll handle the controls, pointing out the various display features to the staff as we run through an actual packaging sequence."

"What do you want me to do while you're at the controls?"

"Just stay in the background, Earl. Try not to pick your nose. Don't worry, I'll give you credit for your part of this effort."

Oh, right, Earl thought. *That would be a first.* "If you ask me, I think the demo's a little premature."

"I'm not asking you. We did a thorough checkout in the lab. It more than satisfactorily demonstrated full and continuous control over the motors and valves."

"Yes, it did, but never with the actual machinery. All we used was a computer-simulated interface."

"What did you expect us to do, bring the ice cream into the lab? That's the difference between you and me, Earl. I think in terms of cost efficiency. It is precisely in this type of situation that the tools of modern simulation technology can make us more efficient. Simulation gives us the ability to bypass all the time-wasting effort of working with the actual equipment while we're debugging the system."

"I don't have a problem with that. But the simulator won't actually do the packaging. At some point you have to marry the computer with the machinery."

"That's already been done, of course." Mike looked at him like he was a slow child. "The equipment crew worked overtime last night hooking it all up."

"Yes, but don't you think we should make a dry run of the actual hookup before the demo?"

"Not necessary." Mike waved his hand in dismissal of the idea. "You've seen the schedule. In fact, you participated in it. Look, Earl, just because it was my idea to do the simulation, you don't have to try and defend your outmoded ideas."

It wasn't your idea, you cretin. You not only didn't think of it, you don't understand the limits of its application. "Sure, Mike. Anything you say. I'll be down there at one."

"Not one. Twelve. You can do a quick checkout of the display. But don't screw around with the controls."

Earl turned into the parking lot of Dairy D-lite at twelve-ten, chewing the last of a tasteless burger that he'd picked up at a convenience store. By the time he had checked out the operator display panel on the screen, Mike arrived.

"You'll have to move your car," Mike said. "We need some spaces to accommodate the management staff."

Earl drove down the street looking for a space. Lunchtime wasn't over yet for the many restaurants. The first open space he came to was several blocks away, and it was metered. He put quarters in the slot and headed back to the factory.

By the time he returned, the management staff was milling about the service area. Mike was seated at the controls, officiously pointing out the display features to a disinterested Walter Jergens, who recently had been promoted to an executive position. The others stood in a self-contained knot, conversing among themselves. The conveyor and packaging system directly in front of them was idle, awaiting the demonstration. In the background a host of other systems were busy whirring, clanking and moving product.

". . .and he still got a hole-in-one!" someone exclaimed, followed by an outbreak of communal laughter.

Mike made a last cursory scan of the setup and stood up. As a final touch, he carefully mounted the camcorder on its tripod and peered through the viewfinder, slowly moving the camera to capture the desired scene. He went over to the vending machine and returned with two cans of pop. He offered one to Earl.

"I'm overwhelmed," Earl said as he reached for the can. "First, you let me see the show. Now this."

"I just want to keep your hands occupied with something safe." He turned to face the chatting executives, but as their interest did not include him, he coughed for attention. Frederick turned, his brows bunched in irritation.

"Gentlemen!" Mike broke in awkwardly. "If I can have your attention, please, the demonstration is about to begin."

The management staff gravitated over to the screen, peering at it as if they understood the contents of the display. "Tell him to go ahead with it, Walter," Jack Guthrie, the company CEO, said. "It's your show."

"Thanks, Jack, but the real credit goes to Mike, here. You'll soon understand why I've been mentoring him so closely." Walter turned back to Mike and nodded his head. Earl studied the exchange, visualizing Walter patting Mike's head, Mike's tongue lolling out of his grinning mouth.

Mike typed in a command and Jack raised his head to watch the empty cartons sitting atop the conveyor belt begin to move toward the cavernous entrance of the filling machine. A pump was turned on and a liquid substance could be seen traveling through transparent tubing into the mechanism.

Earl's eyes followed Jack's. The empty cartons moved inexorably into the machine. A sudden dose of adrenalin surged into his veins. Earl's fears subsided as the cartons moved smoothly along the conveyor. Mike was smiling. *Still*, Earl thought, *I wish Mike had let me use the actual machinery before this first demo.* Mike, of course, had axed the offer, pointing out that verification of the simulator-based checkout was a big part of the demo.

Jack saw his initial consternation. "Mike said that's a tested system," the CEO said, frowning in annoyance. "So what's the problem? Forget something?" The question was purely rhetorical. He turned his head back to the show, dismissing Earl from his mind.

Empty cartons continued to enter the filling station, but none as yet had emerged. The only thing coming out was a strange, liquid noise that steadily grew louder. Finally something tore itself free from some internal restraint and reluctantly emerged from the other side. It was the remains of a carton, still empty but covered in the gooey substance that was intended to become ice cream had the container remained intact. It moved forlornly along the exit conveyor. Soon the filling machine screeched to a halt and unrestrained goo emerged from beneath it to form a puddle on the floor. The puddle quickly expanded, traveling down the aisle to where other machinery, fully functional, was busily making products. An attendant at a nearby machine gave a whoop and fell to the floor. The people standing around the demo simply stared wide-eyed at the debacle. So did Mike and Earl.

"What on Earth. . .!?" Jack asked Walter.

"What in the world are you doing?" Walter shouted to Mike. "Stop this immediately!"

Mike responded at last and stopped the pump. Residual goo spilled out of the system. They stared at the mess. "Why didn't you check out the system after it was connected up?" Mike asked, running a hand through his thinning hair.

Earl let the inappropriate accusation pass. "I think I may know what went wrong," he said.

"As if it matters."

"The equipment inside," Earl pointed to the still-smoldering lumps of metal, "came from Japan. The Japanese use the metric system of measurement. Didn't the simulation use the English system?"

"You mean that your simulator wasn't on the metric system? You craphead, my job is toast! And yours too, if you didn't think of the implications of this fiasco."

Earl walked away in disgust, wondering if he still had a job. It was Friday afternoon. Now he'd have to wait until Monday to find out.

When he arrived back home there was a message on the phone. It was from Mary, the Activities Director at the nursing home. His background check was complete and satisfactory. She welcomed him as a volunteer. *Good thing the checkup was made while I still had a job,* he thought. He decided to go there after a quick meal. It would help him to forget about the day's disaster.

The noise and smell nauseated him at first, but Earl found that he quickly became used to the environment. Mary greeted him warmly and handed him a liability form to sign. "Follow me, please," she said, "we're going to meet a twenty-year-old young man whose name is Buddy. Are you up to it?" Without waiting for his response she walked down the long aisle, entering a room almost at the end. Inside a young lad sat twisted in a wheelchair, limbs akimbo. Food was caked on the front of his shirt. Mary whipped out a handkerchief and wiped the drool from the side of his mouth, watching out of the corner of her eye for Earl's response.

Buddy was afflicted with cerebral palsy, a terrible disability that so thoroughly restricted his movements that his limbs would fight violently with each other whenever he attempted to move, leaving him entangled and grimacing in frustrated effort. Yet in the face of this he persisted in maintaining a basically cheerful nature, a trait that should put Earl to shame as he thought of how much time he spent time focusing on his own relatively trivial problems. Earl forcibly restrained himself from walking quickly out into the hallway and from there to his car. "Hi," he said. "Happy to meet you. What's your name?"

The creature in the wheelchair attempted to respond, legs twisting and arms flying. "aaaAAGH!" he said. Mary answered for him. "This is Buddy, Earl. Earl's your new friend, Buddy."

"aaaOOOH!" Buddy croaked, twisting yet further. An awkward silence followed.

"Buddy's excited to meet you," Mary offered. Buddy actually nodded his head. "Perhaps you might like to read to him," she suggested.

"Sure," Earl said, relieved to have something concrete to do. As he looked around for reading material his eyes settled on a tiny alcove where a few books rested. One was a Bible. Given his motivation for coming here, he immediately selected the Bible. "How would you like to hear a Bible story?" he asked. Again, Buddy managed to respond with a caricature of a nod.

Earl picked up the Bible and sat down on the bed next to Buddy's wheelchair. Mary smiled and left.

He was drawn to the Book of Proverbs, where he began reading from the first chapter. Soon he was immersed in the contents. He sensed that Buddy also was absorbing the words. Time passed quickly, and presently he found himself in Chapter 8, where the words seemed to jump out at him with special significance:

Doth not wisdom cry, and understanding put forth her voice? She standeth in the top of high places, by the way in the places of the paths. She crieth at the gates, at the entry of the city, at the coming in at the doors.

Unto you, O men, I call, and my voice is to the sons of man. O ye simple, understand wisdom; and ye fools, be ye of an understanding heart. Hear; for I will speak of excellent things, and the opening of my lips shall be right things. For my mouth shall speak truth, and wickedness is an abomination to my lips. All the words of my mouth are in righteousness; there is nothing froward or perverse in them. They are all plain to him that understandeth, and right to those who find knowledge. Receive my instruction, and not silver; and knowledge rather than choice gold. For wisdom is better than rubies; and all the things that may be desired are not to be compared to it.

I, wisdom, dwell with prudence, and find out knowledge of witty inventions.

Earl paused, frowning in concentration. *"I, wisdom..." Wisdom is personified, a person speaking. Could it be....?* He continued reading aloud:

The fear of the Lord is to hate evil; pride, and arrogance, and the evil way, and the froward mouth, do I hate. Counsel is mine, and sound wisdom. I am understanding; I have strength. By me kings reign, and princes decree justice. By me princes rule, and nobles, even all the judges of the earth. I love those who love me, and those who seek me early shall find me. Riches and honor are with me; yea, durable riches and righteousness. My fruit is better than gold, yea, than fine gold; and my revenues than choice silver. I lead in the way of righteousness, in the midst of the paths of judgment, that I may cause those who love me to inherit substance; and I will fill their treasures. The Lord possessed me in the beginning of his way...

Wait a minute. The hair rose on the back of Earl's neck. *This is Wisdom speaking, a person. A woman.* An ill-formed image of a beautiful woman at his bedside rushed into his mind. He recalled words about the functional executive role of the Holy Spirit and everything became instantly, beautifully clear. *If the Lord possessed her at the beginning, then she, Wisdom, is the Holy Spirit. The one at my bed.* He continued to read with mounting excitement:

...the Lord possessed me in the beginning of his way, before his works of old. I was set up from everlasting, from the beginning, or ever the earth was. When there were no depths, I was brought forth – when there were no fountains abounding with water. Before the mountains were settled,

before the hills, was I brought forth; while as yet he had not made the earth, nor the fields, nor the highest part of the dust of the world. When he prepared the heavens, I was there; when he set a compass upon the face of the depth; when he established the clouds above; when he strengthened the fountains of the deep; when he gave to the sea its decree, that the waters should not pass his commandment; when he appointed the foundations of the earth, Then I was by him, as one brought up with him; and I was daily his delight, rejoicing always before him, rejoicing in the habitable part of his earth; and my delight was with the sons of men.

Wow! Earl finished the chapter, his heart continuing to race.

Now, therefore, hearken unto me, O ye children, for blessed are they who keep my ways. Hear instruction, and be wise, and refuse it not. Blessed is the man who heareth me, watching daily at my gates, waiting at the posts of my doors. For whoso findeth me findeth life, and shall obtain favor of the Lord. But he that sinneth against me wrongeth his own soul; all they that hate me love death.

Earl closed the Bible with great reverence, awed by the enormity of what he had just learned. He looked down at his new friend Buddy, who nodded his head again. He gave Buddy a hug and told him that he would return soon. He stopped by Mary's desk briefly to say goodbye and that he'd come back within a week. She nodded and smiled. He left in a state of euphoria, having completely forgotten his situation at work.

CHAPTER 7

Earl looked out the window the next morning as he shaved. The pattern of high pressure over the area held steady, which meant that the prevailing wind would be from the north. There was a meadow within an hour's drive that was bordered on the south by a steep, tree-covered incline that was topped by a ridge almost a quarter of a mile high. It would be flyable today. With his glider on top of his car, Earl traveled to the popular site and forked off the highway onto a dirt road that went up the hill. He took the grade slowly, easing over potholes to prevent the bumps from stressing his glider. He crested the ridge, finding it crowded with pilots eager to jump off into the abundant lift. Several gliders had already launched off and were circling the area. He parked the car and walked over to the edge, picking a pathway through the stumps. He peered over the cliff, apprehensive from his cratering-in on his last launch, but was still excited with the anticipation of a good flight. The meadow was clearly visible below, appearing much smaller from this distance. He measured it with his eye and memory, satisfied that he could make a good landing.

His friend John approached as he hauled his glider off the car. "Looks primo, man," he called. "I'm ready to go. See you upstairs." Earl waved in acknowledgment. After checking the repairs, he set it up. Walking to the edge for a final look, he returned and hooked his harness onto the keel strap. Hefting the down tubes onto his shoulders, he trudged over to his imaginary path. He ran immediately, avoiding a prolonged review of everything that could go wrong. Once in the air, he allowed himself a measure of satisfaction that he had refused to let his mishap on the previous flight ground him. Shoving his harness prone and comfortable, he felt the joy of flight return.

The high-pressure system was beginning to disintegrate. The vestiges of the north winds which remained were sluggish and unpredictable. He would not be able to remain aloft above the ridge. He didn't care, for apprehension of the upcoming short-field landing was beginning to eat away at his comfort.

He came in high over the meadow, checking his drift against the pattern of field and trees. Turning for his landing run, he lined up against the direction of his drift and headed in toward the meadow. Over the grass now, he shoved his harness upright and hit the grass with his feet running. It was a perfect landing.

His satisfaction was empty. The brief respite from darkness was over.

That night she returned. "Had a better flight this time. I'm glad. Don't be so down, Earl. Time will heal you. Let the good things come in. And new friends. Buddy will bring you a whole lot of joy, more than you can imagine."

"I read some Proverbs."

"I know. Guess who had you do it."

"You call yourself Wisdom. Are you really the Holy Spirit?"

"Well, actually, I'm a little more extensive than what you see, being God and all, but the me that you see is a manifestation, so, yes, to you I am."

"I'm honored. But how do you find the time to visit me personally, me being just one among billions. I'd think we'd look like ants to you."

She laughed. "That's something that Alicia knows but you'll have to wait to find out. Let's just say that it's a God thing. I came to confirm what you suspected, Earl. I'll be running along now. See you soon."

When the day of reckoning arrived, he drove to work with

mounting apprehension. He could ill-afford to lose his job, but that outcome seemed very likely. He entered the building, managing to get to his cubicle without meeting anyone. When he sat down, the dreaded message was on his screen:

Earl, when you get into work, I'd like to see you in my office –
Walter

He walked toward Walter's office without a coffee cup. The occasion was too serious for that. When he entered the room, Mike was already seated. Walter looked up at him and brusquely motioned for him to sit.

Walter glared at him. "Earl, you and Mike really did it this time. You had a worker slip and fall, you know. What you didn't know is that she's already lawyered up and expecting to sit back and enjoy the rest of her life in Hawaii. Besides the extensive damage to the filling machine and the extra crew they had to put on for the cleanup. And the lost ice cream. And the lost revenue from the lost ice cream. What I'd like to do right now is fire you. Both of you, and apply your last paychecks to offset a tiny fraction of the cost your failure represented."

He sighed, ran a hand through his hair and continued. "But Mike's been sitting here trying to get back in my good graces." He scowled at Mike. "Which will never happen. Mike's been trying to say that our engineering staff is too small for such a project, especially with the short design time. He says that too much was put on your plate. You screwed up because you were overworked. Do you buy that? I don't either," he replied without giving Earl a chance to respond. "But firing you is too good for you. I'm going to keep you both around just to torment you. I'll say more about this later. Now get out and leave me alone."

Much later Earl learned more about what had happened after they had left the demo in disgrace. They had had a row with the plant manager in which insults were exchanged and accusations hurled. The manager had finally demanded that they see the video recording of the incident in order that he might have a solid footing on which to base legal action. They had reluctantly handed over the videotape and watched disconsolately as the drama played out. Then something strange had happened: as the filling machine had begun to break down on the film, the manager let out a chuckle, which quickly escalated into side-splitting laughter. When the video had run its course, the manager had actually become conciliatory, promising to withdraw all charges in exchange for the rights to the video. He thought that the tape might produce excellent footage for a tongue-in-cheek commercial, one that would really grab the attention of the TV audience. He talked about repeating the event with a Lucille Ball lookalike and even offered to share a percentage of the profits. The bottom line was that Mike and Earl were both in line to receive not only additional help, but there was also talk of promotions.

That information was yet in the future. For now, the two men were more than happy to have retained their jobs. Earl left the office for an early dinner, after which he planned to drop in on Buddy.

Before he got out the door he nodded to Patty, who was walking toward Walter's office with file folders in her hand. He did a double-take as he passed her, and called out to her to turn around. When she did, he realized that his initial impression was accurate. She was beginning to show. "Congratulations, Patty," he called out. "When's it due?"

"Oh," she said, "you know. Is it that apparent?" She seemed to have a glow about her. Her flighty attitude had all but disappeared.

"No, I just have good eyes."

"Six and a half more months. It's going to be a while yet."

"Well, congrats. See you tomorrow."

Buddy welcomed him with an enthusiastic greeting, twisting and gyrating in the process. Earl sat again on the bed and continued reading from the Book of Proverbs. As he read to Buddy he learned himself. Everything that he read confirmed the association of Wisdom with the Holy Spirit. By the time he put the Bible down he had read through the fourteenth chapter and felt that his understanding of God had taken an immense leap. It was becoming far more personal, too.

CHAPTER 8

Wisdom didn't show up again since his last encounter with Her. Earl continued to read to Buddy, finishing the Book of Proverbs. In the process they continued to bond. As his association with this terribly encumbered individual developed, Earl began to notice that his intelligence most likely surpassed his own, which just made the fact of his malady even worse: he represented a mind imprisoned in an almost nonfunctional body. That Sunday after Church he went back to the nursing home for some daytime companionship with Buddy. There was a trail nearby in a parklike setting. He wheeled Buddy along the trail, enjoying the outside air. They came to a dip in the trail, and Earl decided to have a little fun with his companion. He released the handles to the wheelchair and told Buddy to go for it. As the unmanned wheelchair began to pick up speed, Buddy flung his arms akimbo and tried to speak. Earl knew him well enough by now to appreciate that Buddy was trying to give him a thumbs-up sign. He ran after the wheelchair and once it was back under control he laughed with joy. Buddy joined in with a croak.

They returned after an hour, but in the meantime Buddy's go-for-it attitude had shoved a novel thought into his mind. *Boy, wouldn't it be great if he could go hang gliding?* But by the time he left, he had dismissed the thought as ridiculous.

Patty lasted three more weeks before the onset of morning sickness forced her to leave her job. Earl glanced at her replacement as he walked past, but her head was down, her eyes apparently focused on paperwork on her desk. All he could discern from the back of her head was that she wasn't Patty. Now that she was gone, he realized that he missed her fresh, vibrant outlook on life. *Oh, well,* he thought, *life goes on.*

A message from Walter was on his screen. It was a command to see him. When Earl came into Walter's office, he motioned him to sit down. He got right to the point. "This is a quickie side job. I need you to cobble together another high-speed Internet connection for the front desk, and I need it done today. We're all going to miss Patty, but Joyce, that's the new secretary, represents an upgrade. She's much more Internet-savvy." He dismissed him with a wave of his hand. "Get going and get it done."

By lunchtime Earl had finished the design of the retrofit, assembled the necessary equipment and tools and had lifted up the floor tiles in front of the now-vacant reception desk for access to the hidden cable system. He was on his knees with a bundle of wires in one hand when Joyce returned to her new desk.

Joyce looked past her desk at the figure kneeling over the bundle of wires. *Kind of a hunk,* she thought, and the thought surprised her, for the feeling was the first of its kind that she'd had since Sam died. As if he'd read her mind, the workman looked up and made eye contact.

Joyce blushed and glanced down at the papers on her desk. But the man's image remained in her mind. *His eyes! They're gorgeous. But they look so very sad.* Her heart melted for a moment, and the emotion annoyed her. She shifted her focus back to her work, but her attention periodically strayed.

Earl continued to check out the system. He had almost completed his continuity test of the wire harness when he heard a voice over his shoulder. He turned to see that the woman behind the desk was now standing above him with a cup in her hand.

"Would you like some coffee?"

"Oh. Sure, that would be fine. Thanks." He reached for the cup, noting the vivid green of her eyes. He shifted his eyes down at the cup in awkward silence, not knowing how to kick-start a conversation.

"Looks like an interesting job you have. You must get around a lot. I wouldn't mind getting away from a desk once in a while. Listen to me. Here I just started a new job and already I want to be out and about."

Earl smiled. "I don't get around much, actually. Not very often, anyway. I work here." He pointed down the aisle.

"Oh?" Her interest picked up. "What do you do? Oh . . ." She looked down at the wires in his hand. "I guess that's obvious."

"Yeh. I'm one of the grunts around here. I'm more into software, but I don't mind getting my hands dirty."

"And if it doesn't work right, you get the blame."

"Bingo," he said, breaking into a wide smile. "Only it has to work. If it doesn't, I work all night until it does."

"Harsh," she said. "Could get you into trouble at home."

"Not really. My TV doesn't talk back much."

"Oh. No ties except for the tube?"

"Not now. My wife passed a few months back." His eyes returned to his cup.

"Sorry. Were you married long?"

"Fifteen years. As I look back on it, I think of how much I could have said to tell her how much I loved her. We had some rocky times but mostly they were good. We liked each other."

His desolate look melted her heart. "I think that I had a good marriage with my husband, but we had our rocky times, too. Sometimes arguments are the only way to communicate."

"You *had* a husband? You're not married now?"

"No." Joyce stared sadly at the floor. "He was killed by a drunk driver. In the prime of his life. In the prime of *our* lives."

"I'm sorry," Earl said awkwardly.

"That's okay. At least I have some good memories... Well, I'd better get back to work," she said, turning back to her desk.

Earl completed his checkout by four thirty. He stood up with a grin of satisfaction and began to put his tools away.

"You look pretty smug," Joyce said behind her desk. "Did you get it working?"

"Looks like it."

"Congratulations!"

"Thanks - I, er, kind of feel like celebrating. Care to join me for dinner?"

Sensing her hesitation, he quickly amended the invitation. "That's okay. Maybe some other time."

"No, no. I was just thinking how I can pick up my car. It's in the shop. Walter was going to drive me over."

"I could take you to the shop myself. That is, if you don't mind riding in a rather tired set of wheels." Driving up logging roads to remote launches had taken a heavy toll on his car.

"Sure. It's a deal."

When the waiter handed Earl a wine list with the menu, he glanced at Joyce and gave it back.

"I know why you did that," she said after the waiter left.

"Did what?"

"The wine list. It was thoughtful of you, but it's okay. Wine isn't the problem. People who can't handle it are, such as the man who killed my husband. If someone knows he has a problem, and I can't see how if he got stiffed by several heavy fines and was at least threatened with some jail time he wouldn't know he had a problem, he has no excuse for driving to a bar with the intent of driving home again."

"A multiple offender, was he?"

"Yes. Given the strange skew in our justice system, he's probably driving again, even as we speak."

"That's very wrong."

"Sure is. Sam was a good man. We were happy together." She forced a smile. "Look, I've had my regrets. Let's forget about it tonight, shall we?" When the waiter came back, she pointedly ordered a glass of the house Chablis. Encouraged, Earl did the same.

They relaxed after dinner, neither wishing to get up from the table. The wine had loosened their tongues, permitting them to drift into easy conversation.

"How are you doing, making a life for yourself?" she asked him. "I quit my last job, but truth be told, I was on my way out anyway. Sam seems to keep coming back into my head at the wrong times. I'm trying to turn over a new leaf with this latest job. You know, focus more."

"Yeh. I've had the same problem." His latest gaffe with the glider came into his head. "Focus. That's what I said to myself the other day when I augered in. It can get dangerous."

"'Augered in'. What does that mean?"

"Oh, it's just a term used to describe an accident. You don't want to know about that. Let's just say that I can be pretty clumsy at times. Just don't ask me to dance."

"That's interesting. Sam was clumsy too. Oh, I didn't mean to insult you."

"That's okay. I'm kind of used to myself."

"At least you didn't burn up the building today. I'm glad. I need the job."

"Yeah, well..."

Joyce's eyes reflected her inward compassion. "Sam was the same way, Earl. His mind wasn't very practical. He was the creative type. I loved him very much, even when he was a jerk." Her mind drifted back to the past.

He caught the faraway look. "Like how?"

"Oh . . . there was a time when we went fishing in the Sound, out of Point Defiance. There were lots of boats around. Ours was just a little open fourteen-footer with a 9-horse outboard, but we'd had a lot of fun in it and caught some pretty big fish. On that particular day I had an epic fight with the daddy of them all. It wasn't a salmon, but something bigger. I remember the big salmon pole bending double and me yelling 'I got something! I got something! Sam offered to help, but I told him off good. This one was mine.

"I remember getting very tired. I must have played him for at least three quarters of an hour. Then, just as the monster fish was getting close to the boat, two things happened. First, the fish didn't like what it saw and broke the pole attempting to flee to the bottom of the Sound. The second thing that happened was that the fish didn't like what it saw and broke my pole attempting to flee. The pole broke off just below the reel, so I lost the leverage I was using to reel it in. I was really tired then, so I just let the tip of the pole go into the water and continued to reel. The exhausted fish finally gave up and reached the surface. I just wanted to lie down in the bottom of the boat, but the sight of the fish kept my adrenalin pumping. It was huge, but it wasn't a salmon, shark or sturgeon. It was a ray.

"Sam got into the act then. Taking hold of the line, he brought the limp fish up and, with pliers in one hand, was about to take out the hook. Something stopped him then, maybe it was me asking him if the fish was good to eat. I didn't know and neither did he. Another boat was nearby observing the drama in ours. Cupping his hands, he yelled out to the occupants, "Is this good to eat?" Their only response was visible, a half-shrug like they didn't know what Sam was trying to say. Cupping his hands again, he really shouted this time: "IS – THIS – FISH – GOOD – TO – EAT?" Still seeing no response of note, George clamped the pliers onto the hook, removed it from the ray's mouth, and bid the fish goodbye. As it slowly swam into the deep, flapping its huge wings, we noted the other boat approaching ours. Turning toward them, I heard one speak out for the first time: "Why did you let it go? It was good to eat." Disgusted, Sam headed for the controls to take the boat away from the area. As he did, I glared at him. I wasn't very happy right then. He knew what I was thinking, too: 'Why did you let it go? It was good to eat.' Apparently, as we found out later, if the meat in the wings is cut out with a cookie cutter and fried, it both looks and tastes like scallops. I didn't let him forget it for a month."

"Yeah, but that was maybe a mistake in judgment. I stumble and make other uncoordinated moves. Sometimes I can be pretty stupid. And get scratches and bruises."

This latest turn in the conversation brought a smile to her face. "Oh, poor Sam wasn't above that. One time we thought we might like to do some trailer camping. We started looking around the RV lots to see what was available." She snickered and it turned into a laugh. "Sam has a brother, Bill. He lives in Florida. He and his wife Paula were on vacation, visiting us at the time. They wanted to go with us, so the four of us went together to look around. We'd just be starting out, so whatever we'd be buying would be pretty small. We went to one local RV dealership that offered a tiny but elegant and cute tow-behind trailer. With a sweeping wave of his arm the sales agent bid us entrance to the interior. Bill and Paula were immediately interested in it. As the trailer was so small, Sam and I waited outside while the salesman followed them inside.

"Quite soon the door opened abruptly. The salesman jumped out and rushed away to the office. Peering inside, Sam and I saw Bill with his right hand raised up in the air. Attached to it were a thumb, three normal fingers and one bloody one, outsretched and rapidly expanding. "What happened?" we asked in unison. With his good hand, Bill pointed to a small fold-down table that was dangling on its hinges. Attached to the wall by two hinges, it was deployed by swinging a leg, also hinged to the table, to the vertical position. In folding it away and then attempting to restore it to the deployed position, Bill apparently had extended the leg to its vertical position without realizing that his finger was resting on the spot that the hinged end of the leg would occupy when the table was set up. In the process he squished his finger. The salesman had gone to get a bandage and maybe tell his buddies what an idiot he had for a potential customer.

"Paula, not fully understanding how her husband could be so stupid, looked at his finger, then at the table, and back to Bill. "How did you manage to do that?" she asked him. The question was sincere. That's when Sam got into the story. He decided to show her how he could do it and bent down to pull out the table. When the salesman returned, there they were, Sam and his brother Bill, right hands extended, both with bleeding index fingers. The salesman stared at them in disbelief." She laughed again at the memory. "'I only have one bandage,' he finally managed to say. Head down, Bill grabbed the bandage, which he wrapped around his injured finger. Head down, Sam went to the tiny bathroom and grabbed some toilet paper, which he wrapped around his injured finger. Then we all slunk away to our car. They didn't look, but us womenfolk following them did so with our heads down too."

She looked wistful for a moment, then brightened. "So...what do you like to do in your spare time?"

"Trust me on this, Joyce. You don't want to know."

Her brows shot upward in alarm.

"You're not doing something illegal, are you?"

Earl laughed. "No, no. Nothing like that."

She looked at him warily. "Or destructive..?"

"Not quite."

"I'd better tell you now, I'm a Christian. A committed one."

"That's good news to me. So am I. As a matter of fact, one of the things I've been doing lately to get my mind off Alicia has been to visit a handicapped individual in a nursing home. I read him the Bible. Buddy's his name. We're becoming friends."

Joyce was impressed. *He is a compassionate man. Just like Sam.* "I've been living with my mother since Sam died. In a way it's nice to be back home. We're close - she's wonderful company. And it's a beautiful place in the country with lots of trees and animals."

"I like getting out into the country, too." He hesitated. He wanted to spend more time with her, but was unsure whether he'd be rushing things if he'd ask her for a picnic date. "I . . ."

"Maybe . . . Oh, I'm sorry. I interrupted you. I was just thinking, maybe you'd like to take a drive out to the country sometime and see the area where we live."

He laughed. "I was just going to suggest that we go for a picnic in that area. I guess it's true – great minds think alike."

"A good plan. I like it."

"Now that that's settled, I'll let you get back home. I just want to say, Joyce, what a great time I've had with you tonight. It seems like it's been so long since I've relaxed and just talked."

"I know what you mean. I've had a good time too. I'll look forward to seeing you tomorrow."

At the office the next day, Mike started to make a play for Joyce. He didn't bother to take off his wedding ring when he hit on her, so that didn't last much longer than a microsecond or two. She quickly invited Earl to join her for coffee and they talked some more in the tiny lunchroom. They had lunch there too, which became a regular thing.

John called him up on a Thursday night. "How about going to Chelan this weekend?" he asked.

Earl's spirits, which had been high all week, were up for the event. "That'd be great," he responded with enthusiasm. "Want to pick me up Saturday morning?"

"Aw, no. By the time we got there the lift would be gone. That would only give us Sunday to sky out. How about tomorrow night? We can sleep on top."

"Sure, I guess." He was hoping to take Joyce out on a date tomorrow night. But the relationship was starting to feel secure, so it wouldn't matter so much if he delayed for a week. "Of course," he added more definitely. "Are you coming over here?"

"Well, uh, I was hoping that you'd pick me up." Earl laughed to himself. Of course he wanted to be picked up. He'd bought a new car recently. He just didn't want to trash it driving on a fire trail. But he wanted John to admit that he wanted to use Earl's car.

"Why?"

There was a long silence. "Aw gee, Earl, you know," he finally admitted.

He laughed again, this time openly. "Okay, John, see you tomorrow after work. We'll pick up a burger somewhere on the road."

He saw Joyce enter the parking lot the next morning and waited for her to park. "Hi," he said as she walked up to him.

"Hi yourself. What's that thing on your roof?"

"I'm going to Lake Chelan tonight for the weekend. I was hoping to ask you out tonight, but something came up. Would you mind a raincheck for next Friday?"

"No, of course not." They were inside and had gone their separate ways before she realized that he hadn't answered her question.

CHAPTER 9

As Earl drove over to John's place after work, he looked dismally at the haze from his exhaust in the rear-view mirror. He was amazed that his car still ran, albeit reluctantly. Beginning a month ago, the engine had refused to start. It had first happened in the parking lot after work. The battery was going senile so he had supposed that was the problem. He had flagged down Fred as he was leaving the lot, cadging the use of his battery and jumper cable. Despite the jumper cables, Fred's battery was unable to get the engine started. In desperation, Earl had Fred run him over to a convenience store, where he purchased the solution to the problem in the form of a can of starting fluid. Like a shot in the rear, the ether did the job by exploding the engine into motion. Now he considered the ether to be an integral part of the car. The ritual of raising the hood, looking around to see that nobody at work was watching, and squirting it in was now as natural as turning the switch. He tended to overdo it on the ether. The rusting floorboards compounded the problem by furnishing a direct path of air from the engine compartment to the inside of the car. The ether made his engine start. It didn't work that way with him. Now his morning habits included the infusion of massive doses of coffee to counteract its debilitating effect on his system.

John was waiting for him when Earl pulled up to his house. "You're looking peaked," he said to Earl as he got out of his car.

"Big day at work. I'll be okay. Got any coffee?"

"Sure. I brought a Thermos along. Want some?" Earl nodded and he brought out the Thermos, pouring hot coffee into styrofoam cups. Then the two quickly tied his glider onto the sagging roof next to Earl's.

"How's Joyce?" John asked when they drove off. He rolled his eyes in a grinning leer.

"Let's change the subject," Earl replied. He didn't want his enthusiastic young friend to cheapen a relationship that was growing into a solid mutual affection. Something else about John's attitude entered his head. It was a new thought, and troubling.

But John had seen the change that had come over Earl's countenance and played it out in fun. "Let's not," he said. "It's too good. "Has she been cooking for you? Doing your laundry?" He got to the heart of the matter. "Sleeping in?"

He turned his head to catch his friend's eye. "I thought you were a Christian, John. If you'll remember, it was you who was pushing me into a deeper relationship with Jesus."

"Oh, wow. You're turning into an old fuddy-duddy. Hey, man, I'm happy for you, okay? And don't start telling me about God. Look around you. The world has changed since granny's days. Now it's the girls who are thinking twice about committing themselves to lifelong relationships."

"Maybe so. But you know as well as I do that the Word is timeless." Glancing over, he saw John's face beginning to register real anger. Conciliation was in order. "We're taking it slow, so it'll mean something. John, I really like her. I think I might even want to marry again."

His features relaxed. "I'm glad for you. As a matter of fact, I think that someone's going to be waiting for me over there." His brows clustered into a frown of sudden concern. "Is this car going to make it all the way to Chelan?'"

"We could have taken yours."

"Yeah, well. . ." John shifted uncomfortably on the seat. They both knew why John preferred to ride in Earl's. His car was almost new. Its shiny polished roof had not been sullied yet with the burden of dirty gliders and the abrasion of fabric and aluminum. If he could manage it, it never would.

Four hours and a food stop later the car labored up the steep dirt firebreak to the summit. It was already dark, and they unrolled their sleeping bags by the rapidly dimming headlights. In the morning after oversleeping they ate doughnuts from a bag they'd picked up on the way in. Others had arrived and were setting up at the launch. Others were already airborne.

Earl's attention was focused elsewhere. He saw a single glider on the top of the bluff, the figure beside it pushing in a final batten. *It's Ray.*

"Well, let's hurry and set ourselves up," Earl said. They helped each other unpack their gliders and busied themselves with the assembly.

Ray left his glider and walked over to Earl. "Wire me off, will you?" he asked. Earl nodded his assent and walked with Ray over to his glider.

"Wind here gets dicey at times," Ray said. "Maybe you'd better sit it out until it gets calmer."

"It's been a while since my accident, Ray," Earl replied with a frown. "A lot of time to gain experience."

"Yeah, well, hitting a cow isn't an experience kind of thing." He chuckled to himself. "And me without a camcorder." He laughed.

Earl started to protest but let it pass. Ray wanted to believe what he wanted to believe, and there was nothing he could do to change it. "Do you want me to help you or not?" he asked. "If you're as good as you say you are, maybe you don't need my help."

"Okay, okay," Ray said.

Earl helped him off, observing the initial leg of his flight as he walked back toward John and his own glider. Ray made an inexpert attempt to stay in the thermal and, running out of rising air, flew downward out of sight around a corner of the bluff.

"Looks like Ray's going to have a wimpy sled ride," John said as Earl approached him.

"Yeah. Might not make the landing field. Serves him right."

The location of launch sites, in general, is dictated by the prevailing winds. Unlike many of the sites in the western part of the state, most of the launch runs on this butte were not true cliffs, making the wind direction an even more important factor. While the slopes were steep enough to allow a pilot to attain flight in still air, running into the upslope gust of an initial thermal gave him a better chance to gain sufficient altitude to catch another series of in-flight thermals and sky out. Earl and John, having set up their gliders and wishing for serious altitude, waited for the next thermal of opportunity.

Earl stood below his companion's glider, facing him as he held the flying wires. When he felt the breeze freshen against his back he saw John's eyes bulge in anticipation and released the wires, freeing the glider to rise into the thermal. It was a weak one and John hovered momentarily, attempting to gain altitude before he tried to turn back into it. Earl went back to his own glider and hooked in, waiting for another thermal. Straining his eyes, he saw one birth far downslope, shaking the trees in the distance. It moved upslope, its motion evident in the rising pattern of windblown branches.

He ran, gripping his down tubes, and felt the gust lift him off his feet. A wing came down sharply and he strained to correct. The ground receded below and he thrust his body forward into the prone position, shifting his hands to the base tube. Above the peak now, he levered himself into a bank, maintaining a turn to stay in the thermal.

The lake came into view, long and narrow. Two boats raced westward, their almost invisible hulls trailing large wakes that sparkled in the sunlight. The town nestled peacefully between the hillsides and the lake. He caught a glimpse of Ray below him and close to the hill. Ray had managed to catch a thermal, but it was a weak one. It would keep him up for a while, maybe buy him enough time to find another one. But at his rate he wouldn't get much farther than the park before he'd have to land. To the east, the barren land spread out in rolling hills, the gentle scene sharply broken in places by local badlands. Earl headed in that direction, following a cloud street to another thermal. He reached inside his harness and turned on his iPod. As Emmylou sang a sweet ballad, he passed over the Columbia River, tracing its winding path through the starkly-defined channel of opposing hills. The banks were lined in places with the lush green of apple orchards.

Despite the soul-satisfying harmony of the scene below, Earl willed himself away from the apples. The worst thing that could happen to a pilot in these parts, aside from losing his wings in flight, was to land in an orchard and run the risk of encountering a wrathful owner. Verbal abuse of incredible vehemence follows such contact; fallen branches are wept over like dead soldiers; shotguns are pointed and fired; lawsuits are hurled; hatred abounds.

Earl maintained his altitude as he traveled eastward, relieved to see the apple trees fade off to his rear. Scanning the sky about him, he saw a glider off to the left and below. It may have been John, but it was too far away to discern the pattern of colors. Three more gliders circled under a cloud in the distance ahead. They were higher than Earl, mere specks. He squirmed about comfortably in his harness and relaxed, empty of thought except for the existential joy of flight.

A sharp bump jolted him, lifting his right wing. He turned into it and felt the elevator tug of a rapid climb. The pattern beneath became less sharply defined as it spread out to encompass a greater area. He entered the altitude domain of powered aircraft. Scanning the sky for potential hazards, he saw nothing but peacefully drifting clouds gently casting shadows across the rolling brown earth. Far below he saw a tiny black dot moving slowly against a background of tan. Nearby was a rectangle that indicated a building. Eventually the dot ceased to move and Earl knew that the glider had landed. He recorded the site in his memory and went back to his lazy scan of the sky.

He couldn't find another thermal. Within fifteen minutes the ground below was visibly closer. He didn't mind. His bladder was beginning to make its presence felt. He turned back to a westerly heading, searching for the spot where the other glider had landed. He found it and headed in that direction as he continued to lose altitude. He had not yet reached it when he saw the dust trail of a vehicle on the dirt access road. It was heading in the direction of the farmhouse near the parked glider, which was in the process of being disassembled. The pilot must have called one of the waiting drivers.

He circled the field in a gentle turn, losing altitude as he observed the pattern of his motion against the ground to discern the direction of the prevailing wind. He set up his approach and pushed himself upright. Grasping the down tubes, he saw the earth rush up to meet him and broke into a run as his feet contacted the ground. *The landing was a good one*, he realized with relief as the down tubes pressed against his shoulders. *And not a snake in sight.*

The car, with the other glider on top, moved toward him. He quickly shed his harness and, turning his back to the car, watered the sparsely-grassed soil.

"Hey, Earl!" a voice shouted from the car. "I was watching, you, man. You specked out." It was John, who got out of the car and trotted toward him. "I missed the last thermal, but I had a good flight anyway."

"Yeah, we both did," Earl replied. He looked toward the car. "That's Betty," he observed.

"Sure is," John grinned. "She pulled the driver duty today." Betty was soft on John. She grinned from her seat and waved at Earl, but quickly returned her eyes to the object of her affection.

"Hey, look, man," John said under his breath. "I know that you drove me out here and all, but I think I'll stay in town tonight."

"Go for it," Earl laughed. "Give me a hand with this, will you?"

"Hi, Betty," Earl said as they lifted his glider onto the top of the car. "Thanks for picking us up."

"No problem. This heat's getting to me. How about a nice cool wine cooler when we get back?"

"Sounds good to me." Earl looked over at Frank, who shrugged his shoulders. He would rather have jumped between a set of nice cool sheets with Betty without the cocktail foreplay, but accepted the *fait accompli* with an equable grin.

"Hot day," Betty commented again, fanning her face with one hand as she drove with the other.

"Makes a good change for me," Earl returned. "I haven't dried out yet." This summer was a wet one west of the Cascades, with a nearly constant pattern of rain-bearing clouds coming off the Pacific. The dry warmth felt good to him, especially after the colder air of his high-altitude flight.

Her hand came down to rest on John's thigh. "How're you doing, baby?"

"Just great. They told me you were coming out here today. Why didn't you call me yesterday?"

"Oh, I thought I'd give you a little surprise." She frowned, thinking. "As a matter of fact, I was kind of hoping you might call me."

John placed his hand over hers. "Maybe I wanted you to surprise me."

"Do I have to listen to this?" Earl cut in. "Can't you make with the goo-goo in privacy?"

Betty laughed. "Sure, Earl," she said with a light-hearted smile of anticipation

In the town of Chelan they stopped for lunch. It was anything but leisurely. John and Betty had another agenda, one that didn't include him. "Hey, look," Earl said to them both. I know you have other plans. Why don't you drive me back up to the top and go do your own thing? I'll be fine on my own."

They enthusiastically agreed, and less than an hour later Earl was back on top. His companions barreled back down the road, leaving him with a trail of thick dust. He was alone, but for the first time since whenever, he realized that he wasn't lonely. He'd brought a book along and was about to get it out to read, but the surroundings were so starkly beautiful that he sat on a rock looking downslope.

He remained there for a long time, grateful to God that the almost unrelenting emotional turmoil of his terrible loss had begun to ease, helped along by the hope of a new relationship. Now he was grateful for the day and the flight he'd just experienced. A light wind ruffled his shirt and with it Buddy pushed his way into his mind. *Might it actually be possible to share this experience with him?* He turned it into a prayer.

As the day wore on, he reasoned how it might be done. *Certainly not by me,* he reasoned, knowing that there were many pilots around who where not only younger and in better shape, but far more experienced. He resolved to ask them, beginning with John.

The daylight softened as evening approached. On a whim, Earl set up his glider and launched into a spectacular sunset of yellow, red and purple. The air was calm and he shivered in delight as he pointed his right wing at the receding launch site and turned to look down at the ground and the lake far below. He turned Emmylou back on and basked in a feeling of sheer joy. Presently he was above the bridge over the lake, which sparkled with lights along with the homes and businesses that lined the shore. His flying companions had remained below, and off in the distance he could see the glow of their fire at the junkyard landing. It was night now, and he lined up on the fire as a guide, executing a perfect landing. After sharing a beer, he hitched a ride back to the top with a bunch who wanted to be on top for tomorrow's flight.

The air became troubled during the early hours of the morning. Several of his companions awoke, dressed, and cast doubtful looks at the sky to the west. *Red sky at morning, sailor take warning,* Earl thought. A car was coming up the fire trail too rapidly for the condition of the road. He could see it slew on the curves and when it got closer he could see that it was Betty's car. John's glider was resting on the top.

When they arrived on top, John hurriedly undid the bungees and yanked his glider to the ground, where he immediately proceeded to start setting it up. The others crowded around, looking at him in disbelief. Their own gliders remained in their bags, as did Earl's. Betty looked down toward the vicious storm front advancing up the mountain. When she looked back at John's enthusiastic motions she began to cry. "What do you think you're doing, John?" she wailed. "Don't I mean anything to you? Was last night *nothing?*" Someone snickered in the background, but she was beyond caring about what others thought. John looked up at her, arose, and put his arms around her. "Nothing's going to happen, honey," he entreated. "I've been in a lot worse before." He kissed her and went back to his setup work.

The front's progress was all too evident by the way the trees were being knocked horizontal as it advanced, the shaking impressive to the onlookers even from their great distance away. The disassembled gliders were safely tucked away in their bags, all except John's, which now was ready to fly.

He inspected it carefully to make sure it was set up properly and asked Earl to wire him off. There they stood, him gripping the downtubes and staring irrationally at the advancing front, and Earl below him with his back to the commotion holding his flying wires. Earl knew from the size of his eyeballs the precise moment that the front was going to slam into his back, and released his hold on the wires just as John shouted "leggo!", whereupon he instantly rose a hundred feet up.

His subsequent flight pattern is most accurately described using a term that physics students acquire in high school. There students learn about Brownian Motion, discovering that air is not motionless, but at the molecular level is constantly subjected to collisions and bombardments from neighboring molecules. Each molecule of air, being subjected to this duress, executes a zigzag flight path, traveling from one impact to the next. The intrepid flyer that Earl wired off Chelan Butte made a perfect macro-level execution of Brownian Motion, zigzagging his way vertically, horizontally, and at all attitudes in-between, downslope to an eventual impact against the side of the mountain. Earl and two others crammed into Betty's car and hurried down the fire trail until they could get close enough to see whether he survived. They could tell that his craft didn't make it, because it lacked the symmetry with which it left the shop. But he not only did survive, he was laughing (despite his torn pants and

the bleeding gash on his forearm) and exclaiming "What a ride!"
over and over again. Betty flew out of the car, screaming insults,
and railed at him with her fists, adding slightly to the impacts he'd
received at the end of his strange journey. Rain drenched them both
as she relented and hugged him. Earl perceived that now wasn't the
time to approach John about taking Buddy flying. Not with Betty
there.

CHAPTER 10

Earl put the phone down, disconsolate. He'd called John with the proposition of taking Buddy flying, but, to his surprise, John gave him a flat refusal. "No way, man. That's your gig. I'll help you, but you gotta do it yourself."

"Think about it," Earl pleaded. "Nobody else has your guts. I don't. And I'm not young either. Besides, I don't have that much experience."

"Stop your whining. You've got enough guts. And you're not that old. As for experience, you have about as much as me. You'll do fine."

John remained adamant. Earl gave up on him and called a few others with more experience but they turned him down too. Earl suspected that they felt affronted that someone would want to take a cripple off the big hill. Earl headed off to work, the problem unresolved.

Joyce confronted him at lunch. "I know what that was on the top of your car on Friday," she said crossly. "Walter told me. Why didn't you just tell me that you like to fly?"

"Aw, gee," Earl responded. I'm a little long in the tooth for that kind of thing. I didn't want you to think I'm acting like a kid. At least 'til we got to know each other better."

"What, you think I'm a wimp? Being a woman, I don't like

adventure? Let me set you straight. We used to take our little boat out in some pretty rough weather, stuff that makes big men want to cry. I handled it darned well. Frankly, though, you are a bit old for tooling around in the sky in a hang glider. You must really love it."

"I am old for it. And sometimes it shows. I'm also basically a clumsy person, which doesn't help. But I manage anyway. I think if someone wants to do something badly enough, he acquires a measure of grace in that endeavor which he might otherwise lack."

"You must really love to fly. But I didn't see you as a self-destructive thrill-seeker."

"It does have its rush moments. There are some thrills. But much of the time it's, well, serene. There are times when the experience is astonishingly beautiful. I just had one this last Saturday when I flew into a beautiful sunset. If you'd been with me, it would have been incredible." Wisely, Earl neglected to mention John's more violent flight.

Her face softened in acknowledgment of the compliment. "And hang gliding can be peaceful? Can you stay up that long?"

"Yes. Even for hours when the conditions are right. Hang flight is controlled by weight shift, fore and aft, and side to side. It's incredibly natural, like people are born for it. I'm lying prone in my harness like I'm on a cloud and I can see everything below. My wings are a part of me and when I will it I'm turning. I'm connected. When I see my wingtip framing a scene below me I'm experiencing what I once dreamed about. Especially at dusk. I look past the high wing to a purple sunset and my joy's as pure as a person can have. I see it as a privilege, Joyce. There's more to life than just existing, that goes beyond the mere person. There's a nobility to the human spirit, a quality that reaches out for more than the routine of survival. It's rare, but when it occurs, we are all enriched because it becomes part of our collective experience."

"What does nobility have to do with hang gliding?"

"Maybe that's not the right word for it. But it's close to the same reason why some people put themselves out to spread the Gospel or to oppose corruption when almost everyone else is indifferent to the many ways to make life richer. It's a chance to participate in a larger world, to go beyond lying on a couch, sucking a beer and watching the game on TV. Some have managed to stay aloft for hours, reaching altitudes where supplemental oxygen is a necessity. They've traveled over a hundred miles without having to land, with nothing to keep them up but their basic senses. And their—no pun intended—high spirits."

"What do you do, hum while you fly?" She face began to register warmth, and the corners of her mouth were twitching upward in mirth.

"No, but I do listen to music. Sometimes when I think I can stay aloft long enough, I take my iPod up with me."

"It seems to me that Wagner might be appropriate." Her grin erupted into laughter.

He chuckled. "As a matter of fact, there *is* a guy who plays "Flight of the Valkyrie" when he goes night flying."

"Night flying?"

"Sure. It's awesome. If there's a moon out you can see the silhouettes from the ground. They look like giant bats. In the air it's almost totally dark. The trick is to wait until a car comes down the road. The headlights show the direction of the edge of the field. There's another trick to it, and that's to keep in your mind the position of the car after it's gone by. Then all you have to do is drag a foot when you think you're close to the ground, and start running when the foot touches something solid." Again, he failed to mention that Saturday's flight involved a night landing. Another wise move.

Maybe it's a guy thing."

"It may have been once. But there are women into it too. Some of them are among the best pilots, and they could just as well be fashion models. They do seem to have a common problem, though." He smiled. "Having initiated themselves into the experience of true flying, they tend to think of themselves as above the rest of the world."

"Enough of that. We women are already above the rest of the

world. You men are just too stupid to understand that."

"*Touche.*" They both laughed.

"Getting serious, aren't there a lot of accidents?"

"Not as many nowadays. At the beginning of their popularity, when many hang gliders were home-built before there were good manufacturers and there were no real standards of construction, there were a number of in-flight failures, yes."

"In-flight failure. That's intriguing. What does that imply?" She asked with a grin.

Earl laughed. "You've got me there. Then gravity rules. The hapless pilot augers in, probably saying 'no no no' all the way down."

"Have you ever seen an accident?" she asked, searching his eyes for signs of untruth.

"Well, of course. But most of them. . ."

"'Of course', you say. Boy, that's loaded with meaning."

". . .weren't serious. A scrape on the knee, a sprained ankle, things like that. Mine was just. . ."

"You? You had an accident?"

"It wasn't much, Joyce. I just did something I knew I shouldn't. I'll know better next time."

She looked skeptical. "Whatever. Maybe I'll come watch you some time."

"Might run the risk of getting hooked yourself."

"Maybe. . .or maybe not." She looked at her watch. "Back to work. See you around." She smiled and squeezed his hand.

"Did you say *hang gliding*? After telling me that he's as clumsy as Sam?" Her mother looked incredulous. "I'm happy that your interest in men is picking up, Joyce, but give yourself a chance. I just can't believe that with all the eligible men in the world, you'd show interest in such poor husband material. Don't waste your time."

"When Sam died, I didn't think I'd ever have a second chance to love someone like him. He was klutzy too. I saw some things in Earl that reminded me of him."

"Sure. Sam wasn't perfect. He had faults just like anyone else. Your problem is, you're fixating on faults like they were the defining qualities. Sounds to me like you're setting yourself up for a relationship with Sam's faults."

"You're sure being judgmental for someone who hasn't even met the man."

"Well, look who's talking. You're giving him all this praise, and you've just met him yourself."

Janet's offhanded rejection of Earl ate at Joyce's emotions during the morning. She chastised herself for telling her mother about him. *How was I to know that she'd focus on the negative?* She thought uncomfortably. *Maybe under the right circumstances mom could see some positive in him. What about Buddy?*

The next day at lunch Earl took the lead. "It's my turn to conduct the inquisition. Tell me more about yourself."

"There's not much to say, really. I like to ice-skate and read. I'd travel more If I could afford the time and money. I love the water. I could lay on a beach all day."

"Me too. I used to dive before I took up the flying. And I was a beach lizard in Mexico once."

"Three years ago I took a trip to Antigua on a two-week vacation. I never forgot it. That's my dream, to go back there, like yours with flying."

"I can appreciate that."

"When my life gets difficult I think of that beautiful white sand against the turquoise water. Walking into the surf like it was a waiting bath, feeling the warmth on my skin. Snorkeling among the beautiful colorful fish. I want to learn to SCUBA dive."

"If you did that I'd go back to it. Maybe some day..."

"Maybe." Her face brightened into a smile. "Maybe some time soon I can meet Buddy."

On Saturday Earl drove alone up to the big training hill. This time after he set up his glider and double-checked the rigging, he strapped on a backpack and then launched off. Inside the pack was twenty pounds of old SCUBA weights, representing his first attempt toward getting up to speed in carrying Buddy. He flew off a second time in the afternoon, having upped the weight to thirty pounds.

Having remained physically intact through the experiment, Earl took a quick shower at home and went to pick up Joyce at her mother's house. Janet met him at the door, extending her hand. "Hello, Earl," she started. "Joyce will be ready in a minute. Why don't you come in and sit down?" Her voice was pleasant, but he sensed a negative undertone. Apprehensive, he picked that very instant to stumble on the landing, falling into Janet's arms. When Joyce arrived at the door she was astonished to see her mother and Earl on the floor, Earl on top. "Not a good start, Earl," she managed, picking her mother up.

The episode turned out to be a good icebreaker. Janet gloated over having her pre-meeting assessment vindicated. It took a full five minutes to calm her hysterical laughter. When she settled down she told Earl that his flight with her was a bit premature. Her stomach continued to jiggle periodically as they all sat down in the living room attempting to make sense out his clumsy entrance. Janet had a great sense of humor. Unfortunately for Earl, it came out that evening at his expense. After they all settled down with glasses of wine, they decided to remain at the house and get to know each other better. Janet improvised, expanding on the dinner she was beginning to prepare for herself, and they ate by candlelight.

"Tell me, Earl," Janet said, a smile forming on her mouth. You probably like thrills of any flavor. Are you planning on taking Joyce to the fair this year? Maybe try the Slingshot? If you do, I want the video." She looked at Joyce and laughed, knowing that the only way she would take the ride would be if she was unconscious. Earl needed to know her limitations.

"I have ridden on roller coasters, but I don't like them," Earl answered shortly. "There are at least two reasons why. The first is that on a roller coaster I'm a passenger. Being a passenger doesn't agree with my stomach. The second reason is more urgent than the first: roller coasters are sinister. I say that because I know. I've seen things."

"That sounds kind of dark," Janet said, hoping that it was, and that it involved a good story. She wasn't disappointed.

"Once, against my better judgment," Earl volunteered, "I joined a 'public service' mens' group, a branch of one of those well-known national organizations. If there was anything that just wasn't 'me', that was it."

"Oh, I don't know," Joyce spoke up in his behalf. "You have a compassionate heart, and those groups seem to do a lot of good."

"Maybe some of them do, but this didn't. From the head man on down, it was all about power, control and manipulation. But the new president was by far the worst. He was just about the most arrogant, obnoxious windbags I'd ever had the misfortune of being acquainted with. As a matter of fact, I almost immediately quit after his election. But the club was in the midst of its semi-annual fundraiser and my conscience forced me to stick around long enough to help out with the event.

Janet was confused. What's he got to do with sinister rides?"

"Believe me, I'm getting there. The fundraising event happened to a fair, the kind of thing that's held in the parking lot of a mall. One of the biggest attractions was a 50-foot Ferris Wheel. This guy, the president, came to the event wearing one of his typical flashy suits. It was so garish it was radioactive. Plaid vest and da-glo yellow pants, I remember it well. A boardwalk huckster would have turned his nose up at the sight."

They both laughed and looked at him expectantly, sensing that they would be well-entertained by what would come next.

"Anyway, one of the members asked him, as the senior official present, to make the symbolic first ride on the wheel. The president accepted the offer as his due. Had he been a bit more astute, he might have noticed that the guy who made the offer had a big grin on his face.

"That's when the fun began. He climbed in at the bottom, a fat cigar dangling out of his mouth, and, with a flourish, allowed himself to be strapped in. I guess that I wasn't the only individual who harbored ill feelings toward him, because another of our members, behind his back of course, slipped a twenty onto the palm of the ride operator with the instruction that our president was to be the only passenger. He put another twenty on top of that with the additional instruction, accompanied with a knowing wink, to "give him a good ride".

The girls began to snicker as he continued. "There were four major components to the system: the passenger, the operator, the wheel, and the engine. The operator was dressed somewhat less formally than the passenger. He was wearing dirty old Levis that didn't completely cover his butt. His face hadn't been shaved for several days and his shifty eyes were red, probably from too much Muscatel the night before. Like the passenger, the operator was smoking, but the contents originated in Colombia rather than Cuba. He didn't even smile when he received the forty. He simply gave a one-eyed Jack Elam trademark acknowledgement and fired up the machine.

"The wheel looked like any parking-lot Ferris Wheel, tall and spindly. It looked as if it needed to be handled with care. The engine was the only bulky component of the entire setup. It was a six cylinder Diesel, probably a Cummins – the kind that goes snorting around in Dodge Rams. The operator yanked open the throttle and it shouted out an angry bellow as a jet of hot gas blew out the exhaust stack. It shook when he popped the clutch. The acceleration was impressive, whisking the passenger up into the wild blue as if he was riding a catapult. We could see his face every time that he'd come back around, and with every cycle it underwent an astonishing transformation. The first time around he still had the cigar in his mouth, but his eyes were registering surprise. He lost the cigar near the top of the next cycle, and when he came back around the surprise had turned into horror. The wailing began after that, and remained for the next several passes. We could tell where he was by the Doppler shift of his screams. That's when I noticed that the legs of the wheel were shaking so bad that they were beginning to walk along the asphalt."

By this time the girls were shaking too. Joyce had to put her wine glass down before she'd spill it all over the carpet.

"At that point some of us began to feel that enough was enough, but the guy with the twenties signaled to wait just a little bit more. The operator didn't respond either way. I think he was ogling some girl in the parking lot while mellowing out on his toke. Soon after that the screams ended and the head was lolling as it passed by. We signaled our demand to stop it before the whole thing came crashing down and someone nudged the operator. He gave a surprised jolt as if the nudge woke him up and reluctantly wound down the speed. The passenger remained quiescent in his seat, his yellow pants now fouled with purple puke. Eventually he collected himself, exited the machine with as much dignity as he could muster, and staggered home. After witnessing that scene I rode an arcade attraction just once more in my life, and I did so very reluctantly and only because it was for an extraordinary cause."

Janet commented after their laughter died off. "That was good, Earl," she said. "I get the feeling that you won't be trying to take my Joyce on the slingshot. I'm glad about that. So you actually think that your glider is safer than a ride at the fair?"

"Not necessarily. But on the glider at least I'm in control. And I have to admit that this ride thing is kind of a phobia. There's not much logic behind it."

"That's perfectly fine with me," Joyce said. "I can do without the rides too."

At the end of a companionable evening Earl asked Joyce if she'd care to join him at Church in the morning. She agreed with enthusiasm. Even Janet nodded her approval.

His time with Buddy settled into a routine, which pleased Mary immensely. Her concern that he might leave Buddy hanging after a companionship had formed started to ebb away. As he read the Gospels to him, his Christianity became deeper yet.

Earl's deepening relationship with God carried over to his growing relationship with Joyce. They began attending Church together on a regular basis, this pattern being interrupted only by Earl's occasional forays to popular flying sites. Soon she became insistent upon meeting Buddy. "Sure," he responded to her latest request. "But there are things there that aren't pretty. Smells. Sights. Even sounds. It can be a turnoff to someone who isn't prepared."

"It has to happen sometime, Earl. Buddy's getting to be a big part of your life. Let's just do it and get it over with."

"Okay, then." Earl drove them directly from Church to the nursing home. She wrinkled her nose a bit when she entered, but weathered the experience remarkably well, looking about her with interest as they headed for Buddy's room. Earl was very proud of her. And when she met Buddy, her smile was warm and friendly. She talked to him of little things, but he listened to her with rapt attention, as if his life depended on her words.

Then Joyce did something quite extraordinary. She wheeled Buddy out of his room and down the hall into the large common room, where a piano stood unused in a corner. Parking Buddy next to her, she sat down at the piano and began to play Gospel songs, singing along softly but very beautifully. Soon other children began to show up and they, too, listened intently to her music. As she finished each song her audience croaked and moaned, demanding more. The commotion brought Mary into the room. After she was introduced to Joyce she urged her to continue and joined into the singing. They sang together for an hour, after which an exhausted Joyce begged off, promising to return the next Sunday.

For several weeks after that the pattern remained the same: Bible reading with Buddy Wednesday evenings, practice launches with increasing weights on Saturdays, followed by Saturday evenings with Joyce, Sundays at Church and then piano recitals by Joyce and Mary at the nursing home. During that time Earl had Buddy weighed at 94 pounds, and Earl had flown with up to sixty pounds. But on the last flight with the weights Earl thought he could sense the flying wires being overstressed. Since he had not heard of anyone else having attempted to fly tandem with two people, he decided that he'd gone as far as he could. *Good try,* he managed to convince himself. *But not in the cards.* He was glad that he hadn't mentioned the attempt to Joyce.

He began to fly more frequently with others, particularly with John. When he told his friend that he'd given up on the idea, John simply shrugged.

His life was full. So full, in fact, that he was beginning to truly recover from his loss of Alicia. And to forget about Wisdom. But She didn't forget about him.

CHAPTER 11

Two more months passed during which Wisdom did not appear as She had earlier, at the foot of Earl's bed. But one morning Earl awoke to a strange peace and the certain knowledge that on that day he would take Buddy up to the big hill and they would jump off together. He had no idea how that might be done, but he was sure that it would, despite the fact that he had never flown in a glider with another person, even as a passenger, and had no idea what to expect. As a Christian Earl understood this knowledge and especially the peace regarding it to be a gift from the Holy Spirit.

The first thing Earl did after getting dressed was to call John, asking him to come with him and help to figure out how they were going to get Buddy into the air. Then he went to the nursing home, told the staff what he intended to do, and picked up Buddy. They met up with John on the big hill, where he was already attempting to figure out how the launch was going to take place. He had a rope slung over his shoulder when Earl arrived with Buddy and was eyeing a big stump. He wrapped the end of the rope around the stump as Earl came up to him, and walked over to the edge. "I think this is gonna work," he said as he wrapped the other end around his waist, cinching it tightly. "Go ahead and set up," he continued as he tested it. He had just enough slack to get him over the edge at a 45 degree angle.

John was strong as well as brave and compassionate, being

exactly the person Earl needed for help. As Earl walked the glider to where he'd run off the edge, John cradled Buddy in his harness. They hooked him into the keel, along with Earl, while he continued to hold Buddy in his arms. When Earl signaled his intent to go, John ran with him to the edge and, just as he felt the tug of the rope around his waist, flung him away in front of the glider.

Earl felt a twist of Buddy's harness on the keel and, having not quite achieved flying speed, they momentarily dove in dubious control. But they had a thousand feet to sort things out, and eventually gained a semblance of normal flight. Buddy's excitement was extreme, his jaw dropping as he attempted to grin, and it gave Earl a wonderful feeling that this strange thing they were doing was being smiled upon by God. This feeling of euphoria continued after they landed, when Buddy gave Earl a look of pure joy.

After their first landing Buddy was totally pumped. He flung his arms akimbo and strained to speak. Earl understood him as clearly as if his speech was perfect. John and Earl were both pumped too. It probably was the most significant moment of his life. No bones were broken, he and Buddy were alive, John hadn't fallen off the cliff and they had acquired the experience of a successful venture. They could, in fact, do it again, and now without the fear of the unknown.

It's best to wait until the adrenalin leaves the system before attempting something that demands logic. They didn't do that. Grinning stupidly at each other, John and Earl both said "Let's do it again!"

They returned to the top of the big hill and set up the glider once more. John wrapped the rope around his waist, tugged on it, and took Buddy and his harness in his arms. Earl signaled and began to run, and John followed and flung Buddy off.

It being later in the day, the wind had changed as it is often wont to do. Earl had checked it before launching and knew about it but it's hard to argue with invincibility. Invincibility and logic, unfortunately, are often at odds with each other. On the other hand, the laws of physics are pretty much always in line with logic, as he now found out. It's about the first thing that hang gliding instructors tell their students, usually expressing the importance of it by shouting: "Don't launch downwind! It won't work!"

Indeed. Human power is notoriously weak. The hang glider pilot needs all the help he can get to attain flying speed. Anything less results in a stall, which means that gravity rules over everything else.

So here they were, heading downward in a stall. Theoretically, they had a thousand feet to sort things out and recover. The cliff, however, had a prominent ledge a couple of hundred feet down. Trees resided on the ledge. Big trees, over a hundred feet tall. By the time Buddy and Earl had attained flying speed, they found themselves below the treetops and rapidly heading toward them. Most fortunately, the wing itself remained above the tops and their combined mass was sufficient to plow through them. They were through the gauntlet, and after that the flight was uneventful. But they didn't fly any more that day.

That night he took Joyce to dinner at a downtown restaurant. It was spendier than the usual places that he had taken her, but he was still high from the flight with Buddy and felt like celebrating. Joyce knew to the dollar what his income level was. She was surprised by this minor recklessness until he told her about his day. She shared in his happiness, even when he ordered a large bottle of wine to go with dinner. The argument started when he ordered an after-dinner drink.

"Earl," she said, frowning, "you're already half-tight from the wine. You didn't need another drink, especially hard liquor. I thought you knew how I feel about that."

"S'okay," he replied. "Just one. I'm not drunk. And don't start ruining my day." The drink came along with his credit card. He tossed it down in one swallow.

"You are drunk. Give me the keys." She stood up and retrieved her jacket.

"No. I said I'm fine." He followed her as she stalked out of the restaurant. He insisted on driving. She sat rigid in the passenger seat. They were silent the entire way back. When they arrived at her home she left without saying goodbye, slamming the car door behind her.

Earl went to Church the next morning with a contrite attitude, expecting to apologize and do whatever it would take to return to her good graces. But she wasn't there. He saw her at work on Monday, but she refused to talk with him. He ate a dismal lunch alone in the cafeteria.

She began to warm up on Thursday. They had lunch together for the first time since the dinner date. She let him have it there. "I didn't believe that you were that kind of person," she said, her eyes moistening with the threat of tears.

"I'm not, really," he responded. "Please believe me. It's just that the Holy Spirit did an extraordinary thing with me, something that happens once in a lifetime if a person's lucky."

"That's a dandy way to thank God for it. Don't you remember me telling you that Sam was killed that way? What if you'd injured us on the way home? Or killed me? How would you have liked that?"

"Joyce, I'm very, very sorry. I can promise you this: it will never happen again."

She glared at him. "You're on probation with me, mister. And don't come around this weekend. I don't know when or even if I'll go out with you again. But if we do, it'll be up to me. If you don't respect my wishes on that, we're definitely not an item. Do you hear me?"

"Yes." There was nothing else he could say. She got up from the table and left without saying another word.

That Saturday Earl and John took Buddy flying again. Like the previous flight it didn't work out too well. The flight itself was fine, but Earl's landing lacked perfection. He was too low in the flare-out, just about kissing the grass. Buddy's chin was lower yet. When he gets excited he drops his jaw. When they land he remains prone, thus making his jaw the lowest part of his body and, in actuality, the entire hang glider system. This would have been acceptable if the field contained nothing but grass. But it didn't. Cows grazed there. They ate the grass. They did other things on it, too, so it was inevitable that Buddy's jaw would scoop up a cow pie.

It wasn't a laughing matter. He was choking and Earl was terrified that he wouldn't be able to breathe. As soon as he could he scrambled to clear his airway by poking his finger into Buddy's throat and pulling out the poop. His gasps reassured Earl that he was able to breathe, and Earl continued to kneel there, thanking God for His mercy in the face of his stupidity.

When they returned to the nursing home Earl felt compelled to tell the nurses about what had happened, because he wasn't sure that Buddy wouldn't need a shot of something to immunize him against infection. The fact that Buddy was there and he was alive and apparently in good spirits lightened up the situation considerably. They asked if there were flies on the poop. When Earl replied in the negative, they said that there was no real problem. Then they began to laugh. They were still laughing as Earl left the building. He was hoping that the evening would be an improvement with a call from Joyce, but it didn't happen.

Joyce was perfectly nice throughout the next week. She talked with him when he went past her desk and willingly shared lunch with him. But a subtle distance remained in her attitude. By the end of the week he was beginning to think that what he had done had created an irretrievable separation between them. It was with that desolate attitude that he flew again with Buddy the next Saturday. He should have stayed home.

To this point they had one very successful flight together, followed by two more somewhat marginal ones. But this time they got into a life-threatening situation. As before, John ran next to Earl with Buddy, flinging him into the air as Earl reached the edge of the big hill. On this launch there was an added spin to the thrust, causing Buddy's right arm to loop around the left flying wire that ran between the left tip of the crosstube and the left tip of the basetube.

If Buddy's arm had been capable of flexing at the elbow, this wouldn't have mattered. The arm simply would have slipped back down, allowing Buddy's harness to come back alongside Earl's when he went prone and put his hands on the basetube for control.

But Buddy's arm was quite rigid at both elbow and shoulder, causing him to remain where he was, on the left side of the glider rather far away from the basetube. The situation deteriorated as fear crept into Buddy's mind. His struggling only tightened the rigidity at his elbow.

If hang gliders had control surfaces common to airplanes like rudders and ailerons, that might not have been so terribly important. But hang gliders are controlled in flight by weight-shift, making control surfaces unnecessary under most conditions. Therefore, most hang gliders don't have control surfaces.

As didn't they. There they were then, flying marginally above stall speed with the glider sensing Buddy's position as a rather stern command for a sharp left turn. A sharp left turn at that point would have brought them back toward their launch point. The problem with that, of course, is that now they were well below the launch point. As they began to turn, the cliff face came back into sight. It wasn't a pretty picture. Although he was fully aware of the situation, Buddy's handicap prevented him from moving his arm. His frustration was extreme, matching the intensity of Earl's terror. All they both wanted then was their mamas.

Earl had no choice. Tugging on the right flying wire, he pulled himself (scrabbled would be more accurate) out to the right to compensate for Buddy's position. They straightened out and Earl was then able to turn them away from the cliff and back into unobstructed airspace. But in that position his control was marginal, especially with respect to pitch. They were flying, but barely. Setting up for a landing and then executing it without compromising their health would be extremely difficult under those conditions.

When they had enough room to recover from a complete loss of control, Earl took a few deep breaths to calm himself and let go from his precarious but relatively stable perch, swinging over toward Buddy. As the glider, under their combined weight on the left side, began a turn again to the left, this time more abruptly than the last,

Earl reached out and attempted to unhook the arm. Failing to do it, he scrambled back to the right just as the glider began its entry into a spiral from which it may not have recovered.

Noting with dismay that they were closer to the ground and were approaching the point where they'd have insufficient altitude to recover from that kind of attitude, Earl took a few more deep breaths and prayed silently to God for some way out of the mess they were in. Then he repeated the maneuver. Spurred on by desperation, he did so more boldly than during his previous attempt. This time they were successful. They returned to stable flight greatly relieved and breathing heartfelt thanks to God for getting them out of that situation. The landing turned out to be good.

A very thankful Earl returned home. He asked John to come over but he begged off, saying that he had a date. Earl was tempted to buy some beer on the way, but, thinking of what alcohol had done to his relationship, he settled for a six-pack of cola. He bought a pizza to go with it. He had settled down in front of the TV when the doorbell rang. When he opened the door Joyce flew into his arms.

"John called me. He told me about what had happened. He knew when you launched that something was terribly wrong. He said he didn't think you were going to make it. When you landed, he thought he'd just seen a miracle."

"It was hairy all right. When they sat down he handed her a pizza and a cola and told her the details. She responded with a long, wet kiss. "Are you ever going to get drunk like that again?" she asked.

"No. Of course not. Have another cola," he said, pointing to the alcohol-free beverage in triumph.

"Well, I guess we're back together, then."

They shared a very pleasant evening together.

Earl continued to fly with Buddy for the next three Saturdays after that, all of which were made without untoward incidents. On the last one, Joyce went along. "How about taking me next?" she asked when she and John came down to the landing field to pick them up. Surprised but delighted, Earl quickly assented. They went back to the top before she could change her mind. He set the glider back up and he fitted her into the harness he used with Buddy. They got Buddy's wheelchair out of the trunk and placed him into it for the show. He struggled and eventually achieved a semblance of an arm-pump. Earl and Joyce walked together with the glider over to the edge, where he hooked in. John stayed behind with Buddy.

"There's just one thing you need to know," he told Joyce. "When I say 'Go', start running and don't stop until there's nothing under your feet but air. If you stop before that, we'll crash and burn. Got it?"

"Y-yeah," she said with apprehension. He could see that she was scared. But he also saw the determination in her eyes. "Go!" he shouted, and ran off the edge. When they were airborne, he pulled her harness next to his and placed her hand on the basetube. She seemed to collect her wits, and presently she smiled. "This is wonderful!" she exclaimed. "I feel like a bird!" Her smile remained throughout the flight and the landing. That evening after they dropped off Buddy, they spent another companionable evening together at Earl's.

For the next five weekends they continued to devote their Saturdays to each other, flying together off the big training hill. Earl was plenty happy with the five-minute sled ride that the thousand-foot drop offered them, thinking that Joyce also was content with the ride. He was startled but elated when she looked up at him after their sixth flight together and said, "When are we going to get some real air time?" Earl had told her that the training hill was just that because it was located where neither ridge lift nor thermal activity were very likely.

"Sure," he responded enthusiastically. If the conditions are right, we'll go over to Dog next week. Dog Mountain, situated west of the Cascades next to Riffe Lake, was known for excellent ridge lift. The next Saturday, the conditions were perfect for sustained flight. Earl flew with Joyce for almost an hour, which was long enough for her to get queasy. After a bumpy flight down to the landing, she recovered quickly and they set off for lunch.

She snuggled next to him as they drove down the highway,

anticipating a good lunch at the next town. She turned her head
to say a word to him, but something caught her attention out of the
corner of her eye. "LOOK OUT!" she screamed.

CHAPTER 12

His mind registered awareness. He dimly recalled like times of consciousness extending into the distant past. Then the awareness subsided into an indistinct gray and faded out into nothing.

Consciousness returned. He opened his eyes for the first time, seeing nothing but white. Eventually a shape became recognizable. It was a ceiling light. He tried to turn his head, but realized that something was holding his head immobile. He wasn't in pain. In fact, he felt nothing and was perfectly comfortable except for the growing claustrophobia in his mind. It remained in the background for now, kept at bay by the cloudiness of his mental processes. He suspected that he was drugged, but was indifferent to that possibility. He stared at the light in the ceiling for a long time, until it, too began to turn gray.

Awareness returned. This time it remained, and his mind was clearer. He looked again at the light. Eventually, after a duration of indeterminate but immense length, an object moved past his line of vision. It was a head. A female, with long brunette hair.

"He's awake now." The voice was low and calm. Another head came into view. A male, bald and red-faced, wearing a green gown and a stethoscope about his neck. He fingered it and bent down. Earl couldn't see what he was doing. Nor could he feel anything.

"Hello, Earl," the male voice said. "Your jaw is wired shut, so don't try to speak. I'm holding your left hand. If you can hear me, squeeze it."

Earl squeezed it. When the man gave no response he squeezed it again. There was still no movement from the doctor and adrenalin shot into his bloodstream with the onset of panic. *Left hand!* he thought with a burst of relief. *He said the left!* He squeezed his left hand and the doctor nodded. "Good," he said. "Excellent. Do you know that you are in a hospital?" He squeezed. "Do you know why?" This time he didn't respond. "You were in a bad automobile accident. Your car was hit on the front passenger side. We had to use the Jaws of Life to get you out of the car. You came out lucky. Do you understand?" He squeezed again. He was assaulted by a sudden return of panic: *Joyce! She was sitting in the passenger seat! What happened to Her?* He frantically squeezed multiple times until the doctor acknowledged his urgent appeal. "Okay," he said. I think I understand. Is it about your companion?" He squeezed again.

The doctor turned away. He looked attentively in that direction and then slowly shook his head. He turned back to Earl. "I'm going to be up-front with you, Earl. The girl got the worst of the accident. But she is alive. Beyond that, only time will tell." He squeezed hard and willed himself to stay awake.

The doctor seemed to understand his thoughts. "You're not in the best of shape yourself," he continued. "The faster you get off the pain meds, the faster you'll recover. What do you say? Shall we start easing off on the meds?" Earl squeezed again. Presently he could sense the return of feeling. His jaw and right arm became noticeable, a mere annoyance at first, but the discomfort soon turned into excruciating pain. His jaw felt like a single enormous pus-filled infection. He heard a moan. It became a plaintive wail. It sounded familiar. His mind suddenly pictured Buddy, but then he realized that the sound was coming from his own mouth. The doctor must have responded, for a comforting warmth flooded in to crowd out the agony.

Wisdom returned later that night. He felt alert and free of pain when he awoke to see Her tender gaze. "Had a bad time of it, didn't you?" she began. He didn't take offense, because above her smile he could see the sorrow in her eyes. "Oh, well, She added, "it gives me a good opportunity to talk with you. You won't remember the conversation, but I do want to reinforce some thoughts that I've planted into your head and introduce you to a few more items."

"How come you weren't around when this happened?" he accused.

Did you think I'd forgotten you?"

"Well, I don't know. It's been a while. A long, long while. Things have happened back at the ranch."

She laughed, a crystal tinkle. "Don't I know it. I was there, of course. The whole time."

"Couldn't You have prevented the accident then?"

"Yes, I could have. Now listen to me. What I'm going to say is very important. It's something that you'll have with you the rest of your life. "What's the purpose of your existence hear on earth, Earl?"

He thought about the question. He started to speak, but then he realized that what he was about to say was embarrassingly self-serving. I really don't know, Wisdom. Maybe You'd better tell me."

"Wise, Earl. Very wise. You almost made me wince. You have one purpose here: to glorify your God. But before you start thinking of God as selfish and vain, let me assure you that He's exactly the opposite. God is Love Personified. When you exhibit love yourself, you naturally glorify God. But it's a special kind of love . . .""

"You mean, not the romantic kind, like I share with Joyce."

"You interrupted me. And don't try to shove your thoughts onto me. It won't work. As a matter of fact, the kind of love that is important to God can very well be romantic. You'd be surprised if you knew how much. But what makes it special to God is that it must be selfless. Its focus must go beyond self-interest. In other words, it must be noble. And, I'm happy to say, you're already showing it. First with Buddy, with My help, of course, and now you will with Joyce, also with My help."

"Well, my ability to work with Buddy has kind of flown out the window."

"Your special work with him is done, but you aren't completely through with him. Not by a long shot, actually." She showed him an enigmatic smile. Even that was radiant. "On the physical side of things, with the start you gave him, he'll go on to excel in the Special Olympics. You'll continue to be in his life. In a less adventurous way, you may think. But then again you may realize . . . whatever. I'll let you find out for yourself about that one. Right now We have other plans for you. Buddy's flying with you represented a short trial period, one of many, most of which you weren't aware. Think of them as kind of a boot camp. You needed to learn to place your trust in Us. You did rather well, as a matter of fact."

"Was Buddy getting caught in my flying wire part of the exercise?"

"Yes, it was. And it was your prayer that got you out."

"What if I hadn't prayed?"

"We knew you would, Earl." She patted his hand. "Let me get to the heart of the matter. Your work with Us is just beginning. If you think that taking Buddy flying with you called for faith, hang onto your hat. Your future's going to be tougher than that, and I won't be around as much as I have been, which means that you and Joyce are going to have to go it alone for the most part."

"That hurts, Wisdom. I love you."

"I know. And I love you, more than you can know. But you'll be putting most of your love onto Joyce, which is the way you were designed."

"Will you be there when I, when we, really need you?"

"Of course. You just may not be aware of it." She continued to smile, but her next words were all business. "Okay," She said without further preamble. Let's get to work. First, let's review what I've already told you. The Godhead?"

"Father, Mother, Son. A divine Family."

"Yes. The centrality of family, not only in God's creation and plan for humanity, but descriptive of the Godhead Itself. The functional roles of the divine Persons?"

"Will, Means, Actuality."

"Good. The Holy Spirit?"

"The third Person of the Trinity, the divine Mother. Also the Means."

"When was Jesus born?"

"At the beginning of creation, of time itself. He was the first Word spoken into existence, the first Light of Genesis 1."

"Yes. He was in the Old Testament as well as the New. How so?"

"Several ways. He was the God of Israel, Jahweh. He was also represented by many Old Testament figures, like Isaac and Joseph. He was the Word of God written by the Old Testament prophets as guided by the Holy Spirit."

"Okay. Fine. I guess your memory still works, then. Any questions about what you just said?"

"I do. It's been bothering me for a while. Some of that, equating the Holy Spirit with Motherhood, isn't taught in Church. I'd say that means it isn't in Scripture either."

"Dear Earl, you couldn't be farther wrong. You've actually read some of the passages yourself, but with your suppositions you glossed right over them. I'll give you another example, a more basic one that we've gone over before. It's that beautiful passage by Paul in his letter to the Church at Ephesus. It's in Chapter 5 of Ephesians. I'll quote you again the relevant passage, but someday you'll have it memorized.

Husbands, love your wives, even as Christ also loved the church, and gave himself for it; That he might sanctify and cleanse it with the washing of water by the word, that he might present it to himself a glorious church, not having spot, or wrinkle, or any such thing; but that it should be holy and without blemish. So ought men to love their wives as their own bodies. He that loveth his wife loveth himself.

For no man ever yet hated his own flesh; but nourisheth and cherisheth it, even as the Lord the church. For we are members of his body, of his flesh, and of his bones.

For this cause shall a man leave his father and mother, and shall be joined unto his wife, and they two shall be one flesh. This is a great mystery: but I speak concerning Christ and the church.

"Earl, this was a mystery only because the followers of God didn't read and understand the Bible in the depth that it deserves. They don't even bother to attempt to reconcile their supposed monotheism with the notion of a Trinitarian Godhead. If they did, they'd soon realize that a reconciliation is possible only in the loving unity of Family. Not only is that apparent conflict a clue, but there's the even more obvious one that they could see just by looking around them, which is the centrality of family to all of life as We designed it. Nor do they appreciate that if Jesus as God will be married to His Church, it would be odd not to extend that same blessed attribute to the other two Members.

"Jesus' marriage, Earl, will be anything but trivial. In Genesis Chapter 24, Isaac, who you should know represented Jesus because of Abraham's attempted sacrifice of him, married Rebekah, a type of the Church. Then there's the Song of Solomon that most preachers won't touch with a ten-foot pole because of its sexually explicit nature. Why do they think that the Song was canonized in Scripture? If it doesn't represent Jesus and the Church, or more fundamentally of the divine Will and Means, then its inclusion in Scripture would be gratuitous. God doesn't do things that way - they should have known that. And then there's Isaiah 54. Isaiah 53 is popular in the Christian community as being a Messianic prophecy. Of course it was – it foretold of Jesus' suffering for our sake. But the next chapter, which is a sequel to it was just as prophetic, foretelling of Jesus' marriage to His Church just as plainly as Ephesians 5. Listen to the words:

Sing, O barren, thou that didst not bear; break forth into

*singing, and cry aloud, thou that didst not travail with child:
for more are the children of the desolate than the children
of the married wife, saith the Lord. Enlarge the place of
thy tent, and let them stretch forth the curtains of thine
habitations: spare not, lengthen thy cords, and strengthen
thy stakes; for thou shalt break forth on the right hand and on
the left; and thy seed shall inherit the Gentiles, and make the
desolate cities to be inhabited. Fear not; for thou shalt not
be ashamed: neither be thou confounded; for thou shalt not
be put to shame: for thou shalt forget the shame of thy youth,
and shalt not remember the reproach of thy widowhood any
more.*

*For thy Maker is thine husband; the Lord of hosts is His
name; and thy Redeemer the Holy One of Israel; the God of
the whole earth shall he be called. For the Lord hath called
thee as a woman forsaken and grieved in spirit, and a wife of
youth, when thou wast refused, saith thy God.*

"As if the Old Testament references weren't enough, there is also
John Chapter 2 in the New Testament, the wedding at Cana. It's
amazing how few people see the significance of this first miracle
that Jesus did. Couldn't they see that if it wasn't applicable to Jesus'
marriage to His Church, it also would be a gratuitous, unnecessary
inclusion in Scripture?

"It's the same situation with the Holy Spirit: man's refusal to look
at Scripture in depth. All throughout Scripture the Holy Spirit is
portrayed as working in response to the Divine Will. Respected Bible
commentators have remarked on the executive functional nature of
the Holy Spirit. But still they failed to grasp the feminine nature of a
responsive function. Again, why couldn't devout people understand
the significance of the Book of Proverbs as a very important message
about the nature of God? That should be the biggest mystery of all
to you, and you'd be surprised at how many people actually did
think about it to the point that they understood. But sometimes the
more shallow among you are the ones with the biggest mouths, who
take it upon themselves to speak for God. Remember when you

read Proverbs Chapter 8 to Buddy? It was these same people who, in their shallow understanding, insisted that it applied to Jesus instead of to the Holy Spirit, the One whom I am privileged to represent to you. Then again, there's the Song of Solomon, which is so in-your-face straightforward that it's more than a clue. And, among other New Testament passages, there's John Chapter 3, where Jesus speaks to Nicodemus of spiritual birth. I'll quote parts:

> *There was a man of the Pharisees, named Nicodemus, a ruler of the Jews: The same came to Jesus by night, and said unto him, Rabbi, we know that thou art a teacher come from God: for no man can do these miracles that thou doest, except God be with him.*

> *Jesus answered and said unto him, Verily, verily, I say unto thee, Except a man be born again, he cannot see the kingdom of God.*

> *Nicodemus saith unto him, How can a man be born when he is old? Can he enter the second time into his mother's womb, and be born?*

> *Jesus answered, Verily, verily, I say unto thee, Except a man be born of water and of the Spirit, he cannot enter into the kingdom of God. That which is born of the flesh is flesh; and that which is born of the Spirit is spirit.*

"Here you have a direct reference to the Holy Spirit as the source of spiritual birth. What is birth if not the essence of womanhood, and more, of motherhood?

"That's very convincing, but yet..."

"Yes. Of course. What you mean is that despite all this information in Scripture, nobody would understand unless God gave it to them to do so. The converse is also true: if God wanted people to understand, He would have brought it about. Very true, and it's an important issue. It's about the ease with which perversions of the notion of a female Deity can arise. It's happened in the past, and the Father simply didn't consider mankind to be ready to handle that knowledge of the

Holy Spirit. Many individuals throughout the long history of the Church Age have indeed possessed that knowledge, but as a general understanding, no. Not until now. We're nearing the end of this age, so mankind doesn't have enough time left to truly mess up the understanding. Just as important, there is so much homosexuality about now and other perversions of the way man was created that Christians need to understand, like they never did before, that God's proscriptions against those practices in Leviticus and Romans were there for the fundamental reason that they are violations of types: for both man and God."

"Then I feel privileged to be in this generation."

"Yes, well, maybe. There's a bit of a downside to it also. But it is the time spoken of by Daniel of the opening of the books. As Daniel wrote in his Chapter 12:

> *But thou, O Daniel, shut up the words, and seal the book, even to the time of the end; many shall run to and fro, and knowledge shall be increased.*

"Earl, you are in that time. The books are being opened. You will see amazing things, but you will also experience hardship and privation. It's part of the gig. Are you up to it?"

"Yes, I think. But right now I seem to have a lot on my plate. And I don't know anything about Joyce."

"You'll see her soon. You won't find her situation pretty, but you'll both survive. You have a fulfilling life together to look forward to. About your work, we'll ease you into it. For now, just focus on getting better. We love you, Earl. Both of you." She faded away.

Chapter 13

He awoke to pain, but it remained in the background, tolerable. He endured it in silence. A long sequence of awakenings followed. He remembered a visit from John during one of those times. His friend had tried to maintain a one-way conversation that quickly degenerated into an awkward silence. He left soon after. But Earl knew that he cared. Eventually he realized that his jaw and shoulder ached less. His right arm began to tingle, an irritating sensation. After another interminable duration a nurse came into his line of vision. She was the same brunette that he had seen at first, and this time she wore a smile. "We're going to take off your body cast today," she said triumphantly. "You'll be able to move around some."

True to her word, two more staff came in with the doctor and delicately cut and peeled the plaster tomb from his body. Relieved, he attempted to move his head and was gratified to know that he could do so. He moved his legs and was even happier to know that they, too were intact. Doing the same with his arms, however, he could move them both but only the left arm came into view. He struggled again to move his right arm, but the nurse quickly intervened. "I'm afraid that's not going to happen, Earl. The arm was beyond saving. We had to amputate." She added defensively "The alternative was gangrene, which would have killed you." Earl nodded, attempting to assimilate this unexpected fact. He pointed to his jaw with a question in his eyes. "Next week." The response came from the doctor this time. Earl made a writing motion with his left hand. "He wants to write something," the nurse said and presently a pencil and a board with a sheet of paper were given to him. Being naturally right-handed, Earl found it extremely frustrating to form words with his left. Eventually, however, he managed to scribble the word "Joyce". The nurse looked toward the doctor and he nodded his head.

He found himself being transferred to a gurney and moved down a hallway to another part of the hospital. Eventually they turned into a room, where he saw a pitiful little creature whose sad eyes peeked out from behind a beehive of bandages. He knew that he was looking at Joyce, but she looked so tiny. With a shock, he understood why she was so dwarfed by the bed. The blanket was empty where her legs were supposed to be. She saw his startled recognition of her loss and turned her head away. He saw her shoulders heave. Despite his inability to speak coherently through his wired jaw he called her name. He tried to rise up from the gurney and fell in the attempt, damaging a rib. The commotion caused Joyce to turn her head. As they lifted him back onto the gurney, he wailed his love for her, but his sounds were undecipherable. He was wheeled away.

Back in his room he asked again for the pencil and paper. After laboring, he wrote "Joyce. I love you. Earl." He urged the paper onto a nurse and motioned for her to take it away. Then he wept. "Dear God," he silently prayed. "I don't know why You allowed this to happen and I won't question Your Wisdom. But don't let me lose Joyce too. Please keep Joyce and me together. Please let us stay together all our lives."

God remained quiet. He was wheeled into Joyce's room two days later. Again, when he arrived, she turned her head away from him. But this time he tugged the gurney alongside her bed and reached out with his left arm. He caught her arm and squeezed, silently pleading with her to acknowledge his presence. Her head turned toward his face and they both wept. She rested a hand on his. He silently thanked God.

He came into her room every day after that. A few days later his jaw was unhindered and he spoke to her for the first time. "Joyce,

I'm so sorry," he began. "I just didn't see him coming."

"Hello, Earl," a voice said from behind him. His nurse turned the gurney to allow him to see who spoke. It was Joyce's mother. "Another drunk," she said. "It was in the papers and on TV."

"I'm sorry, Janet. So very, very sorry."

"Don't blame yourself," Janet said, baring her teeth in anger. He's completely at fault, and I intend to make certain that he receives the justice that's due him. Other than not being within ten miles of him, there's no way that you could have avoided the crash."

Joyce motioned him forward. When his gurney was alongside she reached over and held his hand. She gave it a squeeze. She didn't blame him. But he knew that when he overdid it himself with alcohol, it could have been him who had changed some other persons' lives forever. Or maybe Joyce's. Full of contrition, he begged the Lord for forgiveness.

When the doctor motioned with his watch that they'd been with her long enough, they left Joyce's room together. The aide in charge of Earl began to wheel him back to his own room, and Janet asked "Mind if I tag along?" The aide shrugged and said, "Sure." When they were in Earl's room the aide left and Janet spoke up. "I don't want to pester you, but you're my only connection to her. I'm still trying to sort this thing out in my head. My poor daughter," she said, and began to moan. "I'm glad you're here," he said, attempting to soothe her. Please. A chair's over there. Have a seat."

She thanked him and complied. "I have a feeling that you're not particularly happy with me right now," Earl offered. "I don't blame you. Flaky to begin with, and now look what I've done to your daughter."

"Oh, no." She gathered herself together and strengthened her will. "I told you before, it wasn't your fault. I'm not blaming you, and you shouldn't blame yourself."

"I can't help it," he replied. "I keep feeling that there must have been something I could have done to avoid the accident. I . . ."

"Stop it," she commanded, interrupting his thoughts. "I came in here to be with you, not to accuse."

"Thanks, Janet. I never want to leave Joyce, you know. I don't care what parts are missing, I still love her. I always will."

"I know you do. Leave it be, Earl. Time to get on with the job of living. I'm concerned about the driving, though. For starters, you need a better car. I take that back. You need *a* car. Yours was totaled. Mine is still in good working order, but I've had my eye on a cute little convertible. I was thinking of buying it and trading in the old one, but they don't give much on trade-ins. You're welcome to it."

"Thanks very much. I'll sign over to whatever the insurance company's decided to pay me for my old one, but it won't be much, I'm sure. It belonged in the junkyard way before the accident."

"Not necessary. I'd like to make it a gift."

"You know," he replied with feeling, "you might just make a pretty decent mother-in-law."

In another week the staff removed the bandages from Joyce's head. When he arrived at her room that day, a nurse was combing her hair. She was the most lovely sight that he could imagine. It was her turn to look at him in shock. "Your arm," she said, putting a delicate hand up to her mouth.

"Yeah. The Limb fairy took it away. Didn't leave anything under my pillow, either. But we still have each other. Let's see – that's two legs and three arms between us. We should get by."

She gave a sad little laugh, but a smile remained on her face. "I'm game if you are."

Her bravado lasted as long as she remained under the covers. Eventually they got her out of bed, dressed her and took her down to Rehabilitation Therapy. Her relative exposure made the journey an ordeal. *I must look like a beachball sitting without legs in this wheelchair,* she thought unhappily. *A freak.* She was relieved when they wheeled her through a doorway and she was out of the well-traveled hallway.

In the therapy room they spoke to her with kindness, but treated her as if she was in boot camp. A specialist came into the room and examined the stumps, the left of which extended halfway from her hip to where her knee used to be, and the right of which was shorter by several inches. "You had the engine block in your lap, honey," the doctor said. "Your legs didn't like it too much. Be thankful that you have as much left as you do. Be even more thankful that you still have your life. Many people with injuries like yours don't survive the trauma. Your relative youth helped you there."

I know what, or rather Who, helped me, she thought. But then the doctor had a therapist wrap the stumps in cloth and applied cuplike devices to the ends with firm and constant pressure. The sudden pain frightened her and she cried out in alarm. The therapist brushed her hair back from her forehead and said soothingly, "It'll hurt just a bit, but it won't be long. You need to go through the pain." Joyce noted that despite the kindness in her voice, the therapist had not let up on the pressure. "We're trying to get you ready for prosthetic limbs," she continued conversationally. "It won't be easy, but the more you grit your teeth and learn to handle it, the faster you'll be up and about on your own. My name's Maggie, by the way. They call me Magpie. I guess I know why. You will too, I'm afraid."

For the first time, Joyce focused on something outside of her own pain. She studied the other woman, noting her red hair and freckles. *She's Irish,* she thought. *Cute, too. I'll bet she has a fierce temper. And a good sense of humor.*

"So you got caught in an accident," Maggie said conversationally. "I hear he was drunk. Isn't that the way it goes."

"The ironic thing about it is that we just got finished doing something that people usually think of as more dangerous than riding in a car."

"Oh? What was that?"

"My boyfriend Earl had just taken me along with him in his hang glider. We were up almost an hour. It was a great ride. Then this."

Joyce's face registered the rapid onset of pain. Her sudden change in countenance triggered Maggie's vocal reflex. "Good for you, honey," she said, patting Joyce on the shoulder. I like adventure too.

Under the right conditions, that is. Sometimes Bob doesn't get it. Bob's my husband. He's had a bunch of bikes. Motorcycles. Most of them weren't designed with the input of women's focus groups, if you get my drift. The passenger seats, if you want to call them that, were on the primitive side. Hard as concrete, truth be told. I told him just that. I said, 'Bob, you want me to ride on this thing, you stop every hour or two so I can get a butt rest, you hear me?' Yeah, yeah, he says, but you think he listened? In one ear and out the other. He decides to take me to New Mexico one year. There we were, in the middle of Idaho, just outside of Pocatello, and me, I'm marching down the side of the highway. Bob's behind me on the bike, putt-putting and whining for me to get back on. Oh, boy, was I mad! I was so mad that I was crying, he didn't give me a butt rest for almost three hours. I'll tell you, it turned me right then and there into a mean biker bitch and he could beg all he wanted, I wasn't going to get back on that thing. Then I started to see that we weren't exactly alone. It was a busy highway. People in their cars could see me crying and Bob back behind me whining for me to climb back on. I could see them laughing. We must have entertained a hundred cars until I relented and got back on. But I gave his back a good pounding with my fists. He didn't try that again. Oh, he did, but not on that trip."

Joyce found herself laughing at the tale despite her discomfort. Another girl overheard the conversation. Her name was Cindy; she was black and strikingly pretty. Her clothes and demeanor asserted her wealth. She was undergoing therapy for a badly damaged wrist, but she, too, was laughing with Maggie's story. "Men are such fools," she said. "That's a good one but I can top it. We're water people. We have a sailboat and we love it. But one time when we were just out of sailing classes and completely unaware, outside of our books, of what a storm can do to the water, we took our baby – that's our boat, you know - on a cruise of the San Juan Islands. It's beautiful country and the weather was perfect for the first several days. Stephen, that's my husband, really got into it. One evening we found ourselves on our way from Friday Harbor to Spencer Spit on Lopez Island. We intended to pick up a mooring buoy at the spit and stay there the night. Well, the breeze was warm, almost like the Caribbean, and steady at a decent rate of seventeen knots, perfect sailing weather, really. We were running close-hauled, which means that the wind was nearly blowing into our faces, and we were heeling over pretty hard. The water seemed to be rushing past our hull, and Stephen was in his element. So much that he looked upward to heaven, shook his fist and said to God, 'Is this all you can give me?' Cindy gave a rueful chuckle. "Oh, he shouldn't have done that. We picked up a buoy on the spit and settled down for dinner and cocktails up on the cockpit. It stayed nice that evening and, after a couple of games of Pinochle we hit the sack.

"About three o'clock in the morning I awoke to a loud thumping, which told me that our dinghy was beating itself to death against our transom. I hit Stephen in the back with a fist until he woke up. 'Get up and tie the dinghy like you should have,' I told him. Very reluctantly, I swear that he was going to ask me to do it, he got up, put on his rain slicker and went up to the cockpit. I could hear the screeching of the wind from our berth, and our boat was rocking like a bucking bronco. When he came back I could have read a book from the whites of his eyes.

"The next morning when we went back up to the cockpit the water in the little bay inside the spit was white, and the buoy was completely submerged from the strain of our boat. I don't know how he did it, but Stephen managed somehow to free us from the buoy. We set sail for the shelter of Friday Harbor and eventually reached its safety. We were greatly relieved, I'll tell you. And Stephen never again shook his fist at God, asking for more. If he ever does it again, God won't need to lift a finger, because I'll throw him overboard first."

"That is a good one too," Maggie said laughing. "But I can still do you one better." She looked at her watch. "But it'll have to wait 'til next time. Our time is up."

By the time the session was over, Joyce was sweating from the pain and the exertion of suppressing it. Maggie was right. She continued to feel it after the pressure was released, but she found that she could handle it. She was given some pain pills, but not enough to completely remove the electrical jolts from her protesting nerve endings.

When Earl saw her, he was surprised at her attitude. She wasn't morose in the least. "You look great today," he said.

"It's a girl thing," she replied. "It seems like we're starting up a social club."

By the end of the week, however, she was a whole lot closer to God than she had been before the accident. It was a necessity. She needed God just to get through the daily agony of her therapy sessions. Maggie, with Cindy chiming in, continued to try to get her mind off the pain.

"Oh, yeah," Maggie started as she pushed the cups onto Joyce's legs and tightened the bindings. "On one of our trips Bob found the perfect bike salesman. There we were in the Honda shop when this bike – I'll admit that it was a beauty, in an ugly, in-your-face sort of way – caught his eye. It was a Rune, expensive as all get-out. But Bob kept staring at it, which brought the salesmen over like flies on you-know-what. To his credit Bob saw a problem with it. "There's no seat on back," he said to the salesman. "What about my wife?" The salesman knew the problem. So did the Honda Company. They had a simple solution, the only acceptable one with which the bike's styling could be maintained: "You have this bike, you don't need a wife," the salesman explained, as to a mentally slow two-year-old. I walked out of the shop. It was either that or that stupid salesman got a punch in his oversized beer-swilling gut."

"That was good," Cindy said, laughing. "But what were you doing in the shop?"

"Funny you should ask that. He could have been there for any number of reasons, like to get an oil change on his bike, or a new tire. But that wasn't why he was there. He was there because the alternative would have been a divorce."

"Wow," Joyce said. "Harsh."

"Yeah, well, Bob eventually traded his Yamaha 750, the one we went to Colorado and New Mexico on, for a Yamaha 1100 Special, which he, of course, had fallen in love with within a half block of trying it out. He could have learned from previous experience about upping my feelings to item #1 on the list. But No. Taking a first trip on it from Kent to Spokane, he was tooling up Snoqualmie Pass with me on back and him acting like he didn't have a care in the world. If he'd had just one inkling of my feelings he would at least have armed himself with a gun. Forget the two-hour butt rest. On that thing I needed a butt rest ten minutes after we took off. The seat, if you want to call it that, was hard as a rock. But that wasn't all. The foot pegs vibrated. It hit my nerves like chalk screeching on a blackboard. I gritted my teeth up to the summit, but I couldn't take it any more after that and the jerk wasn't showing any sign of stopping. I let go with my fists against his back and was heading for his kidneys when he finally pulled over. You know what he asked me? 'Oh, do you need a butt rest?' 'Oh, I think I just might,' I told him. I didn't care how many cars we entertained, I let him have it with both barrels. "I'll tell you what," he said after I refused to climb back on after ten minutes, "bear with me for a few more miles, and we'll have breakfast in Cle Elum." So there we were, two grim-faced travelers drinking coffee, getting warm, and not the benign kind – I mean hot under the collar- and discussing the division of our assets. As I saw it, he would be left with one asset: the bike."

After the laughter subsided, Maggie went on with the story. "He managed to talk me into remaining married long enough to continue on to Ellensburg, where he promised to stop and solve the vibration problem. I was a fool to listen to him and expect anything good to come out of his stupid brain. I already knew what a fool he was himself. But even I didn't expect something that weird to come out of his head. When we got to Ellensburg he stopped at a Penney's and ran inside. He came running back out ten minutes later with a pillow and a handful of washrags. He tied the pillow to my seat and the washrags to my footpegs and, with a flourish of his arm like he did something wonderful, he bid me to mount his steed, all silent because we weren't talking just then. I'm here to tell you how wonderful it was. There I was, sitting way above his head like a total nerd. I couldn't wait for him to get us out of there before I got stared at. If he'd so much as cracked a smile, that would have been the end of it right then and there. But things just got worse when we drove off. I was so high up that the windscreen didn't work any more, and I started eating bugs. Worse, the washrags didn't do a thing for the vibration. We had it out on the cloverleaf going back and forth between the direction of the highway out of town and the bus station. Finally we both shut up and he headed east over the river to a town called Quincy. That's where the bike shop was. By that time he knew what was good for him. He finally turned away from the Rune and started looking at Goldwings. We couldn't afford it, but we bought one anyway. At that point I didn't care about money."

"Then what?" Joyce asked.

"Everything was dandy after that. The bike was smooth and quiet, and my seat, in comparison, was like a throne. Not only that, music was piped into my helmet. Any time he mentions a different bike, I bunch up my fists and scowl. That takes care of that."

"I have to admit," Cindy said, chuckling. "That's a hard one to beat, but for sheer male stupidity I think I still might just be able to top it. It happened on the boat, like the time before. This time we brought my mother and sister with us on a sail from Friday Harbor to the lovely Prevost Harbor on nearby Stuart Island. Now my mother, she's a bit on the heavy side, so I told Stephen to be extra careful. Besides that, neither of them knew how to swim. Anyway, when we set out the wind was blowing pretty good, but it was behind us, and on that point of sail there's no heeling and the boat and mast stay upright. It was quieter too, because we were going with the wind instead of against it. Things were so nice and calm that mother decided to go to her bunk in the bow and take a short nap. But as our little journey was nearing its end with our having rounded the island, we changed direction to get into the cove. As we were no longer in the lee of the island, the wind also picked up. Our point of sail also changed from a broad reach with the wind behind us to close-hauled, with the increasing wind maybe 25 degrees off our bow into our faces. As we reset our sails our lady gracefully heeled in response, the mast dipping over and water spraying up over the bow. Sailing close-hauled is altogether more exciting than having the wind push the boat from the rear, and my sister screamed with delight. It was a piercing scream, with her face showing a wide, toothy grin.

"At just about that time, Stephen remembered something that he had forgotten. It was important, because the bilge in our boat is quite shallow. "Did you close the sink drain?" he shouted to me. "Of course not," I shouted back. "That's your job!" Alarmed at his forgetfulness, I resolved to head back down into the saloon in a few minutes, not only to shut the sink drain, which provided a clear path between the sink and the water outside when the boat was heeling on a starboard tack, but to clean up the inevitable pool of water that would be sloshing around the cabin deck. Having gone through that particular routine before, we had bucket and sponges on hand for just that purpose.

"A few minutes later I opened the hatch into the saloon. The wide-eyed apparition that greeted me there reminded me of something else that I had completely forgotten: mother. Her frightened eyes were enormous. 'You're here!' she wailed out. 'We're alive!'

"We pieced together the details of that shift of sail from her completely different perspective that evening, when she had calmed enough to speak coherently. Fast asleep on her berth, she had rolled off it and crashed into the bulkhead as the boat heeled. In her eyes, the boat wasn't heeling; it was listing, as in *Titanic*. The perception strengthened as she saw water coming in over the canted decking. Terrified now, she struggled to open the cabin door. Just as she began to climb through it into the saloon she heard the piercing scream. Convinced that we were abandoning ship, she rushed through the cockpit to join us, even though she couldn't swim. She had the guts that night to laugh about the incident. Mother lived for several years after that terrible event. Oh, am I glad that she did – for Stephen's sake."

Joyce began to call the Therapy Room "The Medieval Chamber of Horrors", and took to reading the Bible for comfort. But she realized that there was much good from the therapy sessions. She could feel her tolerance improving, and smiled often at the things her companions there had shared with her. Its rigors offered her another benefit: she cared nothing about her appearance except for the times that Earl was with her in his daily visits. But he seemed not to notice her disfigurement. She asked him about it once. "How can you stand to see me like this?" she questioned him. "Doesn't the sight put you off?"

"Not at all," he replied without hesitation. "Joyce, I thank God every day that you're still with me. There are a lot worse things than for me to see you without legs. You're alive and that's all that really matters."

Earl also was going through therapy preparatory for being fitted with a prosthetic arm. But as the body doesn't rely on arms for basic things like simply standing upright, his therapy wasn't as intensive or as painful as hers. Nevertheless, his loss of an arm helped to humble him and to exercise compassion toward Joyce for her bigger loss.

CHAPTER 14

Within a month they were ambulatory, with him pushing her wheelchair daily along a quiet path in a tiny park environment within the hospital grounds. An outpatient clinic connected with the hospital offered a driver training course for handicapped individuals. Earl eagerly signed up for it and the additional work occupied much of his time when he was apart from Joyce. He was grateful for the distraction, as well as for the prospect of driving again. Janet drove him to his appointments and, finally, to the DMV, where he obtained a license to drive.

Clutching the certificate in his hand, he waved it to Janet. "You don't know what you just did," he chided her as they drove back to the hospital with him behind the wheel.

"Oh?" she asked.

"Yeah," he said with a smile. "You've just unleashed a monster. I've had experiences before with cars."

"You just had a big one."

"There have been others," he said enigmatically.

"Do tell."

"Okay. You saw my last car before it met its doom."

"True. Not much difference there."

"Yeah. Once in high school I bought a big old four-door sedan with an undersized engine and miserable performance. I got it on the cheap in a deal that I could hardly turn down. It was great for dates because it was roomy. Aw, maybe I shouldn't tell you all this."

"No, go ahead," she laughed. It takes two to tango, so we girls aren't all that different."

"Given that it accelerated at the rate of a freight train, it wasn't that easy to abuse. But I managed anyway. One time when I was leaving a store downtown on the way to a date I started playing around, trying to speed-shift. The tranny didn't like it and decided to go on strike."

"What? It wouldn't go at all?"

"No, it still went all right, but only in reverse. As a result, I had to drive that way seven miles back to the house. There was a lot of honking along the way and, boy, did I see a lot of white teeth, all of which started in anger and ended up in laughter. Some of them I knew from school. Can you imagine what it would be like to come upon the rear of a car at an intersection? Or having one facing you as you pull up to a stop sign? I pulled the transmission and eventually got the gears to mesh properly, after which I unloaded the unfortunate vehicle onto some other poor sucker who bought it on the cheap, thinking that he was getting a good deal from some poor sap who didn't know the value of his possessions. That car passed through a lot of hands and became kind of an inside joke before it finally reached the junky's. There must have been a host of us who laughed inwardly upon seeing it wobble down the street."

She laughed and then became thoughtful. "I'll bet there are a whole lot of cars at the junkys' that would have some pretty good stories to tell if they could talk. By the way, I want to make a stop at the Ford lot before we see Joyce. And try to be more careful with this one than your others. It's yours when we get to the lot. And its passengers – both of them – are kind of special to me."

"Thanks, Janet," was all he could say.

"Joyce," he interrupted her reading during one of their outings in the parklike area, "I don't know a lot about it, but ever since I read the Book of Proverbs to Buddy, I've been having this feeling that people simply haven't interpreted Scripture correctly in a very important matter."

"Oh? What's that?"

"Well, I've been thinking that the Holy Spirit is distinctly feminine in some manner."

"That's an easy one. In John and elsewhere, the Holy Spirit is referred to as 'he'. So you're wrong there. Sorry about that."

"Yeah, I see your point. But somehow..." After he returned Joyce to her room he spent the afternoon grappling with the contradiction. His thoughts periodically took him to the Bible. Within an hour he had grabbed a pencil and a notebook, and busied himself writing down his thoughts and their Scriptural support.

Three days later, as he pushed her wheelchair along the flower-bordered path, Earl spoke to her again about his disturbing thought. "Joyce, somehow I can't let this idea go about the gender of the Holy Spirit. I've been looking up Scripture, and somehow I seem to find passages that suggest an answer."

"I thought you said that you were wrong about that."

"No, you did. I just didn't know. But since then I think I understand the answer. Do you want to hear it?"

"All right," she said doubtfully. "But don't make it too deep. I'm enjoying the sun. And you."

"It's not deep at all. In fact, it's beautifully simple. Remember what Adam said when he saw Eve for the first time? I'll repeat it, because it's extremely important:

This is now bone of my bones, and flesh of my flesh; she shall be called Woman, because she was taken out of Man. Therefore shall a man leave his father and his mother, and shall cleave unto his wife, and they shall be one flesh.

"One flesh, Joyce. In marriage the two become one. If the woman is one with the man in the sight of God, it's as if she was taken out of man in the first place and returns to him in marriage. It's perfectly natural, then, that she should be addressed by the masculine pronoun. That's why a married woman is addressed by her husband's surname."

"But you're talking about people, Earl. That has nothing to do with the Holy Spirit.

"Oh, yes it does. Back in Genesis 1 there's another passage that I memorized for its importance. Here, I'll give it to you.

And God said, Let us make man in our image, after our likeness; and let them have dominion over the fish of the sea, and over the fowl of the air, and over the cattle, and over all the earth, and over every creeping thing that creepeth upon the earth. So God created man in his own image, in the image of God created he him; male and female created he them.

"Don't you see? Mankind is a type of God. God in the plural, you'll note. When He created us in his plural image, He created us male and female. That refers to our gender differences, whatever that might mean in the spiritual realm. It answers another issue, that of monotheism versus the Trinity. In Deuteronomy 6, God through Moses tells us that He is one, and then commands us to love Him with all our hearts, souls and might. This is the Great Commandment that Jesus spoke of, so it's obviously important. But in the Scripture reference I just gave you, God also claims to be plural. The Church has accepted a Trinitarian God from its beginning. How do you reconcile one with three, except in a love so strong that it binds them together? A family, Joyce. The Trinity is a holy Family. That's the Godhead."

Joyce was quiet for a long time, digesting what Earl said. Finally she looked up at him from her wheelchair and spoke. "Earl, that's a beautiful thought. It makes sense, too. But mostly it's beautiful. It makes me see God in a wonderful new way. Please continue trying to justify it, because now that you've given it to me, I don't want to give it up."

Two days later Earl came rushing into her room. "I found some more backup, Joyce!" he said excitedly. "It's huge."

Joyce was all ears. She forgot about the outing she'd been anticipating all morning. "Tell me now. I want to hear it," she said, the excitement in her voice matching his.

"Don't ask me how I found it, but between the Bible and its concordance at the end I got to Paul's letter to the Ephesians. I memorized part of Chapter 5, because it says it all:

Husbands, love your wives, even as Christ also loved the church, and gave himself for it, that he might sanctify and cleanse it with the washing of water by the word; that he might present it to himself a glorious church, not having spot, or wrinkle, or any such thing; but that it should be holy and without blemish. So ought men to love their wives as their own bodies. He that loveth his wife loveth himself. For no man ever yet hated his own flesh, but nourisheth and cherisheth it, even as the Lord the church; for we are members of his body, of his flesh, and of his bones. For this cause shall a man leave his father and mother, and shall be joined unto his wife, and they two shall be one flesh. This is a great mystery, but I speak concerning Christ and the church.

Joyce let the words sink in. "Oh, my!" she exclaimed. "That's nothing short of amazing. Why don't we get that information in church?"

"Don't ask me. But there it is in Scripture. If you can't believe that, what can you believe?"

"Well, anyway, I thank you from the bottom of my heart for the gift you just gave me. I'll cherish it for the rest of my life."

"Don't thank me, Joyce. Thank God for putting it in our Bibles."

"One thing you can say for sure about that, Earl. If Jesus as God marries the Church, it kind of sets a reverse precedent. Why would just one Member of the Godhead participate in marriage and the other two not? That doesn't make sense."

"I know. The implications of that one passage are enormous. Pity that nobody seems to have been interested enough to think about it. For another thing, if Jesus applies to that statement first made by Adam, then He also must leave both Father and Mother to marry the Church. That being the case, to fulfill the statement He'd have to have a Mother to leave. Since He existed before He came in the flesh, that Mother would have to be a spiritual one, not Mary. Then, too, the Bible explicitly states that Jesus has a Divine Father. One would think that if Father and Son were involved in the Godhead, there'd have to be a Mother too."

"You know, you've just convinced me that you're on to something. I'm very happy about it, because that something is quite beautiful. Let's go outside and celebrate by admiring God's flowers and trees."

"You're on," he said. Once they were moving along the now-familiar path, they enjoyed an easy silence, both aware of the other but neither needing to speak. Eventually Earl spoke what was on his mind. "Don't ask me where it's coming from, but this talk of Father and Mother gets me to thinking that each of these Members of the Godhead has a specific role to play. We know that the Father's role is the Will. That part's obvious. It seems to me that Jesus' role is the representation of that Will. The Divine Image, if you will. Or the Divine Reality. That would obviously give the Holy Spirit the role of the Divine Means, so that the Divine Will, in union with the Divine Means, gives birth to the Divine Reality."

"Wow, Earl. You cobbled up a real left-brain idea there if I ever heard one. But it does make sense, too. I think. I need to think on that for a while. Don't feed me any more information until I digest this."

"Okay, but just one more thing. If someone doesn't buy into my explanation of the masculine pronoun for a feminine Person, note this: the Holy Spirit might be a functional female, but if She is part of the Father in love, She might be considered to be of His substance. It's like the Church. As the Bride of Christ, the Church will be a functional female in the spiritual realm, but as redeemed mankind in the collective sense, the Church can substantively be called male. "

She laughed. "Stop, Earl. You're making my head spin." Her happiness was abruptly cut off by an inrush of pain. "I've had a wonderful time with you," she said through compressed lips. "But now I need to get back into bed."

That afternoon Earl had a visitor. It was John, but not the same one that he knew. "Hi," he said to his friend, looking at his gaunt, downcast face with concern. "What happened to you?"

"You were right all along, Earl," he replied. "Betty dumped me. I was just about ready to ask her to marry me. What I didn't know was that she'd been going out with another guy for months, even while we were still together. She told me that when she turned me down. We got into an argument and I haven't seen her since."

They spent the rest of their visit with Earl attempting to comfort John. He talked about how sacred the man-woman relationship was to God, but John wasn't really in a mood to listen. He left before Earl could get too deeply into his discussion, saying that he was going to go into the military for pilot training. They left as friends, but Earl was sad to see him go away with such a cloud over his head. Yet he knew that even in that situation, God was working with him to bring him to Christian maturity.

On one outing Earl kneeled beside Joyce's chair and held her hands. "If you don't mind, Joyce, I'd like to give a little prayer to God for us." When she nodded her head he began. "Lord, we'd like to thank you for keeping us alive. You know what's been on my mind, and I believe Joyce's too. I'd like Your permission to marry her. If it's in your will, of course. I know that if it's not, you will adjust the circumstances so that it won't happen. So in the meantime I'll just go ahead with it. Whatever happens, thank you for it. Amen." She echoed his amen. Still on his knees, he said, "Joyce, I love you. I want to be with you forever. If you consent, I'd like to marry you."

Joyce frowned. "Are you sure you know what you're doing? I'll be quite a handful."

"Believe me, there's nothing I want more than to take care of you."

She smiled down at him. "Of course," she said brightly. Within a week they were man and wife, the modest ceremony having taken place in the tiny hospital chapel with Janet, two doctors and several nurses in attendance. Soon after that they were discharged from the hospital and went to live in his home, having risked a rift between Joyce and her mother over their refusal to live with her. "I wouldn't be so lonely with you there near me," was a familiar lament, to which Joyce consistently replied that it was essential, for a marriage to start off on the right foot, that the new husband and wife should learn to handle by themselves whatever came their way. In the end, Janet had to acknowledge the wisdom of Joyce's adamant insistence on living by themselves. Having won that battle, Earl and Joyce backed off a little, promising Janet that they would welcome her company one night a week.

The accident insurance let them be financially independent, provided that they carefully watched their expenses. The insurance allowed for Joyce to be fitted with rather basic prosthetic legs, which allowed her to stand upright and walk, but she did so with a considerable amount of awkwardness. She could do far better with more expensive prosthetic devices. Determined to provide these for her, he applied for his old job and was relieved but apprehensive to have been offered one. It wasn't quite the level of his old position: the world had turned some since the accident, and the company had replaced him, so he was back where he started before the promotion. But it was a job, and for that he was grateful.

Joyce was indeed a handful, but to Earl her needs were a labor of love. In time, she was able to go to the bathroom and even bathe for herself, and his work also became easier as he grew accustomed to the routine. In return, she gave him her wholehearted love. Their marriage grew synergistic and content.

CHAPTER 15

One night She appeared again. When he saw her beautiful face he pulled back in shock. Then he looked over at Joyce. She was sleeping peacefully. "Let her be, Earl, She said. "It's you I want to speak with. It'll be one of the last chances I'll have to talk with you like this for a long time."

Her words dejected Earl. "Don't look so downcast," She told him. "I told you about this before. I know you'll miss Me, but We gave you Joyce for companionship, comfort and support. It is to her that you now must look. What you two will accomplish together will give Us great joy, for it fits right in with the way We designed you."

"Is that why her therapy was so painful?"

"Sadly, yes. Believe me, We weren't happy letting that happen. But she needed to be strengthened for the sake of what you two are going to do together."

"Will our lives be happy?"

"That's up to you. But I'll give you a little hint." She winked. "Yes. Much of the time."

"What will You have us do, Wisdom?"

"I have given you a rare and precious gift, an insight into Our Trinitarian nature. It is an understanding that, up to a short time ago was virtually unknown in the Christian community. Of course, that also means that the rest of the world doesn't possess it either."

"You mean that I'm alone with this?"

"No. Not at all. Many other people were given this gift at pretty much the same time that you were. But you're scattered about, and each of you has the same job, which is to share this same gift with your fellow men and women."

"But why? Why didn't you just give everybody the same gift that you gave us?"

"Ah, but that's not the way We operate. When you've become more intimately acquainted with Scripture, you'll see a pattern running through it of men performing God's work, like Isaac, Joseph and a host of others representing the Jesus who was to eventually appear in the flesh. You'll like the reason we've done it that way: so that mankind himself gets to participate in God's great plan of salvation and love. We've included you in our game plan, Earl. You're intimately involved in it. But then the gift will propagate, so that those who understand your message will be given other gifts, and so on, so that a very large number of your fellow Christians will also enjoy an intimate involvement with God."

"That's big. Huge, in fact. I'm not sure that a lot of people understand that."

"Many don't. But the ones in whom we're interested do."

"Thanks for the privilege. I'm ready to do it."

"You will. But keep in mind one little item. It's going to be a costly endeavor for you. You're going to come up against opposition, some of it hate-filled. You'll find that you have to lean on us pretty heavily to get through it. But the kind of opposition you'll be experiencing is common to every person who's been given a task like yours. Just remember that you aren't the first to go through the heat. Jesus said that if He did it, and he did, magnificently, His disciples also would. There's a passage in Hebrews Chapter Eleven that's particularly appropriate. Listen well to it:

And what more shall I say? I do not have time to tell about Gideon, Barak, Samson, Jephthah, David, Samuel and the prophets, who through faith conquered kingdoms, administered justice, and gained what was promised; who shut the mouths of lions, quenched the fury of the flames, and escaped the edge of the sword; whose weakness was turned into strength; and who became powerful in battle and routed foreign armies. Women received back their dead, raised to life again. Others were tortured and refused to be released, so that they might gain a better resurrection. Some faced jeers and flogging, while still others were chained and put into prison. They were stoned; they were sawed in two; they were put to death by the sword. They went about in sheepskins and goatskins, destitute, persecuted and mistreated – the world was not worthy of them. They wandered in deserts and mountains, and in caves and holes in the ground. These were all commended for their faith, yet none of them received what had been promised. God had planned something better for us so that only together with us would they be made perfect.

"That little background tidbit brings me to the main reason as to why I'm here. As to specifics: I'm going to move you to read and digest particular passages of Scripture that have to do with your gift, which is knowledge imparted to you about our family-structured interrelationship. Then you'll be moved to write about your findings. After that is the hard part: you'll be sharing your findings with others through a blog on the Internet. You'll get some reactions to it that you wouldn't believe if you didn't experience the rants. Most of them will be coming from those who consider themselves to be good Christians. But you'll also reach those for whom the message is intended."

"I'm ready to do this, but I can't figure out why a person, especially a Christian, would be against learning more about God, and more so because it would help him to love God in a way that wouldn't otherwise be possible."

"Oh, there are reasons. Lots of them. I'll give you a few. There's the 'NIH' factor, for one."

"You mean 'Not Invented Here'? I used to come up against that all the time at work. I wouldn't have thought that kind of self-serving reaction would have any place in the Christian community."

"You'd be surprised. There are lots of so-called 'Christians' who look upon their 'Christianity' as a kind of exclusive social club. They'll be particularly antagonistic to a member of their immediate group who seems to have a message that they themselves didn't receive directly from God, because that would mean that they weren't Number One in God's list of favorites. Despite the negative reaction, a confrontation like you'll be giving them is good for them. Many of them actually are Christians, but they need to get knocked down some so that they'll be useful to Us. Ego just doesn't have a place in Our plan, for Us or for you.

"Another reason why you'll be facing opposition is a problem with the menfolk. It's just plain male chauvinism. Even many women go along with it. The thought here is that a woman's place is in the home and certainly not within the Godhead. Like the 'NIH' factor, its root cause is pride. You'd be surprised, given what Scripture has to say on the subject, that there are so many Christians, among whom are a large number of pastors and other church leaders, who continue to be slaves to pride."

"I'd like to see what Scripture says about pride. Where do I look?"

"The first thing you want to do tomorrow is get on the Internet with the keyword "Bible Concordance". Be sure that you make the selection that tracks your own Bible, the King James Version. Then all you'd have to do is look up the word 'pride' and go to the listed references. You might have to work some and think of different words that mean the same, like 'proud'. For the sake of giving you an answer to your question, I'll start you off with a few representative references. Psalm 101 verse 5 reads

"Whoso privily slandereth his neighbor, him will I cut off; him that hath a high look and a proud heart will not I suffer."

"Then there's Proverbs 16 verse 5, which says

"Every one who is proud in heart is an abomination to the Lord;

though hand join in hand, he shall not be unpunished."

"Mary, in reciting her Magnificat, said, according to Luke 1 verses 51 and 52

"He hath shown strength with his arm; he hath scattered the proud in the imagination of their hearts. He hath put down the mighty from their seats, and exalted them of low degree."

"My all-time personal favorite Wisdom continued, is Paul's description of Christians in 1 Corinthians 1 verses 8 through 31, speaking of those brave souls who endure being branded as the "B" team of society:

For the preaching of the cross is to them that perish foolishness; but unto us who are saved it is the power of God. For it is written, I will destroy the wisdom of the wise, and will bring to nothing the understanding of the prudent.

Where is the wise? Where is the scribe? Where is the disputer of this world? Hath not God made foolish the wisdom of this world? For after that, in the wisdom of God, the world by wisdom knew not God, it pleased God by the foolishness of preaching to save them that believe. For the Jews require a sign, and the Greeks seek after wisdom; but we preach Christ crucified, unto the Jews a stumbling block, and unto the Greeks foolishness; but unto them who are called, both Jews and Greeks, Christ the power of God, and the wisdom of God. Because the foolishness of God is wiser than men; and the weakness of God is stronger than men.

For ye see your calling, brethren, how that not many wise men after the flesh, not many mighty, not many noble, are called; but God hath chosen the foolish things of the world to confound the wise; and God hath chosen the weak things of the world to confound the things which are mighty; and base things of the world, and things which are despised, hath God chosen, yea, and things which are not, to bring to nought things that are, that no flesh should glory in his presence. But of him are ye in Christ Jesus, who of God is made unto us wisdom, and righteousness, and sanctification, and redemption: that, according as it is written, "He that glorieth, let him glory in the Lord."

"God will certainly humble the proud, Earl. But that isn't all bad, because those whom He chooses to humble are also those whom He loves. But pride won't be the only reason for those who will turn against you. Some will get angry because they don't know God very well. They certainly don't have an intimate relationship with Jesus, the Father, or even Me. What's really bad about it is that it doesn't just apply to laypeople, but to theologians as well. So many of them refuse to go beyond the superficial and mundane that it's virtually an epidemic. A big part of that bunch are the self-absorbed people, and I include theologians among them, who don't care whether the rest of the world goes to hell or not, as long as they themselves are safe. These have a squeamish fear of offending the Holy Spirit, maintaining the persistent caution that theologians have exercised against any attempt to change the established understanding of the Holy Spirit, despite the vagueness and confusion attending it. While the general source is the individual's indifference toward God and his selfish attitude toward his salvation, the overt source is related to the warning given in Proverbs 8:36: he that sins against the Holy Spirit wrongs his own soul. There is also a correlation between this caution and the one expressed by Jesus in Matthew 12 verses 31 and 32:

Wherefore I say unto you, All manner of sin and blasphemy shall be forgiven unto men: but the blasphemy against the Holy Ghost shall not be forgiven unto men. And whosoever speaketh a word against the Son of man, it shall be forgiven him: but whosoever speaketh against the Holy Ghost, it shall not be forgiven him, neither in this world, neither in the world to come.

"Earl, you know by now that the only way to love God as He commands is to perceive the Godhead in a family setting. Sadly, some people would rather give up a chance to have that kind of a relationship with God than risk shooting themselves in the foot.

God doesn't take kindly to that kind of cowardice. The problem is made worse by the numerous self-proclaimed expositors of the Holy Spirit. Many of them come to within a hair of explaining the Holy Spirit by means of typically female attributes, and then back off due to this unjustified fear. Through their cowardice they expose multitudes of people to a wrong understanding of the Holy Spirit, one that lacks the love of God that should be theirs to enjoy."

"Thanks for the expose. With that background, I should be well-equipped to withstand the barbs that will come my way."

"Hold on. There's more. If you attribute all the opposition to nothing but the motive of selfishness, you'll be doing yourself and others more harm than good. There are good people out there who'll oppose you. They are a product of the times you're living in. Society's breaking down. So are the churches. It's not just one denomination, or one country. It's everywhere, worldwide. Many pastors try to accommodate Christianity to secular views of the world, coming up with terrible falsehoods like the notion that Noah's flood was local, and that the world has existed for billions of years, and that the earth changes only by tiny increments, and that life arose naturalistically by processes related to chance, and . . . well, I could go on and on, but you get the point. Other pastors have decided that Scripture is not to be trusted, and lead their flocks into perdition. Still others try to mesh Christianity with other religions, in effect saying that Jesus isn't the only way to heaven. That's like you trying to launch off downwind – it won't work, as you well know. Jesus is indeed the only way to heaven, as a great number of self-serving, arrogant humans will learn to their great dismay. Many of these people will get what they deserve, but there are a great many others who were led by them and whose motives are more sincere than their knowledge."

"The big problem is that this falling-away of the churches is affecting good Christians, who see this debacle happening before their eyes and turn away from any new thoughts about God. In their reactionary stance they're refusing to listen to anyone who offers an idea that's different from what they were brought up with. A symptom of this reactionary spirit is a desire to embrace tradition, to return to the God of our fathers, when men were men, women were women, and God was God. It is a time when the introduction of new thought, even if it were a step in the progressive revelation of God to man, would be met with hostility and automatic rejection. The problem isn't new; it's been with you since before the time of Abraham."

"From the very beginning of God's relationship with Abraham, Judaism and its monotheism stood apart from the pantheons of hedonistic gods and the goddess-worshiping fertility cults of the surrounding Gentile peoples. The God who has been handed down to us through Judeo-Christian tradition is far more ascetic and sexually neutral than these shameless pseudo-gods, and for the good reason that He had an altogether different message to give His creation than the self-serving and corrupt fare that man had imposed upon himself. The traditions that man constructed around this message - but not the message itself, having come from God - went to a reactionary extreme in the attempt to distance the faith from the false gods of the surrounding nations and their blatant sexuality. The traditional Judeo-Christian God, then, was essentially emasculated from very early on. That tradition is still very much alive within the Christian community, causing any re-emergence of gender considerations to be treated with skepticism and hostility.

"Reactionary attitudes, despite modern Christians who supposedly embrace them in the belief that they are defending Jesus, had a lot to do with the rejection of Jesus in favor of the traditions of faith; reactionary thought flared up periodically after that, and really got out of hand at the beginning of the Renaissance. This period, the midst of the sixteenth century - Martin Luther lived from 1483, the year that the infamous Tomas de Torquemada was named Grand Inquisitor, to 1546 and in 1517 nailed his 95 Theses of Contention to the door of the Catholic Church in Wittenberg - was in fact in its own state of flux. Indeed, there were elements of that period that were remarkably common to your own. First, the church had its own tradition regarding the cosmos that was coming under increasing challenge by stargazing intellectuals. Despite the fact that the Ptolemaic cosmology to which the church adhered had nothing to do with Scripture but was an outgrowth of Greek metaphysical scholarship, it represented the old order that prevailed when the church establishment was unchallenged.

"As Martin Luther and his adherents spoke out against the Catholic theology, traditions and government, intellectuals also began to seriously undercut the cosmology that was companion to the church for much of its history. With the threat to Aristotle's idealistic cosmology becoming ever more pronounced, the church in 1616 took the reactionary stance of formally embracing it in opposition to revolutionary thinkers as Kepler, Copernicus and Galileo, whose works were declared to be heretical. Despite its secular nature, it would become an issue to be brought before the reactionary Inquisition, which had been active in various kingdoms since the thirteenth century and would continue on to the mid-1700 and even into the 1800s in some areas. The evil sadist Torquemada was appointed Grand Inquisitioner well within this same era. That satan-inspired fiend went so far as to invent diabolical instruments of torture to intensify and prolong his poor victims' agony. These instruments from hell included finger snips and funnels for channeling molten lead into the ear, as well as the more well known racks and chains.

"The bottom line is that during the time of the Reformation and afterward, when the long-established church order was being threatened, the works of new thinkers took a beating from the church. Even Martin Luther, the father of the Protestant movement, took the side of the Catholic Church against Kepler and Copernicus, railing out against their subversive heliocentric ideas which, of course, happened to be true.

"As you can understand by absorbing the news, the reactionary instinct is even more urgent in this time of general moral decline. Many conservative Christians are distressed over what appears to be a wholesale falling-away of traditional church denominations. And well they should be. Major church organizations have not only rejected clear Scriptural teaching by accepting homosexuality as normal, they have openly embraced this heresy, going so far as to ordain practicing homosexuals as ministers and church leaders.

"I could go on, but it would be morning before I finished and you need more sleep. What I've told you so far will give you a taste of what you'll be facing. Remember this: We're with you all the way, and we'll strengthen you as you need us. From now on, though, I'll be working through Joyce for the most part, which is as it should be: man and wife, complementing each other in everything they do. Goodbye, my dearest."

She faded away. He wrapped his arm around Joyce's body and slept.

CHAPTER 16

Joyce greeted him at the door in her wheelchair. There was an excited glow in her eyes. "I've been reading the Bible today, and I came across something that might interest you." Without waiting for a response from him, she opened the Bible on her lap. "It's from John 3, she said. "Jesus is talking to the Pharisee Nicodemus about spiritual birth:

> *Verily, verily, I say unto thee, Except a man be born of water and of the Spirit, he cannot enter into the kingdom of God. That which is born of the flesh is flesh; and that which is born of the Spirit is spirit. Marvel not that I said unto thee, Ye must be born again. The wind bloweth where it listeth, and thou hearest the sound of it, but canst not tell from where it cometh, and where it goeth; so is every one that is born of the Spirit.*

She closed the Bible and backed up to let him inside. "Do you get it? Jesus attributes the function of spiritual birth to the Holy Spirit. Boy, if birth isn't a female function, I don't know what is."

"Thanks for that, Joyce. It sure firms up my case." He kissed her lovingly, thinking that the passage was familiar. He shrugged, thinking that he had read it as a stray passage of interest. Whatever the source, Joyce's reading of it to him reinforced his memory of it, and more firmly implanted in him the conviction that he was correct about the Holy Spirit.

Earl was exhausted when he stepped into their bedroom the next night. He was still learning how to care for Joyce's numerous physical needs. But he wasn't irritated. He was grateful to God for the opportunity of showing Joyce his love for her. Laying her gently onto the bed, he opened the covers and tucked her inside. Before climbing into bed himself, he got on his knees and, holding Joyce's hand, thanked God for preserving her life. When he was finally in bed himself, he put his arm around her and immediately fell into a dreamless sleep.

He awoke unusually refreshed and busied himself preparing for work. When he brought breakfast to Joyce in their bedroom she smiled her thanks. "I'm getting lazy, Earl. This is the last time I want breakfast in bed, and, beginning today I'm going to start pulling my own weight around here."

"Why don't you wait 'til next week? You'll be getting your legs then." She had an appointment the next Tuesday to have her new prostheses fitted. Thanks to Earl's job they'd be able to handle what expenses weren't covered in their insurance with time payments. They both were anticipating the event with excitement.

"No, thanks. There's things I can do in the meantime."

When Earl arrived at work, he was surprised to see that the temp who'd replaced Joyce was no longer at the reception desk. He was more surprised to see who'd replaced her. Patty had come back. He walked up to her, grinning. "Glad to see you back, Patty," he said.

"Well, well, . . . oh." Patty stared at his missing arm. Nobody had warned her, and she didn't know what to say. There was an embarrassed silence, finally broken by Earl.

"Hey, it's not as bad as it looks. I can still do my job. Life is good. Great, as a matter of fact."

"Oh, Earl. First your wife, and now this." For the first time since he'd known her, she showed compassion.

"Time heals. I've remarried, Patty. She's a wonderful woman."

She gave him a hug. "Well I'm glad to be back. And it's good to see you."

He went into his cubicle scratching his head. *Having a baby took some sass out of Patty,* he thought. *I hope she'll still be friendly. I wouldn't even mind obnoxious if some of the old Patty would come back.*

At home that evening Earl found Joyce in the kitchen cooking dinner. He gave her a long kiss and went into the bedroom to change clothes. He discovered there that Joyce had also made their bed. He thanked God for giving her to him and went into the den, where he fired up his laptop and got to work applying his job skills to the creation of a blog site. He was done by the time Joyce called him in to dinner. After dinner they spent a quiet time together reading their Bibles after partaking of the eye-candy offered by the Wheel on TV. For comfort in the hospital, Joyce had also become interested in digesting Scripture. It had since become a full-time enterprise. For that he was grateful.

The next evening at home Earl began in earnest to pursue a new interest in his life, the creation of Christian-oriented blog articles. The first one was addressed to the apparent discrepancy between Judeo-Christian monotheism and the understanding of a Trinitarian Godhead. He entitled it 'A Deficiency'. It took him two evenings to complete it.

Between the two evenings Earl told Patty about his new endeavor and gave her the address of the blog. He didn't hold out much hope, but he thought that perhaps she might read it out of loyalty to a co-worker and pass on the information to her circle of friends and acquaintances. He had no idea that this move would produce the response that it did.

A DEFICIENCY

Among those topics that Christian theologians have been remiss in properly addressing, the number-one item surely must be the apparent conflict between our supposed monotheism and the Trinitarian (three-fold) nature of our Godhead. The issue has implications far beyond intellectual theology, extending down to every last individual who desires to experience a full and satisfying personal relationship with his God.

This problem represents a deficiency so profound that most Christians are unable in their own minds to resolve the conflict between their monotheism and their belief in a Trinitarian Godhead. We usually end up ignoring the whole subject altogether. But if we do that, can we truly call ourselves obedient to God? How indeed can we individuals love our God with all our hearts, souls and might, as commanded by God through Moses in Deuteronomy 6 and by Jesus in Matthew 22, in the face of the prevailing lack of clarity regarding the Godhead? Can we actually love that which we know so little about? Yet the commandments of God are not to be taken lightly. Godly men and women, as Scripture emphasizes time and again, are those who are obedient to our Judeo-Christian God's commandments.

It's not as if our theologians, now and in the past, haven't addressed the subject. There is plenty of literature available from a variety of media, including the Internet and libraries, to occupy for months on end the person who wishes to delve into the subject. The problem with this mass of information is its intuitive meaninglessness.

To be meaningful, any explanation of the Holy Trinity that resolves the issue of monotheism vs. a Trinitarian Godhead must necessarily do so not only at the level of the mind but, first and foremost, it must appeal to the heart. Otherwise, it possesses no value whatsoever toward the achievement of its most important result, a greater love in the heart of the believer.

The answer must be intuitive. It must grab the heart and make the hearer say to himself, "Of course!" It cannot be the product of church councils or pronouncements formulated out of deliberations among august bodies of profound logical thinkers. It must conform to Scripture while making sense to the gut. How, otherwise, can the hearer apply what he hears to the love of his God?

Of the mass of literature created over the explanation of the Holy Trinity, why is it all so sterile with respect to its ability to reach the heart? I, for one, attribute this condition to a lack of courage on the part of those who attempt to be spokespersons on the subject. It isn't as if many of the authors of such explanations didn't know the truth about the matter, because several of them have skirted very close to the essential truth and then backed off short of the mark, as if it represented a cliff beneath which lay a bottomless gorge. As those who engage in a certain mode of flight well know, one must run past the cliff to experience life in all its richness. The present case involves a deep trust in God. (Well, actually, they both do.) Despite the call throughout Scripture for selfless nobility, these self-proclaimed spokespersons for God value their positions and standings within the church community, and the approval of their intellectual peers, over plain truth. The reason why these persons shrink from the truth is that it presents another apparent conflict. Apparently, they have refused to take more than a surface approach to the issue; if they had, they would have realized that this other apparent conflict is quite easy to resolve. I will do my best to do so in this and future postings. Along the way, I will present additional material in support of my vision of who exactly the Holy Trinity is, and of why this vision permits me to embrace my God with a deeper love, a love that makes me think that I am now closer to being obedient to His greatest commandment.

The morning after his first post Earl greeted Patty and was relieved to see that she was beginning to revert back to her old self. Beyond that welcome circumstance he received an unexpected applause from her. "I didn't know you're a real writer," she fizzed. "That's like, wow, I know a writer!" Patty had already been busy at work notifying her fellow-workers of Earl's project. By noon the news had reached the mice in the woodwork. There was a prohibition of using the computers for things not related to the job, but that didn't stop anybody from accessing Earl's first blog. Several people came into his cubicle to congratulate him.

Patty kicked the exposure up a notch on her own. Deciding that if Earl was going to be in the limelight it wouldn't hurt to share in his effort, she called the local newspaper and told them about it. Her bubbly enthusiasm piqued the interest of the columnist, who told her that he'd be sure to follow it.

On Tuesday he took off early from work to take Joyce to her fitting appointment, which was followed by a post-fitting therapy session. He could see the strain on her face on the way home. What was supposed to be a beautiful event was turning out to be not-so-great. Common sense should have told them that it would take much time for Joyce to become comfortable with the prosthetics. But she refused to take them off when they arrived home. Gritting her teeth, she insisted on cooking him dinner and sweeping the floor. When they went to bed she was almost crying.

Wednesday Earl posted his second blog.

FRIEND OF THE FAMILY

It's heartwarming to see happiness shared by close-knit families. In these loving, self-contained environments, each member knows that he or she is an important part of a greater whole. Families like that enjoy a number of advantages. For one thing, all the persons in it have the confidence of belonging to a special group to whom they can turn if for any reason the going gets tough. They also learn that the world doesn't rotate around the individual, which is a very valuable lesson. Beyond that, through their close interaction with several very different personalities, they acquire a variety of experiences that lead to a well-rounded knowledge of what makes people tick.

If the family experiences allow the members to grow in wisdom, the interaction among its members becomes synergistic, wherein they complement each other like in a well-oiled machine. The whole then becomes greater than the sum of its components and acquires its own distinct objectives, personality and method of interacting with the world outside it. It truly has a life of its own. The family, as a matter of fact, is the singular means within our comprehension by which separate individuals may become component elements of a greater whole, a oneness in love that both transcends the individual person and extends his own significance.

Man was designed by God such that family is necessarily an integral part of his life. The baby needs its mother for sustenance, comfort and survival, and its father more indirectly for the survival of its mother. The mother and father, on the other hand, need the child for the continuation of life itself. Without the family setting, mankind simply can't exist. There are totalitarian societies, to be sure, that attempt to play the surrogate parent. But the attempt requires a sophisticated system to be workable at all, and at its best it fails to supply some basic ingredients, both physical and emotional, that have been found to be vital to the proper rearing of a child. In the end the surrogate process can't sustain itself and falls apart. Even then, inferior as it is, the totalitarian state does try to emulate God's family arrangement by attempting to substitute for it.

Genesis 2:24 illustrates God's plan for mankind for which the family is an integral component by noting that when male and female unite, they shall leave father and mother and start their own family as an independent unit:

"Therefore shall a man leave his father and mother, and shall cleave unto his wife: and they shall be one flesh."

The grandfolks may return later as live-ins, but the authority over children rests completely with the parents. Then, too, the fifth of the ten commandments given to Moses by God *(Exodus 20)* is to honor father and mother "that your days may be long upon the land which the Lord your God gives you". Among his exhortations, Paul in *Ephesians 6:2* commented that this particular commandment was the first to carry a promise for its observance, illustrating its importance to God.

A most interesting facet of *Genesis 2:24* is the implication that in the context of the marital union, the male and female become one. When the marriage bears fruit with children, the family unity extends to them. Much more will be said about this later.

Is there a more fundamental reason for the inclusion of family in the design of mankind? Does it also represent a promise to us regarding our relationship with our God? *Genesis 1:27* can be taken to imply just that, for the reason that God created man in His own image and in the process created male and female versions of mankind.

To be fair, many Bible experts think that to attempt to make this connection between man and God is reading too much into the passage. But the more one takes a larger picture in viewing mankind and God, the more he's prone to make that connection. God's design of mankind, which includes his necessity for a family setting, obviously doesn't necessarily impose the same requirement on God Himself. But, as we shall see, both the marriage and family relationship do apply to at least one Member of the Godhead, Jesus.

As before Joyce read the blog before he posted it. She looked up at him and smiled. "Good going. For a geek, you're a pretty good writer."

"I suspect that it's not really me. But I'm grateful for the inspiration. And to you, darling. I never knew that I'd be so happy in a second marriage."

"Me too. Let's go to bed."

The next morning at work Earl was surprised that Patty's enthusiasm hadn't waned. Flattered, he thought that his earlier assessment of her might have been off. *Maybe she's deeper than I gave her credit* for, he thought. But then she spoke. "Now that you've used up the subject of religion, what are you going to write about next? Politics? I can't wait for the next installment."

"No, Patty," he replied. "I haven't used up the subject of religion. There's a huge amount left to discuss. More than I can possibly do by myself."

"Well," she said doubtfully. "Whatever. I'll read it anyway. Maybe if I make a hard copy of it, you'll autograph it. Will you?"

"Sure." Disappointed in the way that the conversation had shoaled up so quickly, he turned and headed for his cubicle. On the way he passed Walter, who patted his back affectionately. It was all he could do to refrain from lifting a leg and piddling on his shoe.

CHAPTER 17

At least the job itself was satisfying and at home Joyce was making progress with her prosthetic legs. It took him three more days to come up with another blog, which he posted Saturday afternoon.

ISAAC'S MARRIAGE TO REBEKAH

Chapter 22 of Genesis describes the greatest test of faith that God would impose upon Abraham or, for that matter, upon any human. In that chapter, God tells Abraham to sacrifice the son whom he dearly loved.

> *And it came to pass after these things, that God did tempt Abraham, and said unto him Abraham: and he said, Behold, here I am. And he said, Take now thy son, thine only son Isaac, whom thou lovest, and get thee into the land of Moriah; and offer him there for a burnt offering upon one of the mountains which I will tell thee of.*

> *And Abraham rose up early in the morning, and saddled his ass, and took two of his young men with him, and Isaac his son, and clave the wood for the burnt offering, and rose up, and went unto the place of which God had told him. Then on the third day Abraham lifted up his eyes, and saw the place afar off. And Abraham said unto his young men, Abide ye here with the ass; and I and the lad will go yonder*

and worship, and come again to you.

And Abraham took the wood of the burnt offering, and laid it upon Isaac his son; and he took the fire in his hand, and a knife; and they went both of them together. And Isaac spake unto Abraham his father, and said, My father: and he said, Here am I, my son. And he said, Behold the fire and the wood: but where is the lamb for a burnt offering? And Abraham said, My son, God will provide himself a lamb for a burnt offering: so they went both of them together. And they came to the place which God had told him of; and Abraham built an altar there, and laid the wood in order, and bound Isaac his son, and laid him on the altar upon the wood. And Abraham stretched forth his hand, and took the knife to slay his son.

And the Angel of the Lord called unto him out of heaven, and said, Abraham, Abraham: and he said Here am I. And he said, Lay not thine hand upon the lad, neither do thou any thing unto him: for now I know that thou fearest God, seeing thou hast not withheld thy son, thine only son, from me. And Abraham lifted up his eyes, and looked, and behold behind him a ram caught in a thicket by his horns: and Abraham went and took the ram, and offered him up for a burnt offering in the stead of his son. And Abraham called the name of that place Jehovah-jireh: as it is said to this day, In the mount of the Lord it shall be seen.

Abraham actually had more than one son, but Isaac was the only son who was born of his wife Sarah, and it was to be through Isaac's bloodline that the promises of God to Abraham eventually would be realized. It was in the sense that Abraham's seed through Isaac would be the one to bear fruit to God that Isaac was considered to be Abraham's only son.

This event in the life of Abraham and Isaac was clearly intended by God to portray the sorrow that would be the Holy Father's lot as his only begotten Son Jesus was sacrificed on the cross at Calvary. What God held back from requiring of Abraham, He Himself had to do in this magnificent expression of His sacrificial love toward mankind. Abraham was blessed for his faith. The importance of it was not just that he was willing to suffer the sorrow of losing his son. The greater part of his faith was that he was willing to represent the drama between the Father and Jesus in the most significant moment in the history of mankind: Jesus' passion on the cross.

Genesis Chapter 24 involves Isaac again, but under considerably happier circumstances. Isaac is now old enough to marry, and his father Abraham is choosy about whom he shall have as a bride. Sarah has died, so the task of selecting the proper wife for Isaac falls on the shoulders of Abraham's trusted servant, who is told to go to the country of Abraham's kinfolk. We pick up the narrative at verse 10:

And the servant took ten camels of the camels of his master, and departed; for all the goods of his master were in his hand: and he arose, and went to Mesopotamia, unto the city of Nahor. And he made his camels to kneel down without the city by a well of water at the time of the evening, even the time that women go out to draw water. And he said, O Lord God of my master Abraham, I pray thee, send me good speed this day, and show kindness unto my master Abraham. Behold, I stand here by the well of water; and the daughters of the men of the city come out to draw water: And let it come to pass, that the damsel to whom I shall say, Let down thy pitcher, I pray thee, that I may drink; and she shall say, Drink, and I will give thy camels drink also: let the same be she that thou hast appointed for thy servant Isaac; and thereby shall I know that thou hast shown kindness unto my master.

And it came to pass, before he had done speaking, that, behold, Rebekah came out, who was born to Bethuel, son of Milcah, the wife of Nahor, Abraham's brother, with her pitcher upon her shoulder. And she was very fair to look upon, a virgin, neither had any man known her: and she went down to the well, and filled her pitcher, and came up. And the servant ran to meet her, and said, Let me, I pray thee, drink a little water of thy pitcher. And she said, Drink, my lord: and she hasted, and let down her pitcher upon her hand, and gave him drink. And when she had done giving him drink, she said, I will draw water for thy camels also, until they have done drinking. And she hasted, and emptied her pitcher into the trough, and ran again unto the well to draw water, and drew for all his camels. And the man wondering at her held his peace, to wit whether the Lord had made his journey prosperous or not. And it came to pass, as the camels had done drinking, that the man took a golden earring of half a shekel weight, and two bracelets for her hands of ten shekels weight of gold; And said, Whose daughter art thou? Tell me, I pray thee: is there room in thy father's house for us to lodge in? And she said unto him, I am the daughter of Bethuel the son of Milcah, which she bare unto Nahor. She said moreover unto him, We have both straw and provender enough, and room to lodge in. And the man bowed down his head, and worshipped the Lord. And he said, Blessed be the Lord God of my master Abraham, who hath not left destitute my master of his mercy and his truth: I being in the way, the Lord led me to the house of my master's brethren. And the damsel ran, and told them of her mother's house these things.

That event led Abraham's servant into the house of Rebekah's brother Laban, where he told them of his mission to find a wife for Abraham's son Isaac. He related how God had led him directly to Rebekah and had confirmed that she was the one whom he had sought. After this, the servant asked for their consent to take Rebekah back with him and present her to Isaac. Upon receiving their consent, the servant lavished gifts upon Rebekah and her family. As he prepared to return home, the family stalled off, asking that Rebekah stay with them for at least ten more days. He, wishing to return immediately, asked them to reconsider the delay, whereupon they called Rebekah into the meeting and asked her for her consent. Having received it from her, the servant then returned home with her and she became Isaac's wife.

At this point, Scripture had already identified Isaac as representing Jesus on the cross. Now, the circumstances of his marriage to

Rebekah just as clearly show him as representing Jesus who will wed a very special bride. Who shall that bride be?

"That's a good idea, Earl," Joyce said after she'd finished reading his post. "Anticipate in this article your next one. Now I can't wait to read the follow-on." Joyce was on the mend and her attitude toward everything was showing new life. Now when he looked into her lovely eyes he could see that the pain was diminishing in intensity. He thanked God for her continued healing.

Patty was good to her word. She told Earl that she'd read his latest blog through and through. "What I don't get, though," she told him with a frown, "is what Isaac has to do with Jesus. Jesus lived in the New Testament, didn't He? That's what I've always heard. Well, no matter. Congrats again, Earl."

"Patty, it does matter, a great deal. The Old Testament is full of accounts of people who represented Jesus before He came to earth. Isaac was one of them. If you have a few minutes, I'd like to explain some things about Jesus to you."

"Oh, hey, that's okay. Don't weird out on me. I've got to get back to work." She returned to her desk and sat down, occupying herself with some papers on her desk. Earl left her desk with sadness.

That evening Joyce told him that a Pastor Frank Wilson had called. "He said he'd be home all evening. Call him any time."

Earl called Mr. Wilson after dinner. "Thanks for returning my call, Mr. Cook. I'm running the Foursquare Church of God downtown. I'm always interested in furthering the Gospel, and I read of you in the paper. I also read your postings. Good work. You're right on. But, ah . . ." he paused, searching for the right words. "perhaps you'd like to run them by me before you print them out. That way I might be able to give you some useful input. This ol' boy still has some notions that might do well in your, ah, column." He ended the sentence with a defensive chuckle.

Earl couldn't define its source, but he had a very strong feeling that, despite Mr. Wilson's undoubtedly excellent academic credentials, submitting his blog to him for acceptance would not turn out well. It didn't help that he felt the man was usurping a function that should be reserved for his own pastor. The thought triggered an image of his Pastor George disagreeing very strongly with some of his statements. While he respected both pastors' superior theological knowledge, he also realized that pastors over the past century had swallowed uncritically some very bad theology dished out by their seminaries. Moreover, the Christian academic system tended to turn out clones who maintained the system's dogma. For the most part, that kind of stability was good. But it certainly precluded the introduction of fresh thought, even if its source was God Himself.

"Golly, I appreciate your offer, pastor. No doubt there's lots of good information you can give me. But for now I'd like to go it alone."

After a significant pause that registered Pastor Frank's deep disappointment with Earl's decision to decline his offer, he negotiated further. "Well, if that's your position, it's your blog. But I'm sure you won't mind my input after the postings. I'll keep in touch." He hung up before Earl could respond.

"Earl, that wasn't very nice of you," Joyce said. She'd been listening to his side of the conversation, and although neither of them was that well acquainted with the pastor, she was appalled that Earl would show that kind of disrespect to a church leader.

"I'm sorry," he responded, "but something is telling me to avoid making this blog a committee enterprise. Beside, I don't know that man well enough to submit to his correction."

"But, Earl, he's a theologian. He probably has a Doctorate in theology. That would put him way ahead of you in knowledge. I'd think you'd welcome a theologian's input."

"I'm not so sure about that. Let me give you a few reasons for my reluctance, okay?"

"Do that. I'm listening." She sat in her wheelchair with her arms wrapped about her breasts, her chin thrust out confrontationally.

"Well, then, I do listen to, I mean read, some pretty deep Christian thinkers through the Internet. It's amazing how much information is at our fingertips through the computer. I've read books, too, so I do know what many very respected theologians think. But on the issue that I seem to be led to address, nobody wants to talk about it, and I doubt whether Wilson would even want to think about it."

"You're assuming. You don't know that."

"Hear me out. There are a couple of reasons for that. First, this thought of mine involves the Holy Spirit, which is a touchy subject because according to Jesus (Matthew 12:31-32), of all the sins that man can perpetrate against God, blasphemy against the Holy Spirit is unforgivable. That little problem takes care of, oh, I'd say about 99.99999 percent of anyone who might otherwise be tempted to discuss the topic. Never mind that the topic is extremely important to one who is engaged in a serious and heartfelt search for the character of God in an attempt to love Him as He asks. I'm reasonably certain that God doesn't mind people asking questions about His nature, but once the subject acquired a taboo, the enthusiasm to pursue it further just wasn't there. Second, among the miniscule group of theologians who might remain available to talk about it, their understanding of God apparently is of such microscopic depth that their collective answers are of the scope of "say wha- - -?" I include in this group seminary graduates. It seems that the only things so many of them have been taught about God are systematic principles developed by men – intellectuals, to be sure, but men - of understanding Scripture, or of how people are to relate to God in order to receive the blessings due the Christian community. As you know, prosperity is a popular subject among Christians. The rest seems to be composed of principles of how to run an effective church organization. If this seems too harsh, let me give you a few examples."

"Go ahead. I'm still listening." Her chin receded somewhat toward its normal position.

"There's the big issue of evolution. How many church leaders have either ignored Darwin or attempted to wicker their theology to conform to macroevolutionary teaching? Answer: most. This despite the fact that evolution trashes Genesis 1. I'll give you a hint about how it does that. According to evolution, a lot of flesh died before the arrival of Adam, which contradicts the teaching of Scripture that death entered into the picture as a result of Adam's disobedience to God. Again, this despite the fact that modern cutting edge science, especially in the fields of molecular biology and applied information theory, has completely unseated Darwin's theory. The worst part of all this is that the general public has been and continues to be seriously misinformed regarding the latest scientific challenges to macroevolution. The liberal media, the National Geographic Society, the National Education Association, the ACLU and the National Park Service have been hugely successful in indoctrinating our children, and we adults as well, in assuming that Darwinian evolution is a proven fact, which it most certainly is not. Nevertheless, this state of affairs furnishes no valid excuse for our Christian leadership, in the face of such a serious Scripture-challenging issue, to have simply assumed that the secular world knows what is talking about or is inclined to tell the truth. It demonstrates a misplaced faith. I can understand why the atheist clings to evolution. He wants to. He will believe anything that comes along that will justify his faith that there is no God. But I am losing patience with those in the Christian community who continue to believe in macroevolution. There are so many good books out there that are accessible to the normal intellect and clearly demonstrate the bankruptcy of Darwin's notion that Christians have no reason to believe in it other than intellectual laziness or an indifference toward God. When a Christian attempts to defend macroevolution to me, I ask him whether he can draw a picture of a string of DNA, labeling its constituents and comparing it to a string of ASCII code. If he can, I then ask him whether he can draw a simple picture of how the cell uses DNA to make proteins, as a side issue asking him if he's acquainted with the concept of chirality. If he can't do these things, and he won't be able to, because if he could he wouldn't be defending evolution, I tell him that he's wasting my time because he doesn't have a clue as to what he's talking about.

"Are you through with that one? Because you're starting to go over my head. But I do understand most of what you're trying to tell me."

"I've said enough for now. Let's go on to other things."

Just then the phone rang. Earl picked it up. "Why, hello, Pastor George," he said after the caller identified himself. "It's nice to hear from you. What's up?" He knew full well what was up, and he dreaded another confrontation like the one he'd just gone through. *This one might be worse*, he thought. The stakes were higher. He and Joyce both liked him and appreciated the nature of his sermons. He was not a shallow thinker, and Earl thought of him as a friend.

"I've been reading your blogs, Earl," the pastor told him. "Looks like you're off to a good start. I just wanted to say that I'm here rooting for you. I won't presume to be giving you advice. Not unless you ask for it, that is. Well, good luck. Better yet, good Providence. See you in Church."

"Thanks, pastor. I appreciate your support. You don't know how much. See you Sunday."

"That was better," Joyce told him after he hung up. "I like George, and I like his preaching. Don't rock the boat there."

"I don't intend to."

Chapter 18

Joyce brought up the subject again on her own. "I'm trying to understand where you're coming from, Earl. I hear you on the evolution thing. But that doesn't justify your turning down a helping hand from knowledgeable people. I just can't go along with your cynicism about religious authorities."

"I wish you were right. But Pastor George might be a rare bird. The problem doesn't end with evolution. There are many, many such issues."

"I'm listening."

"Okay, next issue. How many church leaders remain totally ignorant of the principle of uniformity, which has been so highly regarded within the scientific community, and the impact of its implication of the enormous age of the earth on Genesis 1? I'll tell you: most, if not all."

"Hold on. What's uniformity?"

"It kind of goes hand in glove with evolution, because it demands an enormous age for the earth, giving so much time to the evolutionist that even though the process of evolution is an extremely weak and limited mechanism, evolutionists can claim that it works because the time factor is as large as the probability of evolution is tiny. Here's how it works: in the realm of geology it claims that no process ever occurred on earth that can't be observed today. In other words, with the exception of an earthquake or a couple of volcanoes, the mountains that we see today were essentially created by the miniscule erosional effects of the elements acting over a very large period of time."

"Well, that has been demonstrated, hasn't it?"

"Absolutely not. It's simply conjecture, without any logical basis whatsoever. Actually the whole concept has been overturned lately by the discovery of the dinosaur extinction event by the Alvarez team. So much for that theory. Then there's a general lack of appreciation of just why Scripture stands against homosexuality. How many church leaders fail to understand why Moses and Paul spoke out against society's acceptance of the gay lifestyle as normal? Not a whole lot, Joyce, even those from established and respected Christian denominations. The same can be said of the many sexual perversions that are engaged in by persons who are supposedly devoted to God. But the concept of the Holy Spirit that has been given to me for whatever reason can answer those issues naturally and logically."

"I get that one. It does seem to fit your understanding."

"Sure. And how many Church leaders really appreciate the incredible depth of Scripture? Many of them are so busy trying to wicker Scripture into a handbook for healthier and wealthier living that they can't get below the surface. Examples abound of fascinating, faith-building messages embedded within the more overt stories in Scripture. Many of these are presented in readily-available and highly readable books, so there's really no excuse for such ignorance."

"You're starting to rant, Earl. Calm down."

"I suppose you're right. Then I won't bother to delve into the details of the Church leaders' appalling ignorance of Scripture and what that is doing to the Church as a whole. Like the focus of some on physical prosperity, when Jesus clearly said that His kingdom is not of this world. Real Christianity considers physical wealth to be an obstacle rather than an end, and the quest for it to be idol-worship. Then there's the out-and-out apostasy. A large number of church leaders don't believe in the inerrancy of Scripture. Some have even come to a dead end in their religion, not knowing what or who to worship. Some don't even believe that God exists."

"Are you sure about that? By the way, I thought you were winding down."

"Sorry. Yes, I'm sure. And look at what some Churches are doing, taking the side of the secularists and Islamists at the expense of Israel. Okay, I won't say any more about that now, but some time I'll give you an earful about Israel."

Joyce was subdued by his outspoken opinion. She decided, somewhat reluctantly, to back him for now. "Just tell me that you'll try to get along with George," she pleaded. "And it wouldn't hurt to just listen to someone else once in a while. I really like that church."

"I'll do my best," he promised. "Bottom line, though, Joyce. You'd have to agree that if pastors had been doing their job, the Church wouldn't be in the mess it's in today."

He wrote his next blog that night, and he had decided to continue to submit it to another person for review. Somehow, he knew that it would be the right thing to do. He also knew without a doubt who that person should be. "Joyce," he called. "I've finished another blog. Would you go over it for me, please?"

REBEKAH'S COUNTERPART

In *Genesis Chapter 22*, Isaac obviously represented Jesus. That chapter illustrated the cost to the Divine Father of His Son's sacrifice on behalf of mankind. Isaac reappears in *Genesis Chapter 24*, wherein his marriage to Rebekah represents Jesus in a happier setting. In this particular passage the representation had to do with Jesus' marriage to the special bride who was represented by Rebekah. In the last posting, the question was asked as to whom this honor would be given.

Paul reveals to us in his letter to the Ephesians what he considered to be a mystery, knowledge that was hidden until, through his endowment with Wisdom imparted by the Holy Spirit, he wrote down the answer in Chapter 5 of his letter to the church at Ephesus:

Husbands, love your wives, even as Christ also loved the church, and gave himself for it; that He might present it to Himself a glorious church, not having spot, or wrinkle, or any such thing; but that it should be holy and without blemish.

So ought men to love their wives as their own bodies. He that loveth his wife loveth himself. For no man ever yet hated his own flesh; but nourisheth and cherisheth it, even as the Lord the church. For we are members of His body, of His flesh, and of His bones.

In *Ephesians 5:31* and *32*, he comes to a stunning conclusion:

For this cause shall a man leave his father and mother, and shall be joined unto his wife, and they two shall be one flesh. This is a great mystery: but I speak concerning Christ and the church.

Think about that – in our spiritual form, we're going to marry Jesus! So in *Matthew 22:30* when Jesus said that in the resurrection we neither marry nor are given in marriage, what He meant was that we wouldn't be marrying each other. Instead, we'd be marrying Him.

The notion of our marriage to Jesus opens enormous side issues. For starters, it explains why He reserved His first miracle for the wedding ceremony in Cana *(John 2)* where He changed water into wine. It also explains why He remained celibate during His time in the flesh, having reserved Himself for His future marriage to us.

But it gets deeper. It means that there's an element of romance in our love of Jesus, and that the union will bear fruit, for Paul spoke about it with the authority of earlier Scripture, quoting a passage in Isaiah that mankind wasn't given to fully understand about this future union until Paul clearly spelled it out. Paul had hinted about this relationship in *Galatians 4:24*, where he pretty much directly quoted *Isaiah 54:1*:

For it is written, Rejoice, thou barren that bearest not; break forth and cry, thou that travailest not: for the desolate hath many more children than she which hath a husband.

In turning back to the source, we find that as a sequel to the great Messianic passage, *Isaiah Chapter 53* that illustrates Jesus' sojourn in the flesh as sacrificial for our salvation, Isaiah Chapter 54:1-7 is replete with the promise of our future as Jesus' bride, a union that will bear much fruit:

> *Sing, O barren, thou that didst not bear; break forth into singing, and cry aloud, thou that didst not travail with child: for more are the children of the desolate than the children of the married wife, saith the Lord. Enlarge the place of thy tent, and let them stretch forth the curtains of thine habitations: spare not, lengthen thy cords, and strengthen thy stakes; for thou shalt break forth on the right hand and on the left; and thy seed shall inherit the Gentiles, and make the desolate cities to be inhabited. Fear not; for thou shalt not be ashamed: neither be thou confounded; for thou shalt not be put to shame: for thou shalt forget the shame of thy youth, and shalt not remember the reproach of thy widowhood any more.*

> *For thy Maker is thine husband; the Lord of hosts is His name; and thy Redeemer the Holy One of Israel; the God of the whole earth shall he be called. For the Lord hath called thee as a woman forsaken and grieved in spirit, and a wife of youth, when thou wast refused, saith thy God.*

> *For a small moment have I forsaken thee; but with greater mercies will I gather thee.*

In the context of our marriage to Jesus the book of Ruth comes alive, particularly in the fact that since Ruth was a Moabite and considered to be a Gentile, Ruth's marriage relates to the Church, just as Paul openly declared.

But the issue goes yet deeper. The Church's marriage to Jesus inescapably connotes that redeemed mankind, for which the aggregate gender is plainly masculine, will assume a profoundly female function. In the first place, despite our perverted society's attempts to change the rules to the contrary, a bride is always considered to be female. Secondly, we shall be the complement in marriage to the Son of God, a decidedly masculine appellation for Jesus. Thirdly, according to Isaiah 54, we shall give birth to much fruit, implying our motherhood which, of course, is eminently feminine in function.

Therefore we, being referred to in the aggregate as masculine, will have a female spiritual role. Does this dichotomy exist elsewhere in Scripture? I'll answer that in the next posting.

"I like it, Earl," Joyce said after reading his latest blog. "I must have read that passage a dozen times without really thinking of its significance. It really strengthens your case about the Holy Spirit. I find that very exciting."

After that buildup from his wife, it took Earl about five minutes the next morning to get pruned down to size at work. First off, Patty returned his greeting with indifference. *What's that all about?* he asked himself. He'd been in his cubicle less that a minute when Mike walked in and sat down. "Hi, dearie," he said in a falsetto voice, batting his eyelashes and flopping his wrist. "If we're all going to be girls, I guess we'd better get used to it."

Anger mounted inside Earl. He forced himself to remember what Jesus had said about loving even your enemies. "That's just dandy, sweetie-pie," he replied, matching the pitch of Mike's voice. "You can be a girl if that's your gig, Mike," he said in a more natural tone. "That's not what I said, and not what I meant. Down here in the physical realm, men are still men and women are still women. With a lot of exceptions that have nothing to do with God." Mike waved him off with an under-the-breath dig to the effect that he didn't need any strange theology from him and left his cubicle.

Walter, like Patty, didn't have anything to say to him. Instead he, also like Patty, looked at him with indifference when they saw each other in the cafeteria. Obviously, Walter had been discussing him with a good many of the employees, who rather openly avoided him.

He raised this new issue with Joyce that night. "Look, Earl," she replied. "You knew the score when you started this project, or if you didn't you should have. I certainly did. Think of what Jesus said in the Beatitudes, Matthew 5. He said for you to jump with joy if you're persecuted for His name's sake. You've made me believe what you think, that it's what Scripture has implied all along. You believe that yourself, don't you?"

"Of course."

"Then stick to your guns. Don't let it get you down. According to Jesus, you're supposed to have counted the cost before you started." She read to him Hebrews 11. "Expect the persecution. Rise above it. Now forget about it and let's eat."

"Yes, ma'am." Again, he was grateful for Joyce's presence in his life. He started on his next blog that evening. Three days later, after Joyce's review, he posted it.

SOMETIMES I'M LONELY

I have a lovely wife to whom I am devoted. We spend most of the day together and, of course, the night too, because we're also the best of friends. We have a wonderful pastor whose sermons delve into Scripture quite deeply, and we belong to a small church where everyone is a friend of everyone else.

Our pastor loves Jesus, and it shows in the manner that he conducts his life. He reveres Scripture as the Word of God, and that is plain from his preaching.

Because of these benign circumstances, I am almost happy. But not quite. As a Christian I lack the fulfillment of being able to share openly some insights into the nature of God that I consider to be of the most fundamental importance. The insights, while I understand them to originate with God, are personal, which makes me a bit of a stray. As one of Jesus' sheep, I suppose that I should have been content to graze with the rest of the flock, but I saw a greener pasture elsewhere. I'd very much like to think that Jesus opened the gate for me and led me into it, but a number of Christian brothers and sisters are bleating that I jumped the fence. My pastor knows where I am, but he has the rest of his flock to care for and so he must remain noncommittal about my situation. The upshot is that despite the richness of the grass nobody's coming in to share it with me, and I'm starting to get real lonely.

My situation began innocently enough. I love to read, and when I was born again, I picked up a Bible and read it. Having done that, I simply took Scripture at face value. When I arrived at *Matthew 22*, I read this:

> *Then one of [the Pharisees], which was a lawyer, asked [Jesus] a question, tempting Him, and saying, Master, which is the great commandment in the law? Jesus said unto him, Thou shalt love the Lord thy God with all thy heart, and with all thy soul, and with all thy mind.*

Having taken this Scripture to heart, I attempted to be obedient toward this greatest of commandments. To do so, I continued to read Scripture, this time in greater depth, in order that I might more intimately know this Person who commands me to love Him with all my being. Almost immediately a problem was encountered: God the Father is understandable in Scripture, and so is Jesus the Son, but the Holy Spirit, in the context of how we have been taught to view this Person, is not. Nor, because of the vagueness surrounding this Third Person of the Godhead, is the Holy Trinity.

How then, given this vagueness of knowledge, could I be obedient to the greatest commandment of Jesus? Somewhat frustrated, I set the matter aside as I continued to pore over Scripture. Then, when I happened upon *Ephesians Chapter 5*, I was delighted to discover the plainly-delivered answer to my earlier question. It was noted in the previous posting that, in the fullness of time according to Ephesians 5:31 and 32, Jesus shall leave His Father and Mother to wed the Church:

> *For this cause shall a man leave his father and mother, and shall be joined unto his wife, and they two shall be one flesh. This is a great mystery: but I speak concerning Christ and the church."*

It is conspicuous in this passage that in the process of marrying His Church, Jesus will leave his Father and Mother to do so. This, statement, of course, implies that He has both a Father and a Mother to leave.

Oh, my, what a lot of information is packed into those two verses! One must understand that even if the verses stand alone in the entire Bible as suggesting that the Godhead Itself is a Divine Family, they are unequivocal with regard to that implication. The only way that one can deny the family attribute of the Godhead in the face of those words is to deny that all of Scripture is inspired of the Holy Spirit. I'm certainly not willing to do that, for that constitutes an error infinitely graver than any controversy regarding the nature of the Godhead.

In my previous posting, I described the implications of our future spiritual marriage to Jesus, ending with mention of the dichotomy between redeemed mankind's masculine aggregate designation and the obviously female nature of our role as Bride of Christ. I then asked whether this dichotomy exists elsewhere in Scripture.

I'll answer that emphatically in the affirmative, and add that in its broader form this dichotomy is so profoundly important that I find it difficult to understand how anybody can fully love his God without appreciating its significance. It has to do with another marriage, one that was consummated long ago at the beginning of time.

As noted before, when thinking of the substance of the Church in terms of redeemed mankind, we apply the male gender. We do that because when we use a pronoun to refer to an aggregate composed of both sexes, we always apply the one associated with the dominant gender, which is male. Sorry, ladies, but that's just the way it is, political correctness notwithstanding. But you still get the last laugh, because Scripture openly describes the Church as female in Her relationship with Jesus. A good example of this is Paul's description of the Church in Ephesians as Jesus' future Bride. That makes you and the menfolk components of a spiritual female, a fact that you can goad your husbands with when they make you angry.

What I've written about the Church is not controversial with regard to basic theology. Being in full agreement with mainstream Christianity, I'm still grazing in the big pasture along with the other sheep. Now, in turning to the topic of the Holy Spirit, things begin to get dicey: the rest of the flock is staring at me and I can see the whites of their eyes. Nevertheless, I shall now assert that the gender situation with regard to the Holy Spirit may be very similar to that regarding the church in Her functional role as Bride of Christ: just as the masculine pronoun is used when referring to the Church constituted of redeemed mankind, Scripture uses the masculine pronoun when referring to the Holy Spirit. But redeemed mankind is also the Church as Bride of Christ, and just as the masculine pronoun in reference to redeemed mankind does not contradict a functional reference to the Church as female, I would say that here we have Scripture itself paving the way to considering the Holy Spirit to have a feminine function in the face of a masculine reference. Therefore, the masculine pronoun in reference to the Holy Spirit need not contradict a functional reference to this Comforter as female. But there is a big difference between an implication by similarity and an actuality. Do I make that leap?

I do, and it places me alone in the small pasture. But this pasture is rich in nourishment, for the notion of Godhead as Divine Family fully agrees with Scripture, specifically *Ephesians 5:31* and *32* as noted above, whereas any other possible understanding of the Godhead cannot enjoy that same agreement.

In the case of the Holy Spirit, the male designation simply may connote that this Member of the Holy Trinity, while possessing a unique functional identity that may be of either gender, is composed of the same Divine Substance as the Holy Father who is male. Then, as in the case with the church, the male pronoun would be used because male is the dominant gender, which also applies to the Holy Spirit for having an essence of which both genders consist. The answer to this apparent gender inconsistency may be as simple as attributing it to a common lack of perception in reading the Bible, and that from the very beginning. In *Genesis 5:1* and 2 the creation of man as first presented in Genesis 1:26 and 27 is recapitulated, but with a significant addition:

This is the book of the generations of Adam. In the day that God created man,, in the likeness of God made he him; male and female created he them; and blessed them, and called their name Adam, in the day when they were created.

Note in this passage that both Adam and Eve were named Adam. We don't usually think about the implications, but that same practice is maintained to this day. When a woman marries a man, she takes his name. This is quite significant, for it implies, beyond the notion that God considers the male and female to be one flesh, that the woman (and the man also) was never intended to live apart from her spouse, but to assume his identity as an unbreakable partnership. Therefore, the reference to the Holy Spirit as 'he' may simply and quite logically imply that the Holy Spirit is of the same Divine Substance as the Father as well as being indivisibly joined to Him.

But in an alternative interpretation the male designation also may suggest a very wonderful promise to us: it may mean that the Holy Spirit is also an aggregate of many components, one that in our future spiritual form we actually may be privileged to join, possibly as a Divine Daughter.

The reason for the use of the male 'he' in reference to the Holy Spirit may be identical with the reason why the church, with specific reference to its aggregate nature as redeemed mankind, is described as masculine when, in fact, it is functionally feminine. The possibility exists that the use of the male gender may represent a promise that the church and the Holy Spirit may have a closer relation than mere similarity of gender. In this suggestion, redeemed mankind may, in fact, while being a masculine aggregate, become intimately related to the Holy Spirit by assuming a functional role as a new Divine Means with Jesus serving as a new Divine Will. Is that why Jesus *(John 5:17)*, in performing what the Pharisees considered as work during the Sabbath, said *"My Father worketh hitherto, and I work"*?

I emphasize the following line of reasoning in attributing a female functionality to the Holy Spirit: Judeo-Christianity is generally assumed to be a monotheistic religion; yet, our Godhead is also assumed to be Trinitarian. The basis of our monotheism is expressed in *Deuteronomy 6:4: "Hear O Israel: the Lord our God is one Lord."* On the other hand, Christianity deifies Jesus as well as the Holy Spirit; together, all God, they comprise the Trinitarian Godhead. Adam's statement regarding Eve, repeated by Jesus and Paul, reconciles two back into one: *"Therefore shall a man leave his father and mother, and shall cleave unto his wife; and they shall be one flesh."* Extending this unity of family to the offspring of this union permits the full Trinitarian Godhead to be perceived as one, justifying the monotheism implicit in *Deuteronomy 6:4.*

In this posting I add further justification for a female Holy Spirit by noting in particular in that same reconciliatory statement that in joining with his wife a man shall leave his father and mother. When this notion is applied to Jesus as in *Ephesians 5:31* and *32*, it becomes obvious that Jesus had to have had a Holy Mother to leave in joining with His wife. This can't apply to Mary because the unions that we are addressing are spiritual and because, according to numerous references throughout Scripture, for example *Micah 5:2*, and *John 1:1* and *14*, Jesus existed long before His sojourn in the flesh. On top of that, Scripture and nature both emphasize the sterility associated with any union other than between a male and a female. How, then, could Jesus be the Son of God without a female forebear? Why would Jesus take a Bride if His Father did not?

In this posting I'm not simply attempting to justify a pet thought. In my opinion, the prevailing notion of an all-masculine Godhead is intrinsically profane, representing no less than a repudiation of Scripture itself. I sincerely believe that Paul and other Bible greats knew the truth about the functional gender of the Holy Spirit. If there are just a few who share the little field, remember these words of Jesus in *Matthew 7:13* and *14*, and fervently hope that God will show mercy to the ignorant:

> *Enter ye in at the strait gate: for wide is the gate and broad is the way, that leadeth to destruction, and many there be that go in thereat: Because strait is the gate, and narrow is the way, which leadeth unto life, and few there be that find it.*

CHAPTER 19

At work Earl received a summons from Walter. When he entered Walter's office, his grim-faced boss motioned for him to sit. "I didn't know you were a Jesus freak," he said. The accusation hung heavy in the room. "You know my policy – when you're at work you're here to work. I can't tolerate distraction, so if you can't focus on your job, I'll have to do something about it."

Earl fought to maintain his poise. "I'll make sure I'm focused, Walter," he replied. Anything I do that's not job-related will be done after hours, I assure you."

"Okay. But I'll be watching you." He dismissed Earl with a wave of his hand.

Earl's spirits rose considerably at home when he saw Joyce standing in the doorway waiting for him, her face radiant with joy. "Look at me!" she cried as she reached up to kiss him. "I'm standing! I can even walk a little. See?" She demonstrated her new skill, walking into the kitchen, where she had been preparing dinner. Thankfully, she was so immersed in this hugely important recovery of ability that she didn't ask him how his day went. "I won't throw away the wheelchair just yet," she said, somewhat subdued by the encroachment of pain. But I've been practicing while you were at work for over a month now, and I'm getting pretty comfortable with the prosthetics. I couldn't wait to show you. Are you proud of me?"

"I sure am, darling. Maybe soon we can go to the store together and you can take over the shopping."

"Won't that be a thrill? Let's do it this weekend. Here's something else. I don't want to pressure you, but we seem to be getting on top of our latest setbacks. I thought maybe it was time that we could go back to spending some time with Buddy and maybe a few others. Besides, there's a piano at the nursing home and I'd like to get back in practice."

Earl thought about it for a few minutes. "I'm glad you suggested that. It's been a while since we saw him. I'm with you."

"Good. I thought you'd say that." Her smile broadened. "I've already called Mary at the home. She was happy to hear from me and would love to see us back." The smile remained on her face throughout dinner and as they sat down in the living room for some time together. "Oh," she said. "I almost forgot. Frank Wilson called again. He asked for you to call him back sometime tonight."

Her offhand comment brought with it a pall of gloom. *That's all I need,* he thought. But he swallowed his foreboding and called the pastor.

"Thanks for returning my call," he told Earl with a neutral tone. "I read your latest blog. This is awkward, Earl. You should have taken me up on my offer of help." He paused for a moment, as if he was collecting his nerve. "Earl, you just can't fit what you wrote into Scripture. Besides that, you're bucking centuries, even millennia, of Church tradition in your suggestion that the Holy Spirit is female. I'm embarrassed to even think of the possibility. Why don't you come over tonight, and I'll help you write a retraction in your next blog."

Earl was aware of the probability of this thing happening. But now that it did, this new situation – and the firming of the man's position – depressed him greatly. He just didn't feel like clicking his heels in joy. "Pastor Frank," he replied, "Thank you for your concern. But I believe what I wrote, I certainly think that it fits well into Scripture, and I have no plans to retract any part of it. Besides, you're not my own pastor. I had a hunch that you'd disagree with me on it, but I'm convinced that what I wrote is the truth and that it is consistent with Scripture."

"Why, then," Frank's voice took on an edge of sharpness, "did you write that you thought you were all alone? Don't you think that maybe there's a pretty good reason why you are all alone? That countless theologians with, if I may say it, considerably more depth of knowledge than you, have already addressed that issue and have uniformly come up with a drastically different opinion of the nature of the Holy Spirit?"

"Yes, I understand that, Pastor. Believe me, it's bothered me too. Several times I've wanted to just forget about the issue, but instead I've gone back and reviewed my beliefs, and every time I do that I'm more firmly convinced of their correctness. I will do this, though. I'll take to heart your suspicion of my being out there alone. Perhaps I'll address it in a later posting. I'll also guarantee you that if you can demonstrate through Scripture the falsity of my beliefs, I'll be the first to retract them. But until that time, I plan to continue with my postings on the subject."

"I can't get you to see my position?" Frank was clearly frustrated.

"Like I said before, you can if your position is Scriptural. Otherwise no."

Pastor Frank sighed loudly and hung up. Joyce looked at him. She'd been listening as before. "That didn't go too well, did it?" she stated.

"No. I knew that would happen but when it really did, it's very disturbing."

"At least it wasn't George who dressed you down. I like him. I like his sermons. He uses Scripture a lot, which is good. Let's just hope that he doesn't get in your face like this man. But not only do I love you, I also think you're right on this. Not that I'm an expert or anything, but from what I have read of Scripture, and I'm picking parts that have to do with your thinking to read, what you think makes a lot of sense. So I'll stick by you, for now anyway. Only I want you to know that I'm going to continue going to Church there even if things turn sour between you and George too. At least until we get booted out the door."

"Fair enough. I'll go along with that, and I won't initiate any confrontation. Maybe this evening would be a good time to see Buddy. Get the smell of Wilson out of my nostrils."

Buddy was overjoyed to see them. Squirming in his chair, he pointed upward. Earl understood. "I'm afraid not, Buddy. Something happened to my arm." He pointed to the empty space where his right arm should have been. He pointed a finger at his friend. "But that doesn't have to stop you from doing bigger and better things on your own. Mary tells us that you're preparing for the Special Olympics. Keep it up. Joyce and I would love to see you perform." Buddy's countenance, which registered sadness after he saw Earl's missing arm, brightened. He nodded emphatically.

"From now on, Buddy, we're going to be spending time with you the way that you and I started out, helping you to get to know God better. Joyce will start us off with some hymns."

Joyce responded with a piano rendition of "He Leadeth Me" and "How Great Thou Art". The music brought two other youngsters into the room. They parked their wheelchairs next to Buddy's. "Hi," Earl said. "My name's Earl and my wife here is Joyce. We're glad to see you." Earl opened his Bible and turned to the Book of Isaiah.

"I thought I'd start in with a message from one of the great prophets of the Old Testament. Almost a thousand years before the birth of our Lord Jesus Christ here on earth, Isaiah the prophet spoke of him. He told us why Jesus came to earth in the flesh. Do you know why He did?"

He looked at their blank faces and said, "He came to show us how much God loves us. God knew from the beginning of time that He would have to send His Son Jesus to earth to suffer and die on our behalf. One reason why He did that was to save us from ourselves. When the first people disobeyed God we lost our ability to please him. We became selfish and did bad things. The only way to come back to God was for God Himself to do it for us by dying in our place. But there's another reason why he did this. It was to show us how much He loves us. To God, we are worth the sacrifice of God Himself. Isn't that wonderful?"

He was heartened by their enthusiastic nods. "The prophet Isaiah wrote about what was going to happen to Jesus many hundreds of years before it happened. Here is what he said:

> *Surely he has shouldered our griefs, and carried our sorrows; yet we did think of him as stricken, hurt by God, and afflicted. But he was wounded for our wrongs, he was bruised for our badness; the punishment for our peace was upon him, and with the marks of the lash of the whip on his back we are healed. Like sheep, we have all gone astray; we have turned every one of us to our own way, and the Lord has laid on him the punishment for us all. He was hurt, and he was afflicted, yet he didn't open his mouth; he is brought as a lamb to the slaughter, and as a sheep before her shearers is without voice, so he didn't open his mouth. He was taken from prison and from judgment, and who shall declare his generation.? For he was cut off from the land of the living; for the badness of my people was he hurt. And he made his grave with the wicked, and with the rich in his death, because he had done no violence, nor was there deceit in his mouth. Yet it pleased the Lord to bruise him; he has put him to grief. When you shall make his soul an offering for sin, he shall see his seed, he shall prolong his days, and the pleasure of the Lord shall prosper in his hand. God shall see the agony of his soul, and shall be satisfied; by his knowledge shall my righteous servant justify many; for he shall carry the burden of their wrongs. Therefore will I divide him a portion with the great, and he shall divide the spoil with the strong, because he has poured out his soul to death; and he was numbered with the wrongdoers, and he bore the wrongs of many, and made intercession for the transgressors.*

Earl closed the Bible. "That's why Jesus came to earth. He came to die for us, that we may live. He stood up. "That's all for now.

We hope to see you next week. 'Bye." He and Joyce gave them hugs and left.

"It was nice to say something that's not controversial," he said to Joyce when they reached the car. She agreed with a laugh. "Yeah," she said. "And I really liked being able to play the piano."

"You did very well. I think they may have gotten something out of our visit."

"I'm sure of it. Let's do this every week."

That night when they returned home he started on his next blog. It was posted three days later.

THE GENDER OF THE HOLY SPIRIT

Viewing the Holy Spirit as functionally female opens up Scripture in a wonderful way. Consider, for example, the Book of *Proverbs*, in which wisdom is presented in female form. With an understanding of the Holy Spirit as functionally female, I would suggest that this functionality is indeed that which is represented by Wisdom, and which I would now capitalize in acknowledgment of Wisdom's Godhood. Indeed, it becomes obvious, upon reading certain passages in *Proverbs*, that the traditional application of them to Jesus is way off-base, not the least of which is the attribution of the wrong gender to Him. The following experts from chapters 1 through 4 and 8 speak convincingly of the identity of Wisdom and the Holy Spirit:

> *Wisdom crieth without; she uttereth her voice in the streets: She crieth in the chief place of concourse. . .My son, if thou wilt receive my words, and hide my commandments with thee; so that thou incline thine ear unto wisdom, and apply thine heart to understanding; yea, if thou criest after knowledge, and liftest up thy voice for understanding; if thou seekest her as silver, and searchest for her as for hid treasures; then shalt thou understand the fear of the Lord, and find the knowledge of God. . .The Lord by wisdom hath founded the earth; by understanding hath he established the heavens. By his knowledge the depths are broken up, and the clouds*

drop down the dew. . .Get wisdom, get understanding: forget it not; neither decline from the words of my mouth. Forsake her not, and she shall preserve thee: love her, and she shall keep thee. . .Doth not wisdom cry? And understanding put forth her voice? She standeth in the top of high places, by the way in the places of the paths. . .I wisdom dwell with prudence, and find out knowledge of witty inventions. The fear of the Lord is to hate evil: pride, arrogancy, and the evil way, and the forward mouth, do I hate. Counsel is mine, and sound wisdom: I am understanding; I have strength. By me kings reign, and princes decree justice. By me princes rule, and nobles, even all the judges of the earth. I love them that love me; and those that seek me early shall find me. Riches and honour are with me; yea, durable riches and righteousness. My fruit is better than gold, yea, than fine gold, and my revenue than choice silver. . .The Lord possessed me in the beginning of his way, before his works of old. I was set up from everlasting, from the beginning, or ever the earth was. When there were no depths, I was brought forth; when there were no fountains abounding with water. Before the mountains were settled, before the hills was I brought forth: while as yet he had not made the earth, nor the fields, nor the highest part of the dust of the world. When he prepared the heavens, I was there: when he set a compass upon the face of the depth: when he established the clouds above: when he strengthened the fountains of the deep: when he gave to the sea his decree, that the waters should not pass his commandment: when he appointed the foundations of the earth: then I was by him, as one brought up with him: and I was daily his delight, rejoicing always before him; rejoicing in the habitable part of his earth; and my delights were with the sons of men. Now therefore hearken unto me, O ye children: for blessed are they that keep my ways. Hear instruction, and be wise, and refuse it not. Blessed is the man that heareth me, watching daily at my gates, waiting at the posts of my doors. For whoso findeth me findeth life, and shall obtain favor of the Lord. But he that sinneth against me wrongeth his own soul: all they that hate me love death.

It is of interest to note that among the early Church fathers, Irenaeus was among those who appear to have made a direct link of Wisdom with the Holy Spirit. The following passage is attributed to him (*Against Heresies,* Book 4, Chapter 20) by Paul Copan and William Lane Craig in *Creation out of Nothing*:

"For with Him were always present the Word and Wisdom, the Son and the Spirit, by whom and in whom, freely and spontaneously, He made all things."

As John noted, God is love. Furthermore, as Scripture emphasizes over and over again, love is so intrinsic to His being that this feature dwarfs his attributes of power and knowledge, commonly referred to by the catch-all-descriptors of omnipotence, omniscience and omnipresence.

In *Genesis 1:27*, Moses describes the creation of man, a being who is to possess two fundamental attributes:

So God created man in his own image, in the image of God created he him; male and female created he them.

The first attribute of fundamental importance is that man is made in the image of God. They are to share similarities of character, including the ability of man to understand God sufficiently to love Him. The second attribute is that they are male and female. Some theologians would insist that the gender issue is incidental to mankind's being made in God's image and that it has nothing to do with the nature of God Himself. Given the context of this passage in Genesis and other facts that I intend to bring out later, I would suggest that theologians of that ilk are grazing in some very sparse fields. Instead, I emphatically insist that the gender issue is much more than incidental, being one of the most fundamental concepts one can acquire with respect to God's own nature. Moreover, I assert that the suppression of this concept represents the worst misrepresentation of God that He has ever had to endure at the hands of fallen mankind.

The Godhead Itself, far from being a vague collection of three Beings, represents the very essence of Family. It's a Family that

I'd like to be more than friends with. The context of family makes it infinitely easier to obey God's commandment to love Him with the passion suggested in Scripture, the essence of which is embedded in the Shema of Moses, *Deuteronomy 6:4* and *5*:

> *Hear, O Israel: The Lord our God is one Lord: and thou shalt love the Lord thy God with all thine heart, and with all thy soul, and with all thy might.*

The female form of the Holy Spirit is suggested in numerous other places in Scripture and stands out readily to those with sufficient understanding to look for them. These include *Genesis 1:1-5* and *27*, *Genesis 24*, *Ruth*, *Song of Solomon*, *Isaiah 54*, *Hosea*, *John 2* and *3* and, of course, *Ephesians 5*. There is much more to say about the implications of a female Holy Spirit, which I'll pursue further in the next update.

Despite their vastly different reasons for doing so, Earl's work associates and Pastor Frank embarked on long-haul positions of displeasure with him. For the time being, much to his relief, his job wasn't threatened. They even praised his work when his performance called for it. But their attitudes were always there in the background and they darkened his workday.

Earl kept his peace on Sunday when the pastor interspersed within his sermon almost nakedly overt commentaries in reference to those who "in disobedience stray from the faith". They reddened his face, but he didn't attempt to rebut the pastor. Joyce, fearful that his temper might erupt, was grateful for his silence. The Church experience for both of them, however, took a nosedive. Yet they did their best to absorb the sermon, which was quite good.

To make matters worse, George collared Earl as they were about to exit the Church. "Please bear with me, Joyce," he said, "but I'd like to have a word alone with Earl. It shouldn't take too long."

Earl spoke up, bothered by the thought that perhaps his own pastor would be taking a position like Frank Wilson, but suppressed an open expression of it. "I'll be with you in a moment, pastor," he said, "but first I have to take Joyce to the car. She still can't stand for very long." He turned away and, holding Joyce's arm, walked her to the car. He remained grimly silent on the way. When she was inside, he returned to the pastor, who ushered him into his study.

"I've been holding back from giving you advice on your blog," he began when they were seated. "After reading your latest posting, though, I thought I'd at least give you some friendly advice regarding what theologians generally think about the topic. Are you okay with that?"

"Sure," he said with relief. At least his friend was avoiding a heavy-handed personal confrontation, which he greatly appreciated.

"It's not a huge issue, nor a show-stopper regarding your standing in the Christian community, but I'll just tell you that theologians in general don't associate Proverbs with the Holy Spirit. In other words, we think of the personification of Wisdom in Proverbs as a mere literary device, not an actuality. Wisdom is that which is possessed, in general, by God, whether it be Father, Son or Holy Spirit. Your personification of it might be off track."

"But what of Irenaeus' linkage of Wisdom with the Holy Spirit, as I mentioned in the posting?"

He waved his hand in dismissal. "Granted, Irenaeus is respected as a Church Father, but he had his problems, too. One of which is his commitment to the notion of apostolic succession. Catholics love him for that view, but we in the Protestant community are not quite so happy with it."

Chapter 20

Earl spent the remainder of that Sunday addressing the issue that Pastor Frank had raised. He wrote a rebuttal but held off including it in his next posting, as a continuation of his originally-intended sequence of issues held a higher priority in his mind.

THE MARRIAGE OF GOD WITH GOD

In previous postings I have raised the question of why God's Trinitarian nature, a facet of Him that is accepted without question by mainstream Christianity, is so vaguely defined in Scripture. I also raised a companion question as to why, in the face of this apparently feeble portrayal of the Trinity, both Moses and Jesus declared with passion the oneness of God. I then presented the obvious answer, which was that the loving union of male and complementary female produces unity from multiplicity, a unity that continues with the fruit of the union. In this context and only in it, the description of the Trinity in Scripture isn't feeble at all; it's quite strong. The wonderful truth about the Holy Trinity is expressed openly throughout Scripture beginning in *Genesis 2:23* and *24*:

> *And Adam said, This is now bone of my bones, and flesh of my flesh: she shall be called Woman, because she was taken out of man.*

> *Therefore shall a man leave his father and his mother, and shall cleave unto his wife: and they shall be one flesh.*

To the above I add the following:

God Himself through Scripture has provided man with certain specific images of His nature by which He apparently wishes us to understand and appreciate Him. First among these is His ability to give and to receive love. Fundamental to the exercise of that ability is the family structure, within which we have the ability to intuitively understand a corresponding relationship among the members of the Godhead itself as well as of the relationship between God and mankind. The family is the singular means within our comprehension by which separate individuals may become component elements of a greater whole, a oneness in love that both transcends the individual person and extends his own significance.

As the communication and functional harmony within the family approach the highest ideal of which humans are capable, in the setting of selfless love at an equally ideal level, the individuality of its component members blurs. All become subordinate but vital elements of the greater entity called family, which itself takes on a life of its own. If the love, communication and harmony within this entity are perfect, an impossibility with mankind but perhaps a defining quality for God, one would expect a spiritual unity and mutual identification so complete that the component members could no longer rightly be thought of as separate individuals. The Divine family, in which the various members would identify perfectly with each other as if the individual boundaries did not exist, would have its own unique identity and life.

God, in this context, is truly one God.

It is natural, in the context of the family, to attribute to the Father the functional role of Divine Will. To the Holy Spirit is then attributed the role of Divine Means, such that the Divine Will, in union with the Divine Means, gives birth to the Divine Implementation, Who, of course, is Jesus. A proviso in this is the recognition that the Father, if He so chose, could do it all Himself.

It is my conviction that God chose to have a partner in the process instead of going it alone, voluntarily elevating selfless love above His more fundamental attributes. I believe that Jesus was not the first to humble Himself in love, but that the Father also, at the very beginning, stood alone. I believe further that for the sake of selflessness He willingly parted himself into the Divine Persons of Father and Holy Spirit such that He had a Partner in the process of creation, one upon Whom He could confer His love.

The fruit of this union, Jesus, represents the Actualization of the Father's Divine Will in all of Creation. *Genesis 1:1-5* describes the bringing forth of Jesus as the Word and Light, as I had noted in an earlier posting. This same Word can be viewed as the Implementation of the Divine Will. In that context, this same passage in Genesis 1 also speaks of the operation of the Holy Spirit in response to the Will. In re-reading it, note the formation of Jesus out of the union of Will and Spirit:

> *In the beginning God created the heaven and the earth. And the earth was without form and void; and darkness was upon the face of the deep. And the Spirit of God moved upon the face of the waters. And God said, Let there be light: and there was light. And God saw the light, that it was good: and God divided the light from the darkness. And God called the light Day, and the darkness he called Night. And the evening and the morning were the first day.*

The events spoken of in all these passages took place in God's universe, dimensionally unconstrained unlike our own. Therefore, time and sequence don't have the same meaning. In fact, our incomprehension of the spiritual world does not allow us to make any meaningful statements whatsoever regarding the implications of Jesus' eternal existence. We do know that Jesus is fully God and that He preexisted with the Father before the foundation of the world, because the Bible tells us so.

It should be easy to appreciate how much deeper it is possible to love God with the understanding presented above regarding the Holy Trinity and particularly the Holy Spirit. This insight has given me the ability to love God in a way that I didn't know was possible beforehand.

The Catholic Church has suspected that something of this sort has been missing all along and has attempted to compensate by elevating Mary beyond what Scripture suggests. That the church has missed this point for so long is a tragedy. Unfortunately, they have sterilized her by insisting upon her everlasting virginity when her having children through Joseph after the virgin birth of Jesus is an established fact. Indeed, the James and Jude whose letters are included in the Bible were both half-brothers to Jesus.

I have considered in the past the possibility that it was in the will of God that the female function of the Holy Spirit was overlooked by the church. Here I wonder if it wasn't caused more by a lack of commitment to God and a subsequent focus on the physical world in place of the spiritual. That it may have involved an absence of any indwelling of the Holy Spirit in the church leadership isn't all that difficult to grasp when one considers how terribly anti-Christian has been the behavior of so many well-known church leaders over the past century. This glaringly bad behavior includes an astonishing lack of courage on the part of the mainstream church leadership with respect to their failing to hold at bay all the encroachments of evolution and other godless theories that have been forced into the false public perception of reality that is so prevalent today. It is my opinion that a number of church leaders had arrived at some initial understanding of the female nature of the Holy Spirit, only to discard it as requiring too much effort and threat to their careers to pursue it. If that's true, I wouldn't want to be in their shoes when called upon to meet their Maker.

There you have it. I consider it to be an obligation to my Lord Jesus Christ to attempt to set the record straight on this subject of the female gender of the Holy Spirit. I welcome your comments on this subject.

The issue of the Holy Spirit and the Holy Trinity is not the only one that separates me from the flock and makes me lonely. I'll continue to address these in future postings.

"This looks good. Go ahead and post it. I have to agree with you about Pastor Frank," Joyce said after reading Earl's latest blog. "I don't like bucking an authority, but your conviction makes a lot of sense to me. That man seems to be stubborn about it, making it a personal issue. When he does that, he's going over the top. Furthermore, I've read Proverbs too. I can't picture how anybody can read it and not make the link between Wisdom and the Holy Spirit like you did."

"It wasn't a quickly-formed connection. It took a lot of thinking. As I began to make the association, I suspected from then on that making that link would put me out of the mainstream of theology. I thought I was being cautious."

"I was particularly struck by verses 13 through 20 of Proverbs 3." She picked up her Bible and read the passages aloud.

> *Happy is the man that findeth wisdom, and the man that getteth understanding. For the merchandise of it is better than the merchandise of silver, and the gain thereof than fine gold. She is more precious than rubies; and all the things thou canst desire are not to be compared unto her. Length of days is in her right hand, and in her left hand riches and honor. Her ways are ways of pleasantness, and all her paths are peace. She is a tree of life to those who lay hold upon her, and happy is every one that retaineth her. The Lord by wisdom hath founded the earth; by understanding hath he established the heavens. By his knowledge the depths are broken up, and the clouds drop down dew.*

"My Bible directly links that passage to verse 27 of Proverbs 8," she continued. "You know about that, but I want to read it again, starting at verse 22:"

> *The Lord possessed me in the beginning of his way, before his works of old. I was set up from everlasting, from the beginning, or ever the earth was. When there were no depths, I was brought forth – when there were no fountains abounding with water. Before the mountains were settled, before the hills, was I brought forth; while as yet he had not made the earth, nor the fields, nor the highest part of the dust of the world. When he prepared the heavens, I was there; when he set a compass upon the face of the depth; when*

he established the clouds above; when he strengthened the fountains of the deep; when he gave to the sea its decree, that the waters should not pass his commandment; when he appointed the foundations of the earth, then I was by him, as one brought up with him; and I was daily his delight, rejoicing always before him, rejoicing in the habitable part of his earth; and my delight was with the sons of men.

"Earl," she went on, "as you said, that relates directly to Genesis 1." She quickly turned to the front of the Bible and continued reading:

In the beginning God created the heaven and the earth. And the earth was without form, and void; and darkness was upon the face of the deep. And the Spirit of God moved upon the face of the waters. And God said, Let there be light: and there was light. And God saw the light, that it was good: and God divided the light from the darkness. And God called the light Day, and the darkness he called Night. And the evening and the morning were the first day.

"How can anyone not see that the Holy Spirit in Genesis 1 and Wisdom of Proverbs are one and the same Person?"

"Hey, you're on a roll, Joyce. Maybe I should say 'Welcome Aboard', because whether you like it or not, your commitment to that viewpoint is going to give you a bumpy ride."

"I don't care. At least we're together on this. Maybe it'll be fun."

"But scary, Joyce. Remember what you told me before in quoting Jesus: Count the cost."

"I'm in. That's that."

"Well, to continue on your roll, think about that light in Genesis, keeping in mind that that light was the first word spoken by God, and that the sun and moon were made on the fourth day."

"Jesus? Do you think that light was Jesus?"

"I do. Note that the Light came about by the operation of the Holy

Spirit upon the Father's Will. Now I'll read you some Scripture. It's from John Chapter 1:"

> *In the beginning was the word, and the word was with God, and the word was God. The same was in the beginning with God. All things were made by him, and without him nothing was made that was made. In him was life, and the life was the light of men. And the light shineth in darkness; and the darkness comprehended it not.*

"John goes on to say, '*that was the true light, which lighteth every man that cometh into the world.*' A bit farther on, he says '*And the Word was made flesh, and dwelt among us, and we beheld his glory, the glory of the only begotten of the Father, full of grace and truth.*'

"The clincher, of course, is what Jesus called Himself in Revelation 3 verse 14: '*the beginning of the creation of God*'."

"Oh, my. Well, that settles that also. I appreciate the insight."

"There's more. You might want to look up Psalm 104:30 and Job 26:13. Both of those passages link creation with the Holy Spirit. I have also read some books on the Holy Spirit to find out if the popular authors had anything of substance with which to refute me. One of these authors was Benjamin Warfield, a highly respected Christian theologian. He claimed that both Testaments depict the Holy Spirit as the executive of the Godhead. I agree wholeheartedly with that assessment, as an executive function is a responsive one. On a war ship, the executive role is responsive to the dictates of the commanding officer. It's the same thing in the Godhead, with the Holy Spirit being responsive to the Father's Will. But a responsive function is also typically a female one, which bolsters my conviction about the female nature of the Holy Spirit. At least functionally. Irenaeus, commonly accepted as a Church Father, also directly equated Wisdom with the Holy Spirit, and he did so at the dawn of the Church age. Oddly, Joyce, I got that little tidbit from a book that Pastor George loaned to me."

"About your last blog. Before you consign it to history, what you wrote about Mary and the Catholic Church intrigues me. Maybe you should say more about it. At least I'd like to know more about the link you suspect between Mary and the Holy Spirit in the Catholic understanding of God."

"Catholics themselves have collected their traditions surrounding Mary under the label of Mariology. It's a rather large field of study in itself. Let me get to my next blog and think about how I can give you the best picture of it in ten thousand words or less. You should know about it and I'll be sure to feed what I know to you when I can give you a coherent picture."

Earl spent the remainder of the evening on his next blog. This time, having read another book suggested by George that supported his position, he decided to address Frank's comment about being out there alone. In his emotional involvement with the issue he wrote it quickly. He turned it over to Joyce to read before they both went to bed.

CHAPTER 21

I'M NOT AS ALONE AS I THOUGHT

As I learn more about the early Christians and the Church Fathers, I'm beginning to appreciate that there have been more sheep than I first thought who have been feeding in my little field.

Not long ago my pastor loaned me a little paperback book entitled *Creation out of Nothing,* written by Paul Copan and William Lane Craig and published in 2004. The primary issue for Drs. Copan and Lane is the question as to whether God created the heavens and earth from nothing (*creatio ex nihilo*) or whether He did so from pre-existing matter (*creatio ex materia*). Admittedly, I hadn't given the matter much thought because I had simply assumed that God, being God, wouldn't have the need to start with something already at hand. I found the topic fascinating, however, and was intrigued with the necessity of addressing it, which, it seems, began with the Gnostic view of matter as evil and thus outside of the realm of God's creative effort. I was also intrigued with the arguments that the authors presented in favor of *creatio ex nihilo,* which covered a range of source material from the Old and New Testaments, as well as information from extrabiblical sources, including religious texts and scientific data. The source that most impresses me is *John 1:3*:

"All things were made by him, and without him was nothing made

that was made."

As far as I can see, that statement pretty much covers it all. That, and the fact that if God had to rely on pre-existing material to perform His creative work, He couldn't exactly be called omnipotent.

Interested as I became in the main theme of the book, what really grabbed my attention was a side issue, one almost but not quite confined to the footnote region. On page 23 of the book, the Church Father Irenaeus is said to have essentially equated Wisdom with the Holy Spirit. Nor was this association trivially presented, for on page 24 Wisdom is described by Copan and Craig as a Craftsman at God's side, with a reference to *Proverbs 8:27* and *30*:

> *When he prepared the heavens, I was there: when he set a compass upon the face of the depth... Then I was by him, as one brought up with him: and I was daily his delight, rejoicing always before him;*

The association of Wisdom with the Holy Spirit immediately exposes a gender issue, for Wisdom in Proverbs is identified as a female personage. It is precisely the same issue that led so many "experts" to pasteurize their attempts to offer "explanations" of the Holy Trinity into cold and ultimately empty logical sophistries. One can only conclude that such "explanations" are products of self-interest and fear. Irenaeus, on the other hand, seems not to have been so burdened with socio-political concerns; apparently, he seriously entertained the thought of associating the Holy Spirit with a female function.

The reference to *Proverbs 8:27* and *30* again associates Wisdom with the Holy Spirit, and this time it sets the record straight as to whom this passage refers. The prevailing preference is to associate this passage with Jesus, despite its obviously being out of context for that identification. I was most happy to note that the authors of *Creation out of Nothing* understood this and properly associated the passage with Wisdom. I think that the authors understand the unstated implication of attributing the verses to Wisdom: again, that the Holy Spirit and Wisdom are one and the same, and in the context of the nature of Wisdom presented in Proverbs, the Holy Spirit thus possesses a female functionality.

The authors go further, noting on page 25 the self-sufficiency of an intra-Trinitarian love relationship. Love relationship indeed, and one that we can readily identify with on an intuitive level.

I'm more than happy to share my little turf with others. I just wish that they'd come on in, rather than just poking their heads through the fence.

Joyce laughed when she got to the last line. "That was good, Earl. Maybe I should read Irenaeus too."

"You should. You'd get more than information regarding the Holy Spirit. You'd get a real kick out of him, because he has a great sense of humor. Wait, let me get the copy of his *Against Heresies* that I got off the Internet."

When he returned, he showed her a paper in his hand and told her that in that part he had been mocking all the odd words produced by the Gnostic proclivity toward sophistry, and the absurdity of their strange constructions that came out of their interpretations of Scripture. "He also noted that the transmission of this information to the uninitiated involved the exchange of large sums of money. This one," he said pointing to the paper in his hand, "was against the heresies of Marcion and his AEons." He started reading from the paper in his hand:

"'And when she [Achamoth] could not pass by Horos on account of that passion in which she had been involved, and because she alone had been left without, she then resigned herself to every sort of that manifold and varied state of passion to which she was subject; and thus she suffered grief on the one hand because she had not obtained the object of her desire, and fear on the other hand, lest life itself should fail her, as light had already done, while, in addition, she was in the greatest perplexity. All these feelings were associated with ignorance. And this ignorance of hers was not like that of her mother, the first Sophia, and AEon, due to degeneracy due to by means of passion, but to an [innate] opposition [of nature to knowledge]. Moreover, another kind of passion fell upon her, namely, that of desiring to return to him who gave her life.

'This collection [of passions] they declare was the substance of the matter from which this world was formed. For from [her desire of] returning [to him who gave her life], every soul belonging to this world, and that of the Demiurge himself, derived its origin. All other things owed their beginning to her terror and sorrow. For from her tears all that is of a liquid nature was formed; from her smile all that is lucent; and from her grief and perplexity all the corporeal elements of the world. For at one time, as they affirm, she would weep and lament on account of being left alone in the midst of darkness and vacuity; while, at another time, reflecting on the light which had forsaken her, she would be filled with joy, and laugh; then, again, she would be stuck with terror; or, at other times, would sink into consternation and bewilderment.'

"All that I've read to you so far, Joyce, is a preamble to set the stage for the expression of wit that I'll read next:

"'Now what follows from all this? No light tragedy comes out of it, as the fancy of every man among them pompously explains, one in one way, and another in another, from what kind of passion and from what element being derived its origin. They have good reason, it seems to me, why they should not feel inclined to teach these things to all in public, but only to such as are able to pay a high price for an acquaintance with such profound mysteries. For these doctrines are not at all similar to those of which our Lord said, 'Freely ye have received, freely give.' They are, on the contrary, abstruse, and portentous, and profound mysteries, to be got at only with great labour by such as are in love with falsehood. For who would not expend [all] that he possessed, if only he might learn in return, that from the tears of the enthymesis of the AEon involved in passion, seas, and fountains, and rivers, and every liquid substance derived its origin; that light burst forth from her smile; and that from her perplexity and consternation the corporeal elements of the world had their formation?

'I feel somewhat inclined myself to contribute a few hints towards the development of their system. For when I perceive that waters are in part fresh, such as fountains, rivers, showers, and so on, and in part salt; such as those in the sea, I reflect with myself that all such waters cannot be derived from her tears, inasmuch as these are of a saline quality only. It is clear, therefore, that the waters which are salt are alone those which are derived from her tears. But it is probable that she, in her intense agony and perplexity, was covered with perspiration. And hence, following our notion, we may conceive that fountains and rivers, and all the fresh water in the world, are due to this source. For it is difficult, since we know that all tears are of the same quality, to believe that waters both salt and fresh proceeded from them. The more plausible supposition is, that some are from her tears, and some from her perspiration. And since there are also in the world certain waters which are hot and acrid in their nature, thou must be left to guess their origin, how and whence. Such are some of the results of their hypothesis.'"

At the last few sentences Joyce held her stomach in laughter. "Good, huh?" Earl commented with a chuckle. "That's but a tiny sample of his witty, on-the-money dismissal of the ill-conceived, pompous and thoroughly heretic Gnostic sophistries. He was a very intelligent theological giant who put many of the more well-known Greek philosophical thinkers to shame. Catholics love Irenaeus because he interprets Matthew 16:18 in favor of Christ identifying Peter as the rock upon which the Church is to be built, leading to the notion of apostolic succession. Protestants, who identify the rock of Matthew 16:18 as Christ himself, sometimes shun him, but those who do that do themselves a disservice. For one thing, despite what Protestants might think of him regarding apostolic succession, he was a great theologian. For another, he was just a human. There isn't one of us humans who isn't without some oddity or another. Look at Martin Luther himself. Despite the fact that many Protestants revere him as a theological great, he and John Calvin both viewed Jesus' mother Mary as a perpetual virgin, another Catholic tradition that has been rejected by Protestants long ago as being contradictory to Matthew 13:55."

"That sounds kind of hypocritical to me, rejecting one theologian and accepting another when both have questionable notions of equal weight."

"Yeah. Especially when the topics aren't show-stoppers."

"Well, get your last blog posted."

Earl did that. Then he started the next one and didn't get up from the table until he'd finished it.

Once they'd gone to bed and turned out the lights, Earl turned to Joyce. "I'm proud of the way you're handling your new legs. Is the pain going away at all?"

"Yes. Enough that I want to take my recovery to the next level. I need your help for that."

"Sure thing. Just tell me what it is."

"I want to drive again, Earl. Don't get me wrong. I like you being around and helping me with what I need. But I'd like to be more independent. Useful."

"We'll start tomorrow after work. You can drive us to see Buddy."

"Thanks, but maybe that's a little ambitious. I'll probably need to take some baby steps first."

"We'll see. Goodnight, darling." He kissed her tenderly and rolled over.

Left to himself in the cafeteria, Earl pondered over the many hazards the Lord had brought him through so far. Of these, he knew that with Joyce's help he could weather the present cold-shoulder he was getting at work. The most potentially deadly were created by the churches that he attended. While most of them were pointing accusing fingers at each other and some of the more well-known cults, these same churches had no idea whatsoever how blind they were themselves in some very significant areas. He decided to devote his writing that evening to that topic, emphasizing the necessity of personally reading Scripture with common sense, an open mind, and much prayer.

THE ONLY BEGOTTEN SON OF GOD

When I first accepted Jesus Christ as my Lord and Savior, I went to a number of churches in an attempt to find one that I could call home. I was disappointed several times over, and I revisit the problem here as a caution to new Christians: a good church is worth the effort of finding it. The first church I visited was a charismatic one, which is fine with me provided that the church maintains a reverence for Scripture as inspired of the Holy Spirit, that it judges spiritual encounters by means of Scripture, and that if the Holy Spirit decides to leave that church for a while, the members let it go at that and get on with their lives until they have another valid encounter not called forth by the church membership. That church didn't adhere to any one of those conditions, so I left it abruptly. The second one I visited was a "Jesus Only" church in which the membership defined God as Jesus alone, thereby rejecting the Scriptural concept of a Trinitarian Godhead. I had read Scripture to completion before attending this church; out of my reverence for Scripture as the inspired Word of God and its implication throughout of a Trinitarian Godhead, I declined to darken their doors after that one visit. The third church that I encountered wanted to play games and have communal dinners. It was difficult to find any reference to Jesus. I think they wanted to be a social club. I left there too. The fourth was excessively dispensational, considering the Old Testament to be of no theological value to Christians and focusing exclusively on the New Testament. I was really taken aback at that thought, which leads me to suggest to the new Christian that he read the Bible before attempting to find a church home. At least then he can weigh a church's creed and activities against Scriptural standards before he commits his time and thoughts.

My wife and I eventually found a good church that fit in well with Scriptural standards. We're happy there. Like a good church should do, it helped us grow in our faith and Christian maturity. Among its good features is its treatment of Scripture as an integral whole, emphasizing the amazing harmony that exists between the two Testaments. It is a true saying that "The New is in the Old Concealed, and the Old is in the New Revealed". What that means is that Jesus is actually defined in the Old Testament through the acts and words of numerous people as they were led by the Holy Spirit. Put another way, the Old Testament, in the lives of people like the Patriarchs, Joseph, Joshua, Samuel, David, Isaiah, Daniel and Jonah, established the credentials for the Jesus to come in the flesh, so that any person who truly understood the Law and the Prophets with a circumcised heart should have had no problem recognizing Jesus when He came in the flesh. In fact, I'm convinced that the first Gospel of Jesus Christ is not the book of Matthew but rather the book of Genesis. I shall present but one example below.

The beginning of Creation is described in *Genesis 1:1-5*:

> *In the beginning God created the heaven and the earth. And the earth was without form, and void, and darkness was upon the face of the deep. And the Spirit of God moved upon the face of the waters. And God said, Let there be light: and there was light. And God saw the light, that it was good: and God divided the light from the darkness. And God called the light Day, and the darkness he called Night. And the evening and the morning were the first day.*

What was that first light that was also the first spoken word of Creation on the very first day? It wasn't the sun, the moon or a star, because according to *Genesis 1:14-19*, these were made on the fourth day. Turning from Genesis in the Old Testament to John in the New, we come upon a remarkable correspondence in both style and content between *Genesis 1:1-5* and John's Prologue (Chapter 1, verses 1 through 18):

> *In the beginning was the Word, and the Word was with God, and the Word was God. The same was in the beginning with God. All things were made by him; and without him was not any thing made that was made. In him was life; and the life was the light of men. And the light shineth in darkness, and the darkness comprehended it not.*
>
> *There was a man sent from God, whose name was John. The same came for a witness, to bear witness of the Light, that all men through him might believe. He was not that Light, but was sent to bear witness of that Light.*
>
> *That was the true Light, which lighteth every man that cometh into the world. He was in the world, and the world*

was made by him, and the world knew him not. He came unto his own, and his own received him not. But as many as received him, to them gave he power to become the sons of God, even to them that believeth on his name: which were born, not of blood, nor of the will of the flesh, nor of the will of man, but of God.

And the Word was made flesh, and dwelt among us, (and we beheld his glory, the glory as of the only begotten of the Father,) full of grace and truth.

John bare witness of him, and cried, saying, This was he of whom I spake, He that cometh after me is preferred before me; for he was before me. And of his fullness have all we received, and grace for grace. For the law was given by Moses, but grace and truth came by Jesus Christ. No man hath seen God at any time; the only begotten Son, which is in the bosom of the Father, he hath declared him.

In this profound theological summary, John specifically links the Light and the Word together in Jesus Christ, thus openly declaring what was suggested in *Genesis 1:1-5*: that the beginning of Creation was the calling forth of Jesus Christ, the Word that was Light.

Some theologians disagree with this point of view. They seem to have the weight of logic on their side, as they point out the Jesus, being God, must have existed from eternity past. But here they get themselves wrapped around the axle of semantics, because man, being a dimension or so short of understanding what time really means to God, is simply unable to fully comprehend the meaning of the eternity that God inhabits. Jesus indeed could have been called forth by God the Father, as being the Son implies, without contradicting His existence from eternity past. How? Because, inhabiting at least one dimension beyond our own, the Godhead and each of its Members are also beyond time regardless of the sequence of their beginnings.

Besides, those who deny that Jesus was that First Light of *Genesis 1:3* do so at the peril of denying the inspiration of Scripture, because Jesus clinched this association in *Revelation 3:14* by describing Himself in the same terms to the Laodicean Church:

*And unto the angel of the church of the Laodiceans write;
These things saith the Amen, the faithful and true witness,
the beginning of the creation of God.*

Thus, Jesus is there right at the beginning of the Old Testament. As the Word develops throughout the Old Testament narrative, it is Jesus who is being fleshed out in its verses.

CHAPTER 22

When Earl drove into the driveway, Joyce came out of their house, closed the door, and walked over to the car. "Remember?" she asked.

"Sure." He got out and motioned her to take the driver's seat. She'd been full of anticipation until she sat down behind the wheel. Now the excitement had morphed into fear. Earl saw her consternation as he got into the car and sat in the passenger seat. "Don't worry, honey," he said, patting her hand. "I'm right here with you."

Despite his reassurance, the lack of feeling in her legs disappointed her. They seemed to be extremely awkward, and she had difficulty sensing the brake and accelerator pedals. Oblivious to this development, Earl turned the key and started the engine. "Okay, honey," he said, "there's no time like now to begin."

Gritting her teeth, Joyce shifted from "Park" into "Drive" and released the brake. She thought that her shoe was on the brake pedal, but it wasn't. It was on the gas. When the car started to roll backwards down the gentle slope, she stepped harder on the pedal. The car responded with a jerk, plowing into the garage door and buckling it. With a scream she removed her legs from the pedals as Earl switched off the engine and jammed the shift lever into "Park".

She turned to him with saucer eyes. "I'm so sorry. I guess I wasn't ready. Maybe I'll never be ready." She broke down and wept.

With his hand, Earl turned her face toward him. "Don't blame yourself," he said. It was more my fault than yours. Do you realize how lucky we are?"

"Lucky?" She laughed wryly, pointing to the damaged garage door. "How can you say that?"

"Your first mistake was putting it into drive instead of reverse. Oh, am I glad that you did. Look in the rearview mirror. Do you see how busy this street is at rush hour? Better to smash into a garage than hit a car. Far better. But now I see that I was pretty much helpless to correct your mistakes. I wanted to tell you to put it into reverse, but, thankfully you hit the garage before I could get the words out of my mouth." He looked up. "Thank you, Lord," he breathed.

"What about our car?"

He got out and motioned for Joyce to extricate herself. When she did, he got behind the wheel and backed the car into the driveway. After engaging the parking brake he got out and looked over the front end. "We're lucky there too," he said to Joyce. "Looks like our garage door's flimsier than the bumper. We'll probably want to forget about calling our agent. It'll be cheaper in the long run to call someone to replace the door. I'll go inside and call."

Despite his gratefulness that the accident hadn't been more serious than it was, the incident was still a letdown for both of them. He called a repair service, who said they'd be out in the morning.

"There's nothing more we can do about the garage door tonight, Joyce. Let's go see Buddy. Maybe it'll get our minds off the damage. I'll call Mary and let her know we're coming."

"Well, okay. But I'm not in the best of moods. I'll try to be brave and smile through my tears. But what about the garage being open? Are you afraid someone will try to rip us off?"

"We'll leave that in the Hands of God. Besides, the door to the house inside the garage is still locked. There's not that much in the garage that's valuable."

"How true." She got into the car by herself as Earl called, her spirits lifted a little by that ability.

When they reached the nursing home, Mary was at the door waiting for them. She carried a wide grin. "Hi, y'all," she said, "come right on in."

Sweeping a hand in welcome, she led them into the common room, where their mouths gaped open in surprise. Waiting for them were what he guessed about thirty attentive faces. Among them was Buddy, who squirmed and waved in happiness. A Bible was in his lap.

"It's Buddy's doing," Mary told them. "When I told him you were coming over, he dashed around in his wheelchair collecting his friends and pointing to his Bible. He wouldn't take 'no' for an answer.

Joyce was speechless. Eventually she recovered and walked over to the piano, where she sat down and played "And Can It Be That I Should Gain", a beautiful hymn penned by John Wesley. She sang the words as she played and became immersed in the song. Within moments the audience was held in rapt attention. *Thank you, Lord*, Earl breathed. He had been planning on sharing with Buddy the love embodied in Isaiah 54, but decided on a simpler message. When Joyce finished the hymn, he asked her to play a child's hymn, "Jesus Loves Me, This I Know". They sang together as she played, beckoning for those who felt like it to join in with them. Mary, who was in the background, sang the simple tune, as well as a few of the audience. When the hymn was over, Earl began speaking.

"Jesus loves me, this I know," he began slowly and softly. "For the Bible tells me so." He picked up his Bible and opened it. "For God so loved the world that He gave His only begotten Son, that whosoever believes in Him should not die, but have everlasting life. What does it mean to give up your only begotten Son? It means that you must look on in pain at your Holy Child as He dies on a cross. But He didn't just die. It took him hours of pain to reach that point of death."

He pointed a finger at Buddy. "Do you know pain? The pain of not being able to move as you wish? The pain of muscles that stay

too tight? He thought of Buddy being entangled in his flying wires.
"I know that you do. I've seen it. There's someone else who knows
your pain, Buddy. It's Jesus. He knows because He went through it
Himself. Why did He do it? He did it because He loves you. He did
it so that he could take on Himself the cause of all the sickness and
suffering of a helpless human race and put it to death. He was God
but He became a person like you and me just for that reason." He
pointed to another child in a wheelchair, disfigured like Buddy with
Cerebral Palsy. "You too. He gave His life for you out of love." He
pointed around the room. "And for you, and you, and you."

"Because of Jesus and His love for us, we all have something to
look forward to. He told us that if we believed on Him we could
have life forever. He tells us that this life isn't all there is. There's
another one waiting for us after we leave this earth. In bodies that
aren't sick. In bodies that work like we want them to. In bodies
without pain. Wouldn't you love to live in such a body?" He saw a
dozen heads nod fervently. "Well, you can. You can make sure that
will happen tonight, because after Jesus died on the cross for our
sakes, God gave us a free gift. All we have to do is ask for it."

Earl saw the avid attention he was getting from the audience.
"How do we ask for it? It's very simple. Jesus can hear our hearts.
All we have to do is tell Jesus that we believe He can do what He
promised us, and ask Him to come into our hearts. Would you like
to do that?" A number of heads nodded in affirmation. "All right.
Let us all bow our heads and talk to Jesus. Say my words after me.
If you mean them, then you have been born again. Dear Lord Jesus.
I know that you died for my sins and I thank you. I ask You right
now to come into my heart and give me your love. I want to be with
you forever. I thank you for coming into my heart and making me a
new person. Amen."

Earl looked up and saw that several in the audience still in an
attitude of earnest prayer. One of them was Buddy. Another was
Mary. He nodded to Joyce, who played "Amazing Grace" on the
piano. Buddy looked up at him and squirmed in his wheelchair with
enthusiasm. He went over and gave him a hug.

"Goodbye, everybody," he said when Joyce finished playing.

"We'll come back next week. We hope to seen you then."

On the way home Joyce patted his cheek. "That was wonderful," she said. "I think we've made ourselves another home."

"Right on," he replied. "We make a good team."

When they arrived back home, Joyce went into the kitchen to fix them a simple dinner. The phone rang. Earl picked it up. "Hello," he said. "What can I do for you?"

"This time you've really gone over the top," Pastor Frank said without introduction or preamble. "First you come up with a female Holy Spirit. Now you write about a Jesus who had a beginning in time. You know full well what the Christian thinking is on that one, that Jesus existed with the Father from eternity past. I'm afraid that this call is a formal warning, Earl. As an ordained pastor, I'm commanding you immediately to stop publishing anything relating to the Church or theology that hasn't first been approved by an authority on theology. If you persist, I will do two things. First, I'll initiate a dialogue with your own pastor. Second, I have contacts at the paper. People who respect me and God. I'll start writing articles to counter the damage you're doing to the community. Do you understand this?"

"I'm afraid I do. However, Mister Wilson, I haven't received the one thing from you that would get me to stop or at least think about it."

"What's that?" he asked warily.

"A Scripturally-based refutation of my position."

"How many times do I have to tell you about the numerous times in Scripture that the pronoun "he" or "him" is used in reference to the Holy Spirit? Are you blind?"

"Please. And I've responded to that objection with the observation that male and female together are one; as the female is part of her male, she can be addressed as male without contradiction. Look what Jesus said about marriage in Matthew 19: that we were made in the beginning male and female with the intent that a man shall leave his father and mother, and shall cleave to his wife, and they two shall be one flesh. He repeated that fact, saying again that they are no longer two, but one. He said rather directly that the marital union is something that God Himself joined together. Again, look at redeemed mankind: male in the aggregate, and yet female as the Bride of Christ. Beyond that, I can also add my favorite reason for the use of the masculine pronoun, which is that God is actually giving mankind the promise that we, as the Bride of Christ, will serve as His Body in a role that reflects both the substance and the functional office of the Holy Spirit, just as Jesus Himself reflects the Father's Will."

"And what about the little fact that in Galatians redeemed mankind will be neither male nor female?" he shouted, ignoring Earl's answer to his previous accusation.

"I addressed that too, pastor. I fully acknowledge that each individual within the Church, in his spiritual state, will be neither male nor female. This has nothing to say about the Church Herself, who is a much larger composite of all the little redeemed individuals comprising the Church. Don't you remember what Paul had to say about each of us being little pieces of this much larger Body, with a little cellular function as the Holy Spirit determines for us? Now, since you refuse to listen to me, I'll add another condition for listening to you: I'm going to send you my own list of Scripturally-based reasons for adhering to my own position. Unless you can refute them all, and do so with Scriptural backup, I'll simply continue to write my blogs and post them."

"I don't need a lecture. And I sure as heck don't need any ultimatums from you. Just remember my warning." He hung up on Earl.

Earl laid aside his thoughts for his next posting and focused on writing down those items from Scripture that supported his position regarding the female function of the Holy Spirit. He came up with the following items and addressed the letter to Frank:

> Dear Pastor Frank Wilson,
>
> Having taken a primarily defensive position up to this point, I am confident that my answers

regarding the female function of the Holy Spirit are sufficiently logical that they justify my taking an offensive stance hereafter. In that vein, I respectfully invite any individual who objects to my view of the female functional nature of the Holy Spirit to respond with rebuttals of the following Scripturally-based items that support my viewpoint.

Marriage of Christ with His Church as representative of the family nature of the Godhead.

The rebuttal must take into account the fact that Jesus claimed that He is the Image of the Father, as well as address the oddity that while one Member would have a gender-based relationship, the other Members would not.

The linkage in John 3 of the Holy Spirit with spiritual birth.

Birth, whether it is physical or spiritual, is a profoundly female function. John 3 directly links this function with the Holy Spirit.

The linkage of the Holy Spirit with Song of Solomon.

Many respected Bible commentators agree that Song of Solomon represents the future relationship between Christ and His Church. Well they should make this claim, for if it did not say something about God or His relationship with mankind, it wouldn't belong in Scripture. But if Jesus is the Image of the Father (John 8:19, 14:7,9), then Song of Solomon should also describe the relationship between the other two Persons of the Godhead, Father and Holy Spirit. Moreover, Song of Solomon confirms the romantic nature of which God (Jesus and Church and/or Father and Holy Spirit) is capable in the spiritual domain.

The linkage of the Holy Spirit with Proverbs.

Any attempt at rebuttal must address Proverbs 3:19 in the context of Genesis 1:1-5, Proverbs 8:22-36, Job 26:13 and Psalm 104:30. The attempt to attribute Proverbs 8 to Jesus rather than the Holy Spirit must explain the out-of-context insertion into material descriptive of Wisdom, to whom Scripture invariably attributes a feminine nature.

The attempt at rebuttal must also avoid taking the Jungian notion of the human psyche, both male and female, as containing both masculine and feminine elements, and extrapolating it to arrive at a similar notion of the Trinity. There are logical difficulties in doing so, as described below.

Scripture rather exclusively associates the Father with the Divine Will, which, as an initiating role, also is exclusively masculine. Similarly, Jesus the Son is presented in Scripture as the Divine Representation which, as the perfect image in reality of the Father, would also be predominantly masculine. The masculine predominance of Jesus is given further weight by Paul's characterization in Ephesians 5 of Jesus as the Bridegroom of the (functionally feminine) Church. **In Family of God** I simply noted what to me was an obvious connecting function of the Holy Spirit between Father and Son: the Divine Means which, in union with the Divine Will, gave birth to the Divine Implementation in reality (Divine Representation). Obviously, this Divine Means, being so closely linked with the other two Members, is also Deity. Because the Divine Means performed a function that was responsive to the Will, an obviously female role, I attached a female gender to this Person. Scripture and Christian tradition both understand this third Member of the Trinity to be the Holy Spirit.

Another difficulty, and it is a big one, that I see in the notion of each Member of Godhead possessing elements of both genders is that such a state of affairs would promote self-adoration, a characteristic that I sincerely hope is lacking within the Godhead. Love and adoration require **otherness**. The alternative is narcissism. I truly believe (and hope) that both Father and Holy Spirit are as selflessly noble as the Son demonstrated on the cross, which, for the reason given above, would preclude a hermaphroditic gender arrangement.

A family-based Godhead in which the Holy Spirit is functionally female, united in love, naturally and intuitively resolves the apparent discrepancy between monotheism and a Trinitarian Godhead.

Assuredly, a union within the Godhead involving love of a non-romantic nature can be proposed. However, a rebuttal alternative should carry as much intuitive and love-inspiring force as a relationship in which a family setting is central. A rebuttal should also explain in functional terms why there is a proscription against the gay lifestyle as presented in Leviticus 18 and Romans 1. Furthermore, a rebuttal should also address the centrality of family in Scripture as well as in life in general.

Linkage of the Holy Spirit with an executive

function.

This executive nature of the Holy Spirit was proposed by respected theologian Benjamin Warfield as well as others. It is certainly suggested in Scripture. An executive office is responsive to higher orders, this being within the Godhead the Father, or Divine Will. A responsive office, in turn, is a distinctly feminine one. This creative response is distinctly different than Jesus' role as the Divine Representation, or Divine Implementation, which is, as a perfect Image of the Will, the result of creative response to the Will.

Sincerely,

Earl Cook

Having completed this response to Pastor Frank's rant, he printed it out, signed it, stuck it in an envelope after Joyce's review and approval, and addressed it to the pastor.

Seeing his frustration, Joyce attempted to calm him down by offering some reasons as to why the pastor himself was so distraught with Earl's position.

"Earl, you were the one who was telling me that we've come into times when all the violence and the crime and corruption of society has spilled over from society into the churches. That has caused the Churches that have remained faithful to go on the defensive about anything that can possibly be interpreted as a further threat to the order. These Churches are taking a reactionary stance more and more. You have to expect it of them. Any new idea is going to suffer in that atmosphere.

"We are faced with a rapidly-expanding state of spiritual chaos. It would take an idiot not to see that. Given that situation, the committed Christian has little difficulty applying Scriptural admonishments to our present age. I'm familiar with the Bible too, you know. We're witnessing right before our eyes the fulfillment of several prophetic warnings, of which 2 Thessalonians 2:1-12 is particularly appropriate." She opened her Bible and started to read from it.

Now we beseech you, brethren, by the coming of our Lord Jesus Christ, and by our gathering together unto him, that ye be not soon shaken in mind, or be troubled, neither by spirit, nor by word, nor by letter as from us, as that the day of the Lord is at hand. Let no man deceive you by any means; for that day shall not come, except there come a falling away first, and that man of sin be revealed, the son of perdition. Who opposeth and exalteth himself above all that is called God, or that is worshiped, so that he, as God, sitteth in the temple of God, showing himself that he is God. Remember ye not that, when I was yet with you, I told you these things? And now ye know what restraineth that he might be revealed in his time. For the mystery of iniquity doth already work; only he who now hindreth will continue to hinder until he be taken out of the way.

And then shall that wicked one be revealed, whom the Lord shall consume with the spirit of his mouth, and shall destroy with the brightness of his coming, even him whose coming is after the working of Satan with all power and signs and lying wonders, and with all deceivableness of unrighteousness in them that perish, because they received not the love of the truth, that they might be saved. And for this cause God shall send them strong delusion, that they should believe a lie, that they all might be judged who believed not the truth, but had pleasure in unrighteousness.

"You can see all around us people taking pleasure in unrighteousness. The debacle in the churches is just one symptom of a general decline in society as a whole. From what I've been reading on the Internet, children are no longer being taught what used to be considered the essentials of education. All this illicit sex, abortion, wholesale drug use that we see and hear about on

TV, and the prevalence of self-interest in interpersonal relationships all lay bare our society's descent into madness and violence. Jesus Himself warned of a return of the violence prevailing in Noah's day. A description of that time is given in Genesis 6." She picked up the Bible again and started reading.

> *And God saw that the wickedness of man was great in the earth, and that every imagination of the thoughts of his heart was only evil continually. And it repented the Lord that he had made man on the earth, and it grieved him at his heart. And the Lord said, I will destroy man whom I have created from the face of the earth; both man, and beast, and the creeping thing, and the fowls of the air; for it repenteth me that I made them.*

"There's more and it's creepy. People everywhere seem to be acquiring the nature that Paul spoke of in 2 Timothy Chapter 3, the passage that Pastor George spoke of in his sermon last week:

> *This know, also, that in the last days perilous times shall come. For men shall be lovers of their own selves, covetous, boasters, proud, blasphemers, disobedient to parents, unthankful, unholy, without natural affection, trucebreakers, false accusers, incontinent, fierce, despisers of those that are good, traitors, heady, high-minded, lovers of pleasures more than lovers of God, having a form of godliness, but denying the power thereof; from such turn away.*

> *For of this sort are they who creep into houses, and lead captive silly women laden with sins, led away with diverse lusts, ever learning and never coming to the knowledge of the truth.*

> *Now as Jannes and Jambres withstood Moses, so do these also resist the truth, men of corrupt minds, reprobate concerning the faith. But they shall proceed not further; for their folly shall be manifest unto all men, as theirs also was.*

"Paul devotes the rest of the chapter to marching orders, just as pastor said.

> *But thou hast fully known my doctrine, manner of life, purpose, faith, long-suffering, love, patience, persecutions, afflictions, which came unto me at Antioch, at Iconium, at Lystra, what persecutions I endured; but out of them all the Lord delivered me. Yea, and all that will live godly in Christ Jesus shall suffer persecution. But evil men and seducers shall become worse and worse, deceiving, and being deceived. But continue thou in the things which thou hast learned and hast been assured of, knowing of whom thou hast learned them, and that from a child thou hast known the holy scriptures, which are able to make thee wise unto salvation through faith which is in Christ Jesus.*

> *All scripture is given by inspiration of God, and is profitable for doctrine, for reproof, for correction, for instruction in righteousness, that the man of God may be perfect, thoroughly furnished unto all good works.*

"We have to listen to him. When the going gets tough, we have to rely ever more on God and His Word. But you know as well as I do what's going to happen. There'll be a whole lot of committed Christians who will have great difficulty maintaining a balanced perspective as they witness the world collapsing around them. I'm sure that this is exactly what's happening to Frank Wilson. This difficulty represents another side to the problem of the falling-away churches. The churches that hold fast in the face of this debacle may tend to become ever yet more conservative, casting away their most important imperative in their haste to react to the moral chaos engulfing society, that of a loving nature reflective of the indwelling Holy Spirit and the light of Christ. In addressing the church of Ephesus (Revelation 2:1-7), Jesus spoke of this problem:

> *Unto the angel of the church of Ephesus write; These things saith he that holdeth the seven stars in his right hand, who walketh in the midst of the seven golden candlesticks; I know thy works, and thy labor, and thy patience, and how thou*

canst not bear them which are evil: and thou hast tried them which say they are apostles, and are not, and hast found them liars: And hast borne, and hast patience, and for my name's sake hast labored, and hast not fainted.

Nevertheless I have somewhat against thee, because thou hast left thy first love. Remember therefore from whence thou art fallen, and repent, and do the first works; or else I will come unto thee quickly, and will remove thy candlestick out of his place, except thou repent.

But this thou hast, that thou hatest the deeds of the Nicolaitanes, which I also hate. He that hath an ear, let him hear what the Spirit saith unto the churches; To him that overcometh will I give to eat of the tree of life, which is in the midst of the paradise of God.

"I hear you, Joyce. I'm sure glad that you're on my side. With your help, like now, I think I can handle the barbs okay. I don't know how I'd handle arguments about this subject without you. So thanks."

Earl became concerned that he may have come close to losing the ability to communicate with Pastor George. Before getting off the computer, he decided to address in his next blog Frank Wilson' concern over his having implied that Jesus had a beginning in time. For all he knew, George might have the same concern that Wilson expressed. If he rebutted Wilson now, it might save him from having George chime in on the reprimands.

Chapter 23

Dreading the uproar that his next posting would generate, Earl grimly wrote what he had to say. He knew what Scripture said about the matter, and as far as he was concerned that was the only valid judge of his work, assuming that his interpretation was reasonable. He knew also that his attitude was hardening toward others, so he passed it over to Joyce to read and approve before he put it out on the Internet.

"Go ahead with it," Joyce responded. "I just wish that you'd done a better job preparing for it."

"What do you mean?" he asked.

"Well, you could have dug us a bomb shelter, Earl. But no. Here we are, all above-ground and exposed."

They both laughed. But the laughter was soon replaced by dour expressions.

THE GREAT I AM

I can't read about Moses and the burning bush without having the movie *The Ten Commandments* pop into my head, complete with the image of Charlton Heston listening to the very deep voice of God saying "I AM WHO I AM".

The account given in *Exodus Chapter 3* is just as dramatic. The awesome power of Jehovah God is still there in the reading:

Now Moses kept the flock of Jethro his father-in-law, the priest of Midian: and he led the flock to the back side of the desert, and came to the mountain of God, even to Horeb. And the Angel of the Lord appeared unto him in a flame of fire out of the midst of a bush: and he looked, and, behold, the bush burned with fire, and the bush was not consumed. And Moses said, I will now turn aside, and see this great sight, why the bush is not burnt. And when the Lord saw that he turned aside to see, God called unto him out of the midst of the bush, and said, Moses, Moses. And he said, Here am I. And he said, Draw not nigh hither: put off thy shoes from off thy feet; for the place wherein thou standest is holy ground. Moreover he said, I am the God of thy father, the God of Abraham, the God of Isaac, and the God of Jacob. And Moses hid his face; for he was afraid to look upon God.

As a side note, the commandment to remove one's shoes is a sign that God Himself is speaking, rather than an angel. This appearing occurs multiple times in the Old Testament, and is called a Theophany. When an angel appears to a person, he will refuse all attempts to worship him. Having said that, I'll return to the narrative:

And the Lord said, I have surely seen the affliction of my people which are in Egypt, and have heard their cry by reason of their taskmasters; for I know their sorrows; and I am come down to deliver them out of the hand of the Egyptians, and to bring them up out of that land unto good land and a large, unto a land flowing with milk and honey; unto the place of the Canaanites, and the Hittites, and the Amorites, and the Perizzites, and the Hivites, and the Jebusites. Now therefore, behold, the cry of the children of Israel is come unto me: and I have also seen the oppression wherewith the Egyptians oppress them. Come now therefore, and I will send thee unto Pharaoh, that thou mayest bring forth my people the children of Israel out of Egypt.

And Moses said unto God, Who am I, that I should go unto

Pharaoh, and that I should bring forth the children of Israel out of Egypt? And he said, Certainly I will be with thee; and this shall be a token unto thee, that I have sent thee: When thou hast brought forth the people out of Egypt, ye shall serve God upon this mountain. And Moses said unto God, Behold, when I come unto the children of Israel, and shall say unto them, The God of your fathers hath sent me unto you; and they shall say to me, What is his name? What shall I say unto them?

And God said unto Moses, I AM THAT I AM: and he said, Thus shalt thou say unto the children of Israel, I AM hath sent me unto you. And God said moreover unto Moses, Thus shalt thou say unto the children of Israel, The Lord God of your fathers, the God of Abraham, the God of Isaac, and the God of Jacob, hath sent me unto you: this is my name forever, and this is my memorial unto all generations.

Thus began Moses' years of service to the Lord, a time that occupied the latter third of his life. He had to wait a long time for it, because he was forty years old when he fled Egypt after killing the abusive overseer, and had left a pastoral life as a shepherd for the next forty years. He was eighty years old when he received the commandment from God to speak to Pharaoh.

Scripture provides no other direct reference to Jehovah as the Great I AM in the Old Testament. For a few years I thought that God's intent in calling Himself by this strange name was to convey to us the majesty of His awesome power, something like the exchange of the bandido with Humphrey Bogart in *The Treasure of the Sierra Madre* when the bandido realizes that he's holding all the cards. "I don' gots to show you no stinkin' bodges!", he responds to Bogart's request for identification.

Later, I learned that while the name still may have conveyed some sense of God's power, there was much more to it that that. The real reason for the name is far more awesome in a beautiful way. The next Scriptural reference to the name I AM is in John's Gospel, where in Chapter 10 Jesus fleshes out its meaning:

Verily, verily, I say unto you, He that entereth not by the

door into the sheepfold, but climbeth up some other way,
the same is a thief and a robber. But he that entereth in by
the door is the shepherd of the sheep. To him the porter
openeth; and the sheep hear his voice: and he calleth his
own sheep by name, and leadeth them out. . .Then said
Jesus unto them again, Verily, verily, I say unto you, I am
the door of the sheep. . .I am the good shepherd: the good
shepherd giveth his life for the sheep.

In *John 6:48, 14:6 and 15:1* and *5,* Jesus fleshes out the name I
AM further with additional characteristics, all intended to display the
intimacy of His relationship to mankind:

I am that bread of life.

Jesus saith unto him, I am the way, the truth, and the life: no
man cometh unto the Father, but by me.

I am the true vine, and my Father is the husbandman... I am
the vine, ye are the branches. He that abideth in me, and I
in him, the same bringeth forth much fruit; for without me ye
can do nothing.

Do these words of Jesus imply that it was Jesus Himself who
talked to Moses from the burning bush? Is Jesus the Great I AM,
the Jehovah of the ancient Israelites?

Yes. The connection is made clear in at least two places in John's
Gospel: Chapter 8 verses 56-59 and Chapter18 verses 3-9:

Your father Abraham rejoiced to see my day: and he saw it,
and was glad. Then said the Jews unto him, Thou art not
yet fifty years old, and hast thou seen Abraham? Jesus said
unto them, Verily, verily, I say unto you, Before Abraham
was, I am. Then took they up stones to cast at him: but
Jesus hid himself, and went out of the temple, going through
the midst of them, and so passed by.

Judas then, having received a band of men and officers from
the chief priests and Pharisees, cometh thither with lanterns
and torches and weapons. Jesus therefore, knowing all

things that should come upon him, went forth, and said unto them, Whom seek ye? They answered him, Jesus of Nazareth. Jesus saith unto them, I am he. And Judas also, which betrayed him, stood with them.

As soon as he had said unto them, I am he, they went backward, and fell to the ground. Then asked he them again, Whom seek ye? And they said, Jesus of Nazareth. Jesus answered, I have told you that I am he: if therefore ye seek me, let these go their way: That the saying might be fulfilled, which he spake, Of them which thou gavest me have I lost none.

Note also that *John 8:58* confirms the pre-existence of Jesus in the Old Testament. That it was Jesus who spoke with Moses out of the burning bush may also be inferred in John 1:18:

No man hath seen God at any time; the only begotten Son, which is in the bosom of the Father, he hath declared him.

Jesus Himself commented that the Old Testament is replete with references to Him. Note what He says, for example in *John 5:39-47*:

Search the Scriptures; for in them ye think ye have eternal life: and they are they which testify of me. And ye will not come to me, that ye might have life. I receive not honor from men. But I know you, that ye have not the love of God in you. I am come in my Father's name, and ye receive me not: if another shall come in his own name, him ye will receive. How can ye believe, which receive honor one of another, and seek not the honor that cometh from God only? Do not think that I will accuse you to the Father: there is one that accuseth you, even Moses, in whom ye trust. For had ye believed Moses, ye would have believed me; for he wrote of me. But if ye believe not his writings, how shall ye believe my words?

"Good again," Joyce said the next evening. "But expect the digs, maybe even from other Church leaders on this one. While you were writing this blog, I was busy on the Internet digging into the Middle Ages, when reactionary thinking was really rampant. Talk about over the top!

"The sixteenth century was especially bad," she continued. "The reactionary atmosphere at that time virtually ensured that perfectionists would enter the religious scene. Their theological precepts constituted a complementary philosophical companion to Ptolemy's geocentric cosmology of perfection. God, they claimed, being the Creator of that perfection, was Himself of a like nature. Listen to these characteristics, Earl. To them, God was the Embodiment of simplicity, perfection, unchangeability and independency of being. These qualities, in turn, implied to them that God was above some of the defining characteristics of lesser beings such as the human race. Passion is included among these 'lesser' characteristics constituting the human nature that don't belong to God."

"Ouch. God above passion? That's not what I get out of the Bible. Think about it. The consequence of a passionless God is a Deity possessing neither romance nor intimacy within or outside the Godhead. That would make the Godhead void of any gender-driven feelings, which is essentially equivalent to a genderless God. But if gender is not involved in the Godhead, God being above that kind of thing, we would end up with a passionless God incapable of experiencing for Himself that which He fashioned in His creation and asks of us to respond toward Him. That would give us an experiential edge on God as well as to suggest hypocrisy in His nature.

"I'm with you," Joyce replied. "Beyond that problem, the perfectionists' definition of God not only suppresses love, His most important attribute, but inhibits those to whom Scripture was written from loving Him back. This is a serious issue because it runs counter to His Great Commandment to love Him with all our hearts, and our souls and our minds.

"Their God was instead, in His perfection, of a remote grandeur.

This notion gave rise to a God whose primary attribute is his majestic greatness. By defining God with majesty in mind, love became a secondary attribute, despite John's emphatic identification of God as the very embodiment of love. They went too far. The perfection embodied in their eulogies renders them sterile.

"The perfectionists' Pasteurization of God has led them to a view of God as residing in absolute flawlessness, so void of blemish that, like the smooth and featureless moon of their era, their statements of position approach the theological equivalent of Aristotle's perfect cosmos, which was embellished upon by Ptolemy and published in his *Almagest* in 150 A.D. Although the medieval church commonly held this viewpoint, it had nothing whatsoever to do with Scripture. In their application of Ptolemaic principles of perfection in the cosmos to their theology, the perfectionists' God, then, is a perfectly round, gigantic, cold and opaque marble."

"That's pretty good, Joyce. Did I marry a philosopher? Maybe you should be writing the column. At least contributing."

"I'd be glad to, although you seem to be doing pretty good yourself. But I really got into this, Earl. I've always wanted to know about the Church in Medieval times. It was a dark place. I think Catholics would like to erase the memory of it altogether."

"There is a utility in that history, black as it was. The Church wrongfully thought that since the Jews had rejected Jesus, God had replaced the Jews with the Christian Body as the apple of God's eye. They had overlooked the fact that the promises given to Abraham, Isaac and Jacob were both unconditional and everlasting. Besides, it was primarily the Jewish leadership, the Sanhedrin, that fomented the hatred against Jesus. The excesses of the Catholic Church at the beginning of the Enlightenment proved that they could be as bad, or worse, than these. And again, the culprits there were, as with the Jews, the Church hierarchy, the self-proclaimed elite."

"Maybe the Protestant Church is the only Christian outfit with truly clean hands."

"Are you kidding? Martin Luther could be called the Father of the Protestant movement, which took place in the sixteenth century.

He may be thought of as a saint by the Protestant Churches, but I certainly wouldn't consider him to be anything close to one. For one thing, he was a rabid anti-Semite. He also had a foul mouth. For another thing, he considered himself to be a true Catholic, and despite his cleanup act of the Church, he continued to believe in things that clearly contradicted Scripture, such as the perpetual virginity of Mary. The problems didn't start or end with him, though. They only got worse over time. I won't even begin to describe how terribly the modern Protestant Churches are spitting in God's face."

"So you're saying that there's really no Christian organization that's truly above corruption?"

"I certainly may be wrong, but that's my take. I'm not talking about the level of the rank and file, but at least at the top level where there's a hierarchical structure, yes, I do believe corruption is rampant. I haven't seen any evidence to the contrary. Look, despite the indwelling of the Holy Spirit in Christian believers, we all are human. Remember the saying about power and corruption. Whoever gets to be treated like royalty will eventually act like it belongs to them. Anyway, I appreciate the history lesson. It's been very helpful. In the context of reactionary thinking, I can begin to understand Frank Wilson's anger. I'll try to be more forgiving of him."

"Don't go nice on me now. I've got a lot more to say about the absurdities of reactionary thinking."

"It'll have to wait, Joyce. I'm getting tired. And I need to be fresh tomorrow to fend off tomorrow's assaults."

Earl had called it well, but it took another day for it to happen. Given the respite of calm, Earl came home from work in good spirits, particularly after seeing that the garage door had been fixed. "Come on outside, he said to Joyce. "Let's get moving on your driving lessons."

"Do you mean it?" she asked in surprise. "Are you sure you want to take a chance?"

"Sure I'm sure. Come on." Earl had her sit in the driver's seat and go through the motions of operating the brake and accelerator pedals with the engine off and the parking brake firmly set. After a half hour of it, she complained of being tired and they switched positions. He started the car and drove off to a huge parking lot. The store had gone into bankruptcy and the lot was empty. He set the parking brake, turned the engine off, and had them switch places. "There's not a whole lot of damage that you can do here," he said. "The pavement's level and flat, and there isn't anything you can hit before I grab for the keys. So have at it."

Despite her nervousness, she gamely started the car, released the brake, and put the shift lever in the 'Drive' position. The car coasted along slowly and she touched the brake pedal with her foot. It turned out to be the right pedal, but she'd applied way too much force and the car came to an abrupt halt, throwing them against their seat belts. She repeated the maneuver, this time applying the brake more cautiously, and was rewarded with a more gentle stop. They continued this process until she was tired. They hadn't gotten around to her use of the accelerator pedal, but she ended the session in the passenger seat both relieved and proud of herself.

CHAPTER 24

Patty shook her head in disgust when he walked past her desk, a gesture that boded ill for the day ahead. The assault began with Walter stomping into his cubicle red-faced in anger. He held the newspaper in one hand and pointed to it with the other. "Did you see the article about you in the paper?" he demanded.

He had caught Earl off guard. "No," he replied. "I didn't have a chance to read it. Can I see it?"

"See it? I've got a good mind to shove it down your throat. It's a tell-all article written by a pastor named Frank Wilson. Claims that you've gone off the deep end. That you are trying, without credentials of any sort, to create a cult. He says that you're trying to create a feminine God, like the goddess religions of the ancient world. Can't you even stay loyal to your own sex? What are you, a bleeding fag?" Walter quieted down after that outburst. Doubtless, he was thinking of the legal ramifications of what he'd just said.

"Listen, Earl," he continued in a more moderate tone, attempting to exude the impression that he was the quiet voice of reason, "every employee in this company has an obligation to represent their employer to the community to the best of his ability. You've just blown it out of the water." He gave up on being the voice of reason; his rant rose by several decibels. "I won't stand for an effing Guru in this building. I'd toss you out into the street right now if I didn't think you'd come back with a lawsuit. So I'll hear you out. But be quick about it. The sight of you turns my stomach."

"Thanks for the vote of confidence, Walter. You take the word of a stranger over one of your beloved employees."

"Don't get uppity with me, Cook. This guy holds a doctorate in theology. You're nothing but a pissant. I've read your articles. Frankly, I didn't get most of it, so at least I haven't been sucked in myself. But I thought something was strange, you bucking the system like that."

"In the first place, Walter, I have no interest in creating a following, much less a cult. I simply have an idea that I want to get off my chest. That accusation is baseless. So is the accusation that my thinking is in any way connected with an exclusively feminine God, as he is trying to imply, and most certainly has nothing in common with the ancient Egyptian God called Isis. The God I worship is the same as the One all Christians worship, a Holy Trinity, of which two of the members, the Father and the Son, are fully masculine. I am only suggesting that the third Member of this Trinity is functionally a female, as in Mother. I see the Godhead as a Holy Family. Even if I'm wrong, which I don't think I am, there's nothing outrageous in that belief. Besides, I have a lot of Scriptural backup."

"Don't try to snow me, Cook. It won't work. I'll give you two weeks to get Wilson to retract his statement and exonerate you. If not, out the door you go. In case you think I can't do that, I know your strengths and weaknesses as an engineer. I may not be able to kick you out on the grounds we've been talking about, but I can give you some jobs that'll make you weep. Then I'll kick you out for lack of performance. And I've got that fiasco with the filling machine to back me up. How'd you like to see that little video in court?" He stalked out of the office.

Earl sat in front of his desk and rested his head on top of his remaining elbow. The now-familiar desolation of spirit was returning. No wonder Wilson hadn't been pestering him lately. He'd simply decided to destroy him. Without this job they would be left without the excellent medical plan this company offered. He'd just begun to think that now, with Joyce's visits to the hospital for her legs being nearly over, he could maybe get an upgrade on his prosthetic arm. That was certainly out the door now, thank you Mister Wilson. He began to think ahead to how they would survive the future.

When he returned home he decided not to bother Joyce yet with the day's catastrophic event.

"You look tired, Earl. I'll fix you an early dinner." He didn't have much to say at the table, so she took the cue and delved back into the topic of reactionary thinking within the Church.

"Earl, I didn't finish last night," she began. "I want to give you the best part. Or the worst, whichever way you want to look at it."

"Go ahead," he replied somewhat indifferently.

"The seventeenth century was pretty bad for knee-jerk reactionary attitudes in defense of the faith. In 1617 the Roman Catholic Church formalized its position with regard to the cosmos by declaring the earth-centered Ptolemaic system to be the correct one as opposed to its Copernican rival. That cleared the way for Galileo's Inquisition trial in 1632. Although Galileo himself did a great deal to get himself into hot water with the church, his violation of the Ptolemaic order led to the censure of his work, never mind that he was actually right.

"Part of Galileo's problem with the church was his attitude, which evoked a reactionary response from the church elite. Another part of the problem came from his status in church: despite his devout Christianity, he was but a lay person and therefore presumptuous in the extreme for daring to interpret Scripture."

"What did he have to say about the Bible, Joyce? I didn't know that he was a Christian."

"Most people don't. They just assumed that since he was pitting science against the Church, he wasn't a religious person. The fact is that he was a devout Christian. Our schools prefer to cast him as a champion of science against religion, and they've been pretty successful at it. Anyway, he had an encounter with the Grand Duchess of Tuscany, who had the misguided notion that the Bible was the source of the Ptolemaic, or geocentric, view of the solar system. If she was right, then Galileo's heliocentric view would constitute a heretical stance. But she wasn't right, as Galileo pointed out in a letter to her. That's what got him in trouble – not what he wrote to her, but his audacity, as a member of the Great Unwashed Masses of laypeople, to write it. The sufficiency of his knowledge of God to interpret the Bible on his own was considered to be presumptuous in the extreme.

"Earl shook his head. "The Catholic Church itself was presumptuous in the extreme to deny people knowledge of the Word, and to do so in the name of God."

"Don't get too carried away, Earl. It's the human condition, not the Catholic Church. The problem began when Constantine made Christianity the state religion. Secular power is a hugely corrupting influence. Look at what it did to the Jewish Sanhedrin at the time of Jesus. Look what it's doing right now in the name of science. The Catholic Church, as a matter of fact, acknowledges her errors in the past. At least she's apologetic about it. But because the Church insisted upon clinging to the Aristotelian and Ptolemaic notion of heavenly perfection, it allowed a monstrous theological error to creep into its notion of God. At the time when reactionary attitudes were rampant there emerged some Christian scholars who insisted that God himself was of a Ptolemaic order of perfection. I've already told you about them and their denial of passion within the Godhead."

"That, she continued, "and the superlatives of perfection with which they endowed God. That may be true, of course, but it shouldn't go so far that it makes God alien to us and crowds out the truly important qualities of God that allow us to relate to him in love. I think, Earl, that it is perfectly proper to humble oneself before God. But I also think that one can go to excessive lengths in this. An excess of humility reeks of self-concern, rendering it false and useless. Worship involving perfectionism represents adoration less than mere groveling. As for my own relationship with God, I would prefer to participate in a loving Wife that as a dog who can only communicate via whines, wags and a slobbering tongue. The perfectionists' God is remote from us and by nature very different. That makes Him alien to us. That kind of entity plays right into the hands of secular society, which, according to the numerous movies dealing with that genre, considers anything beyond humanity to be a threat from outer space bent on swiping its resources, taking over the bodies of humans or eating them."

Earl laughed. "That's good. You're getting colorful."

"Thanks. To continue. In opposition to the medieval perfectionists, Scripture paints a far more beautiful picture of God, depicting His majestic glory as His willingness to give up the majesty of greatness and power in favor of a love of great fullness and depth. The Gospels appear to support this view, depicting Jesus Christ (as God) as a Being full of the attributes of love as we know it, including passion. Examples that come to mind include His weeping over Jerusalem and Lazarus and His ordeal in the garden of Gethsemane.

"We know from Jesus' post-resurrection walk with the mourners on the road to Emmaus as described in Luke Chapter 24 that Jesus was not above the feelings with which we were endowed. Can anyone deny the affectionate, intimate, compassionate warmth of Jesus in the following statement?

> *Then he said unto them, O fools, and slow of heart to believe all that the prophets have spoken: Ought not Christ to have suffered these things, and to enter into his glory? And beginning at Moses and all the prophets, he expounded unto them in all the scriptures the things concerning himself.*

"In sharp contrast with the perfectionists' construction of God, Scripture is replete with passages like the one presented above that amply display God's passion, both positive and negative, and His yearning for a close relationship with mankind, the masterpiece of His creation. Consider, for a famous example, Jesus' agony in the Garden of Gethsemane according to Luke 22:39-46:

> *And he came out, and went, as he was wont, to the Mount of Olives; and his disciples also followed him. And when he was at the place, he said unto them, Pray that ye enter not into temptation. And he was withdrawn from them about a stone's cast, and kneeled down, and prayed, Saying, Father,*

if thou be willing, remove this cup from me: nevertheless not my will, but thine, be done. And there appeared an angel unto him from heaven, strengthening him. And being in an agony he prayed more earnestly: and his sweat was as it were great drops of blood falling down to the ground. And when he rose up from prayer, and was come to his disciples, he found them sleeping for sorrow, And said unto them, Why sleep ye? Rise and pray, lest ye enter into temptation.

"No matter how you slice it, you just can't take the passion out of Christ. Therefore Christ, as God, directly contradicts the perfectionists' presentation.

"Where is all this heading? Unfortunately, a reactionary attitude is firming up among those churches that are holding steadfast. And they're looking for a Ptolemaic idealism in their theology, even to the extent of embracing the perfectionists' remote, alien and basically indifferent God. The notion of gender-driven passion within the Godhead will not sit well with this mindset. So don't be too surprised to face opposition to your ideas. As a matter of fact, you'd do well to think of it like stepping on a hornets' nest."

"Gender is the big bugaboo, isn't it? Somehow sex has acquired the baggage of impurity. I think that's how the Catholic Church got wrapped around the axle of Mariology."

"Oh," Joyce responded. "You were going to tell me about that."

"I will, because it's an important element of reactionary thinking, now that we're on the subject. But before I do, I want you to know that I'm not at all at odds with much that has to do with Mariology, because I think of it as an attempt to get around the numerous problems, logical, moral and emotional, associated with a belief in an all-male Godhead. The Protestant Churches don't even address the issue, preferring to bask in their ignorance and claiming that it's a mystery beyond us. Baloney. The Catholic Church associates Wisdom with Mary, which complements my own association of Wisdom with the Holy Spirit, as I strongly feel that Scripture intended Mary to be a human type of the Holy Spirit, just as Abraham's son Isaac and Jacob's son Joseph, among a host of other human Old Testament figures, were types of Jesus Christ. Perhaps that is what many theologians within the Roman Catholic Church have been aiming for all along. If so, and it is reasonable to expect that it is indeed the case, I find myself highly sympathetic to its Mariology, although I think that the Catholic Church often goes too far in attempting to attribute to Mary what properly belongs to the Holy Spirit.

"But there's one facet of Mariology that I can't go along with, because I can't see any way to interpret Matthew 13 that doesn't directly contradict it. Jesus had half-brothers and sisters, one of whom was the James whose writing is included in the New Testament. In opposition to that, many Catholics, theologians included, insist on Mary's perpetual virginity. It's a purity issue with them, implying that sex itself is unclean. That attitude is in itself a perversion. But we're all infected with it. The mere discussion of sexuality hovers on the boundary of good taste among committed Christians. But to attempt to associate sex with God Himself - - - !" He made a gesture of horror.

"In the first place," he continued, "the insertion of the notion of gender into our perception of the Trinity does not necessarily have to evoke corresponding thoughts of sexual paraphernalia and activities involving such. How can we know what that even means in the spiritual realm? What we can perceive is the relatively benign thought of gender as 'complementary other' which serves to provide a mutual comfort, a harmonious relationship and a creative force. A functional description as this should evoke nothing but noble thoughts.

"Nevertheless," Earl said, continuing the discussion he was having with Joyce on the attempt to neuter God, "lurking just beneath such thoughts are images of a more tacky nature. Somehow, the notion of sex seems to evoke pictures of steamy illicit bedroom encounters in the Notel Motel between passion-crazed cheaters. Such thoughts are distressingly familiar to many, if not most, of us. But such corruptions of nobility are simply manifestations of our fallen natures. Sex as it was designed by God is a magnificent thing, having nothing to do with the many perversions of it that are currently rampant within our society.

"That's a big problem in today's society, and apparently it's a worldwide one. The kind of sleazy sex that we're increasingly bombarded with on TV and in the movies has cheapened something intended to be breathtakingly beautiful. But not only that, it has greatly cheapened femininity itself in a terrible distortion of God's original intent. One can readily see its effect on women everywhere: in their tattoo-disfigured bodies, in their clothing that goes beyond suggestive allure to blatant seminakedness, in the hard, aggressive look of their eyes, and in the disregard, even the distrust, of chivalry. Sexuality and femininity are both so much better than this."

"I'll go along with that. And I appreciate your outlook on the issue."

"One of my Bibles is a Schofield. Despite my feeling that Christianity in general has misguided views on gender, the Schofield Bible's commentary on Song of Solomon is very wise. Let me read it to you." He went into the bedroom and came back with a Bible. Opening it, he read the commentary to Joyce.

"'Nowhere in Scripture does the unspiritual mind tread upon ground so mysterious and incomprehensible as in this book, whereas saintly men and women throughout the ages have found it a source of pure and exquisite delight. That the love of the divine Bridegroom, symbolized here by Solomon's love for the Shulamite maiden, should follow the analogy of the marriage relationship seems evil only to minds that are so ascetic that marital desire itself appears to them to be unholy.'

"'The book is the expression of pure marital love as ordained by God in creation, and the vindication of that love as against both asceticism and lust – the two profanations of the holiness of marriage. Its interpretation is threefold: (1) as a vivid unfolding of Solomon's love for a Shulamite girl; (2) as a figurative revelation of God's love for his covenant people, Israel, the wife of the Lord; and (3) as an allegory of Christ's love for His heavenly bride, the Church.'

"As I see it, the author of this introductory commentary is right on the money. I particularly appreciate his inclusion of asceticism along with lust as a perversion. The bottom line is that any offense that we might take against an association of gender with God is more a product of our own fallen natures along with our numerous perversions than gender itself. It's past time for a correction of that awful mistake, so let's have at it. Is it so difficult to comprehend that it was God Himself who designed and implemented the whole sexuality business? And the fact that He did it while in His transcendent mode, as if there was a difference between that and immanence anyway, makes one wonder how, if He is so far above the sexual experience that He entertains no passion or even thought or feeling in that regard, that He could have gotten it so right. In actuality, if God was truly above "that sort of thing", He would have been faced with a design challenge akin to attempting to explain color to a blind person.

"And then there's the thing about circumcision. Many, if not most, theologians would have you believe that the ritual of circumcision instituted by God upon Abraham's people was intended as a demonstration of cleanliness. What a childish thought! That wasn't the primary reason. The main reason was to increase the male sensitivity to enhance the sexual experience. It is as if God was telling us, I made this beautiful thing. Now let me make it even better.

"If God truly equated purity with a lack of sexuality, Mary really would have remained a virgin after the birth of Jesus, as many Catholics insist, instead of being a good wife to Joseph and mother to a larger family. If God were thus minded, He probably would have instituted a ritual wherein, instead of being circumcised, the priests would have been castrated.

"Better yet, He may well have designed the human body to engage in some sort of, ah, less direct pollinization, wherein birds and bees actually get involved in playing, ah, transport roles. Or, if He did insist on working with the paraphanalia He ended up designing, maybe He could have ramped up the purity factor by easing back a bit on the pleasure. If I could most humbly offer the following suggestion to God, perhaps He might have designed the human body such that the male seed was expelled by something akin to puking, with all the discomfort pertinent to that bodily function. If

God had a patent office to accept ideas like that, maybe I'd apply for a patent."

Joyce laughed. "If you were to attempt such an action, and if the office employed human beings, I doubt if anyone would consider that to be an improvement. Actually, I doubt whether you'd escape with your life."

"Anyway, for a very long time the Roman Catholic Church, almost certainly sensing that the feminine has been missing in the traditional view of the Godhead, has attempted to embellish upon the basic Trinitarian view of God by inserting Mary into the central core of the Christian faith. With the passage of time Mary has increased in stature in the Roman dogma, until now her veneration approaches actual deification so closely that reminders are carefully pronounced to the effect that she must still be considered to be fully human. Regardless of such disclaimers, the laity within the Catholic Church makes little differentiation regarding her between veneration and worship. Mary is prayed to; she has taken her place alongside Jesus as Co-redemptrix; she was conceived without the original sin of Adam; and she was even perceived as having been assumed bodily into heaven at the end of her life. She has been venerated, if you want to call it that, as Mother of God, sometimes even Queen of Heaven.

"But in doing this, right or wrong, they have added something good to the Church's understanding of God that Protestants lack. I think that there's a basic dignity and nobility of love that Catholics express in far greater measure than their Protestant associates. While I don't go along with some of the elements of this veneration, I applaud it as the next best thing to what I really do believe, that what they venerate in Mary should apply to an actual worship of the Holy Spirit. Yet they're not that far off-base, as Mary makes a beautiful type of the Holy Spirit, just as Isaac and Joseph and a host of others served as types of Jesus.

"Not too long ago, in attempting to firm up my own thoughts as to the family nature of the Godhead, I read a book regarding Mary by a professor of Divinity at Oxford University. Father John Macquarrie is his name, and the book was *Mary for all Christians*. Borrowing from some Jungian notions that gender is more ambiguous in us than we are used to thinking, he takes a stab at settling the mystery surrounding the Godhead. He starts out acknowledging that the role of the Holy Spirit in the creation epic of Genesis 1 is a feminine one. He ends up with a concept that is shared by a number of other respected theologians, both Catholic and Protestant, who have attempted to explain the Holy Trinity and found in the process that they must address the issue of gender within the Godhead. The concept that they arrive at is that all Members of the Godhead have elements of both genders. The best that one can say about it is that it's safe. It doesn't conflict with the traditional interpretation of Scripture."

"Gee, I don't know about that," Joyce said. "Paul mentioned effeminate men as being excluded from the kingdom of God. It's in First Corinthians. That suggests a human malady known as hermaphroditism. I seriously doubt in the face of that passage the viability of the notion of a Godhead in which all the members exhibit facets of both genders in anything close to equal proportions."

"Yes, and there's other problems with the thought, including logical difficulties. Scripture pretty much exclusively associates the Father with the Divine Will, which, as an initiating role, also is exclusively masculine. At the same time, Jesus the Son is presented in Scripture as the Divine Representation which, as the perfect image in reality of the Father would also be predominantly masculine. The masculine predominance of Jesus is given further weight by Paul's characterization in Ephesians 5 of Jesus as the Bridegroom of the functionally feminine Church. I see an obvious connecting function of the Holy Spirit between Father and Son, which gives me a picture of a Divine Means which, in union with the Divine Will, gave birth to the Divine Representation. Obviously, this Divine Means, being so closely linked with the other two Members, is also Deity. Because the Divine Means performed a function that was responsive to the Will, an obviously female role, I naturally attach a female gender to this Person. Scripture and Christian tradition both understand this third Member of the Trinity to be the Holy Spirit.

"But that's not all. Another difficulty, and it is a big one, that I see in the notion of each Member of the Godhead possessing elements of both genders is that such a state of affairs would promote self-love, a characteristic that my reading of Scripture indicates is attributable more to satan than to God. As I wrote to Pastor Wilson, love itself, to possess the noble quality that I associate with God, demands otherness. I truly believe and hope that both Father and Holy Spirit are as selflessly noble as the Son demonstrated on the cross. It's interesting to note also that Macquarrie attributed the Wisdom presented in the Book of Proverbs, especially Chapter 8, to Mary. Here again, he like other Catholic theologians, is trying to place onto Mary what properly belongs to the Holy Spirit."

"Well, that's enough for now, Earl. I think we've beaten the subject to death. We're preaching to each other. By this time, you should be fully reinforced in your convictions."

"I am. And thanks. But there are a couple more beautiful aspects of the Catholic Church's understanding of Mary that I'd like to share with you."

"Okay. I'm getting tired but I'll listen to you for a while."

I read a little book written by Dominican Father Gerald Vann, in which he addressed the hatred and suffering in the world during the Second World War. The book was called *Mary's Answer for our Troubled Times*. Like the title suggests, he wrote about Mary's own suffering while Jesus was on the cross. I can't say that Father Vann was always Scripturally accurate down to the last detail in all he wrote about Mary, but I do think that he captured the essence of Scripture in a magnificent way in presenting a stunning demonstration of nobility on Mary's part during that time. It deeply moved me."

"So share it."

"He talked of Mary's concentration of gaze and rapt, exclusive focus on Jesus as He endured His suffering. He contrasted the mutual sorrow-laden silence between her and Jesus with the noisier, more self-serving lamentations of the other women, developing a picture of Mary of stoic determination. She had a task, Vann claimed. This task involved the double sorrow of the mother as she watched the torments of the Son, and of the girl who flinched at the sight of naked evil and cruelty destroying innocence and beauty and love. She remained silent, because it was not for her to find an emotional outlet for her grief, for she is here because of Him, to fulfill her vocation as mother by helping Him to fulfill His as Savior. In her, as Vann claims, there are two conflicting agonies: the longing to save Him from His agony and the effort to help Him to finish His work. It is the second that she must do, giving Him to the world on the Cross as she has given Him to the world in the stable."

"Oh, my," Joyce exclaimed, wiping a tear from her eye. "I didn't expect that. What a beautiful description."

"I'm glad you agree. One can easily include the Holy Spirit in that picture. There's a more famous picture of Mary in Catholic tradition, and it's also very beautiful. Oddly, I came across it a long time ago, in reading Jacques Vallee's book *Dimensions,* in which he speculated on the spiritual side of UFO encounters. But Father Macquarrie mentioned it too. It involves Mary in an appearance in the year 1531 to one Juan Diego, a peasant who lived just outside of Mexico City. According to Vallee, Juan's uncle was very ill, to the point of near-death. He spent a day trying to relieve his uncle's sufferings and left him only on Tuesday, to get a priest. An apparition of Mary barred his way. She told him,

'My little son, do not be distressed and afraid. Am I not here who am your Mother? Are you not under my shadow and protection? Your uncle will not die at this time. This very moment his health is restored. There is no reason now for the errand you set out on, and you can peacefully attend to mine. Go up to the top of the hill: cut the flowers that are growing there and bring them to me.'

"As Juan's uncle was awaiting the priest, his room was filled with light. A luminous figure of a young woman appeared. He was indeed cured, but that's not the essence of this story. The main event occurs with Juan, who obeys the order to go to the flowers on the hill.

"Juan Diego didn't expect to see flowers on the hill because it was the middle of winter. But he did indeed find flowers there. They were Castilian roses. He cut them as Mary had instructed and carried them back to her in his crudely-woven cape. She spent some time arranging the flowers, and then tied the corners of the cape behind his neck to prevent the roses from falling out. She told him to let only the bishop see the sign that she had given him.

"When he reached the bishop's palace several servants made sport of him, pushing him around and trying to snatch the flowers from his cape. But the flowers dissolved when they reached for them. Amazed, they let him go. When he reached the bishop, Juan Diego untied the corners of the cape and as the ends dropped the flowers fell out in a jumbled heap. The disappointed peasant became confused as to the purpose of his visit. But then he was astonished to see that the bishop had come over to him and was kneeling at his feet. Soon everyone else in the room had come near and were kneeling with the bishop.

"Juan Diego's cape now hangs over the altar in the basilica of Our Lady of Guadalupe in Mexico City. Over eight million persons were baptized there in the six years that followed this event. Many millions more of people since that time have knelt before the two-piece cape, coarsely-woven of maguey fibers, for imprinted on it is an intricately detailed, beautiful figure of Mary. In her graceful posture she appears kind and lovable. She is surrounded by golden rays. Fifteen hundred persons a day still visit the shrine. I saw the image myself just by Googling on the Internet. It's awesome."

"Darn you, Earl Cook. Now my eyes are all puffy. But I want to see it for myself before we go to bed."

CHAPTER 25

For the next week Earl's workdays were individual eternities, each descending further into a black hole of misery and dread of impending doom. His work associates treated him with an indifference befitting a pariah. Their attitudes reeked of the expectation that he wouldn't be bothering them for much longer. He made a few unhappy, half-hearted attempts to search for job openings on the Internet, but was discouraged by the inevitability of his being asked for references. He pictured Walter's response to such a request, which would probably consist of a copy of Wilson's article about him with a comment, executed with a thick, red felt-tipped pen at the bottom saying something like "Nuff said".

Toward the end of the week Earl and Joyce went to the nursing home for another session with Buddy and his friends. They were surprised yet again, for this time the crowd was twice as large as it was at their last visit. After they greeted an enthusiastic Buddy, Mary explained it to them. According to her, Buddy had spent hours with her attempting to communicate a simple message, which he had then asked her to copy. She showed him one. It read "Come to my Church". "Then he took the copies and went off on his own to the shopping center down on the next block," she added. "So here they are, waiting for your sermon."

"Why don't you play a hymn, Joyce," he said. "I'll be along before you finish."

When she had left them, Earl spoke to Mary. "I haven't told Joyce yet, but I'll be out of a job week after next."

Surprised and concerned, Mary put her hand to her face. "I'm so sorry, Earl," she replied. "Have you found another?"

"No," he said dejectedly. "I'm not sure that I can around here. We may have to move."

"But why?" she asked.

"I have a blog, you know. One of the pastors in town, Frank Wilson, made a big deal out of what I had written. It got into the paper and my boss didn't like it. He's tossing me out for the publicity headache he thinks it's going to give the company."

"That's terrible. Is there anything that I can do?"

"Not that I know of. I just wanted to give you a heads-up in case we have to leave."

"I'm so sorry. I'll be praying that you don't have to do that."

"Thanks, Mary. I'd best go over and give them a talk."

"Last week," he began when Joyce finished the hymn, "we found out about the free gift that Jesus gave us in dying for us on the cross. We also discovered that when we're through with these bodies on earth, we'll get fresh new ones that will work perfectly." With that, Buddy gave a whoop of joy. Several others joined in.

"But that's not the best part of what's waiting for us," he continued. "We'll be with Jesus in the most loving relationship that you can imagine. Let me give you a taste of it from the Old Testament." He opened his Bible and turned to First Samuel Chapter 1. He began to read:

> *Now there was a certain man of... Ephraim, and he had two wives. The name of one was Hannah, and the other, Peninnah. And Peninnah had children, but Hannah had no children. And this man went up out of his city yearly to worship and to sacrifice unto the Lord of hosts in Shiloh. And the two sons of Eli, Hophni and Phinehas, the priests of the Lord, were there. And when the time was that Elkanah offered, he gave*

portions to Peninnah, his wife, and to all her sons and her daughters. But unto Hannah he gave a worthy portion, for he loved Hannah: but the Lord had shut up her womb. . .And as he did so year after year, when she went up to the house of the Lord, so the other wife provoked her, which made her cry, and she did not eat. Then Elkanah said to her, Hannah, why do you cry, and refuse to eat? And why do you grieve? Am I not better to you than ten sons? So Hannah rose up after they had eaten in Shiloh, and after they had drunk. Now Eli, the priest, sat by a post at the temple of the Lord. And she was in bitterness of soul, and prayed unto the Lord, and wept bitterly. And she vowed a vow, and said, O Lord, of hosts, if you will look on the affliction of your handmaid, and remember me, and not forget me, but will give to your handmaid a male child, then I will give him unto the Lord all the days of his life. And as she prayed, the priest Eli looked at her closely. Now Hannah, she spoke in her heart; only her lips moved, but she was silent. Therefore Eli thought that she was drunk. And he said to her, How long will you be drunk? Put away the wine from you. And Hannah answered and said, No, my lord. I am a woman of a sorrowful spirit. I have drunk neither wine nor strong drink, but have poured out my soul to the Lord. And Eli said, Go in peace, and the God of Israel grant you your request. And Hanna's . . .countenance was no longer sad.

And the Lord remembered Hannah. And she bore a son, and called his name Samuel, saying Because I have asked him of the Lord. And when she had weaned him, she took him up with her along with sacrifices to the Lord. And they brought the child to the priest Eli. And Hannah said, O my lord, as your soul lives, I am the woman who stood by you here earlier, praying to the Lord. For this child I prayed; and the Lord has answered my prayer which I asked of Him. Therefore also I have lent him to the Lord; as long as he lies he shall be lent to the Lord. And he worshiped the Lord there.

And Hannah prayed, and said, My heart rejoices in the Lord, my horn is exalted in the Lord; my mouth is enlarged over my enemies, because I rejoice in your salvation. There is none holy like the Lord; for there is none beside you, neither is there any rock like our God. Talk no more so exceeding proudly; let not arrogancy come out of your mouth; for the Lord is a God of knowledge, and by Him actions are weighed. The bows of the mighty men are broken, and they that stumbled are girded with strength. They who were full have hired out themselves for bread; and they who were hungry no longer hungered; so that the barren has born seven; and she who has many children has become feeble. The Lord kills and makes alive; he brings down to the grave and brings up. The Lord makes poor and makes rich; he brings low and lifts up. He raises the poor out of the dust, and lifts up the beggar from the dunghill, to set them among princes, and to make them inherit the throne of glory; for the pillars of the earth are the Lord's, and he has set the world upon them. He will keep the feet of his saints, and the wicked shall be silent in darkness; for by strength shall no man prevail. The adversaries of the Lord shall be broken to pieces; out of heaven He shall thunder upon them. The Lord shall judge the ends of the earth; and He shall give strength to his king, and exalt the horn of His anointed.

And Elkanah went to Ramah to his house. And the child did minister to the Lord before Eli , the priest.

Earl looked at the people. Despite the length of the Scriptural passage, they remained attentive. "Here was this poor woman who desperately wanted a baby to love and fulfill her womanhood, but she couldn't get pregnant. The Bible says that she went up to the priest over many years and still didn't have a baby. Finally she made a deal with God. In her prayer request, she promised God that if He would give her a baby, she would turn him back over to God, to be raised up as a prophet.

"Now I'll give you a question. Think hard before you answer. Did

God answer her prayer because He liked the deal that she made?" He paused and looked over the assembly. Nobody came forward with an answer, not even Joyce or Mary.

"Nobody answered the question," he said in mock sadness. "Not one." He looked at each of their faces, then grinned. I'm glad. Nobody should have answered, because it was the wrong question." A ripple of laughter passed through the assembly. "The real question is this: why did God prevent her from getting pregnant in the first place? It's a question that you all should be asking. Why were you born with difficulties?" He went over to Buddy and looked fondly at him. "Why, Buddy?" He turned back to his place at the front. "The answer to that question is that God had a mission for Hannah, and He was preparing her heart to receive it. When her heart was ready, He acted on her prayer. It wasn't up to her. It was up to Him." He pointed back to Buddy. "God's not done with you, Buddy. He has something He wants you to do. I'll be willing to bet that it's a very important one." He pointed to others. "The same goes for you. And you. And you. To all of you.

"Here's the rest of the story. Hannah gave birth to the boy Samuel. She gave him back to God as she promised. Samuel was raised among the priests, where he learned much about God. Then God used him in a mighty way. He became a great prophet, one of the greatest in Israel.

"Listen to the words that Hannah spoke in thanksgiving to God for His gift of Samuel: *'The bows of the mighty men are broken, and they that stumbled are girded with strength.'* God humbles the proud and lifts up the humble. Hannah was a prophet herself. She foretold another woman's prayer, far into the future. Listen to Mary's 'Magnificat' in Chapter 1 of Luke's Gospel, which she spoke after learning that she was to give birth to our Lord Jesus Christ:

And Mary said, My soul doth magnify the Lord, and my spirit hath rejoiced in God my Savior. For he hath regarded the low estate of his handmaiden, for, behold, from henceforth all generations shall call me blessed. For he that is mighty hath done to me great things; and holy is his name. And his mercy is on them that fear him from generation to generation. He hath shown strength with his arm; he hath scattered the proud in the imagination of their hearts. He hath put down the mighty from their seats, and exalted them of low degree. He hath filled the hungry with good things; and the rich he hath sent empty away. He hath helped his servant, Israel, in remembrance of his mercy; as he spoke to our fathers, to Abraham, and to his seed forever.

"We can learn something from this. God is our maker, and He loves each of us with a very great passion. He made us how He wanted to make us. Perhaps we should think less about how God should make us as perfect as possible and more about how we can be used by God and for His purpose the best that we can with what He has given to us to use. Should I ask for my arm back? Not if its loss glorifies God. Should my wife ask for her legs back?" Joyce proudly displayed her prosthetics. "Not if God wants to use her just as she is. It is a lesson of hope, for our purpose in life is to serve God, and in doing that we will be filled with joy."

The visit ended with Joyce playing "Just As I Am" on the piano. Several people came up to Earl, who guided them through salvation prayers and told them to follow up with regular attendance and seek baptism at the Churches of their choice. Joyce held onto his arm as they drove home. "I really liked the talk, Earl," she told him.

"So did I," he responded. "It wasn't up to me. I was going to talk about Isaiah 54, but the Lord changed it on me."

She snuggled next to him. He enjoyed it for a while, but became uncomfortable with what he had to say. "Joyce," he began, "I have something serious I have to tell you." She looked at him in surprise, but before she could talk, he launched into what he had to say. "I'm going to lose my job after next week. Walter got very angry with me over Frank Wilson's article in the paper. He thinks I'm giving the company a bad image. So, despite your buck-me-up pep talks, which I still appreciate very much, I'm out of luck. I guess that makes us both out of luck."

She remained silent for several minutes. Finally she spoke. "It's

not as bad as all that, Earl. We still have the Lord. And each other.
We'll manage. Besides, I have a feeling about this that doesn't seem
appropriate. Earl, I'm thrilled with something that God has in the
works for us. Keep the faith, and we'll be fine."

Joyce's faith picked up Earl's spirits. He decided to be happy in
the face of the impending disaster.

Chapter 26

Sunday at Church, Pastor George spoke to the notoriety afflicting one of the members of the Church. Maintaining a discreet silence about who that individual was, he developed the notion of Christian charity in his sermon, taking as a point of departure the Scriptural text of 2 Samuel 12. Without preamble, the pastor opened his Bible and began to read:

> *And the Lord sent Nathan unto David. And he came unto him, and said unto him, There were two men in one city; the one rich, and the other poor. But the poor man had nothing, save one little ewe lamb, which he had bought and nourished up; and it grew up together with him, and with his children. It did eat of his own food, and drank of his own cup, and lay in his bosom, and was unto him as a daughter. And there came a traveler unto the rich man, and he was not willing to take of his own flock and of his own herd, to prepare it for the wayfaring man who was come unto him, but took the poor man's lamb, and prepared it for the man who was come to him.*
>
> *And David's anger was greatly kindled against the man; and he said to Nathan, As the Lord liveth, the man who hath done this thing shall surely die; and he shall restore the lamb fourfold, because he did this thing, and because he had no pity.*

And Nathan said to David, Thou art the man.

"Most of us know the story of how King David lusted after Bathsheba when he saw her," Pastor continued. "She was married to a soldier named Uriah, so David, being commander-in-chief of the army, sent Uriah to the front lines and certain death, intending to marry Bathsheba herself after the inevitable happened. David committed murder in carrying out that despicable act, and he did it for a despicable motive. He violated the commandments of murder, adultery and coveting his neighbor's wife in the process. God punished him for it, to be sure. Bathsheba had a baby out of her union with David, and the Lord caused it to die. But yet He forgave David, who had repented with heaviness of heart, because even through that terrible act He still loved him. He and Bathsheba had another son, Solomon, who built the first and greatest temple of God, penned the Books of Ecclesiastes, Song of Solomon and most of the Book of Proverbs and under whose reign Israel became the wealthiest nation on earth. Both Mary and her husband Joseph came out of David's loins. Jesus Christ was called the Son of David, a title that He Himself acknowledged in Matthew 22.

"The point is that if God possesses the mercy to forgive such a great sin, who are we to deny forgiveness for those who sin against us, and particularly if the sin amounts to nothing more than a difference of opinion? Now the person to whom this latest notoriety is attached, and his wife, have been subjected to merciless attacks on their character for possessing some beliefs that we all don't share. Frankly, I don't have an answer to those beliefs. On a Scriptural level I can't seem to put my finger on anything I can use in refutation. I'd like to, because on a personal level I find the ideas less than appealing. But I truly can't say in my heart whether the lack of appeal is based on a knowledge of God, or on ignorance. Furthermore, the issues aren't so large that they threaten to separate Christianity from anti-Christianity. One can be a Christian on either side of them. The end of all this is, as the Bible tells me, not to judge. That privilege is God's alone. So I won't judge, and I urge you not to either.

"There's another message embedded in Nathan's charge against

David. That's the issue of hypocrisy and intolerance, traits that go hand-in-hand. Do you not find it odd that, just as the noose of intolerance is tightening around the necks of all us Christians *in the name of religious tolerance,* we should show the same intolerance against one of our own? I end my message with that thought."

"You're a courageous man, Pastor," Earl said, shaking his hand. "More important than that, you're kind. I appreciate that more than I can say."

Earl cringed at the thought of going to work on the last day of his employment, only to leave forever at the end of the day. But that time inevitably arrived. Walter entered his cubicle and sat on the edge of the desk. Well, this is your last day, Earl," he said conversationally. "Mike, of course, wishes you the best." Mike, of course, hadn't felt the need to see him off in person. Walter handed him his severance paycheck. "It's too bad that things had to end this way. But my word is my word. If it'll help, I think that your work was pretty good as a whole. You'll be pleased to know that if you need a reference, I won't screw you over. You'll be okay as long as you stick to engineering, doing what you know." He hesitated, reluctant to say what was on his mind. "Security will be over at the end of the day to see you off." He extended his hand. "No hard feelings?" he stated as he shook Earl's hand. He left the cubicle before Earl could answer.

Earl couldn't answer right then anyway. He was speechless at the humiliation of being considered so untrustworthy that Security had to be involved. The implications of that act of dehumanization were horrific. He opened a drawer and started to remove items. He started two piles on the desktop. One was for his personal belongings, and the other for those that the company owned. He decided to make the piles visible to Security, so he moved them over to the small table.

The phone rang. It was Joyce. "Earl, something big is happening," she said breathlessly. "I was watching the news on TV and, you won't believe this, but Buddy and his friends have circled Wilson's Church. They're holding signs. Protesting on your behalf! Some of the more ambulatory kids have put up a stake and piled wood underneath. They're suggesting that Wilson is wanting to burn you at the stake."

Earl's heart leapt with the news. "What do the signs say?" he asked.

"One says 'Save the intolerance for the secularists'. Another says 'Suppression isn't Christian'. And, oh, that one is good. It says 'Welcome back, Torquemada'. Oh, my!" she exclaimed suddenly. "Here comes the news!"

Joyce filled him on developments as they happened. The reporter held a mike up to Mary's face and asked, "Are you the spokesperson here?"

"Just one of them," she responded. She pointed to Buddy and said, "Buddy's the instigator of this event. He truly loves Earl."

"Earl?" the reporter asked into the mike. "Who's Earl?"

"He's the person who this is all about. Remember the newspaper article that Pastor Frank Wilson of this Church printed against Earl's beliefs, accusing him of forming a cult?"

"Why, yes I do. Are you people trying to say that isn't true?"

"Most definitely. Earl has been very open about his beliefs. He's put them out in his blog. They may differ from the norm, but they certainly aren't show-stoppers like Wilson suggests. There's nothing in them that might challenge basic Christian beliefs. It's ironic, as a matter of fact, that just at a time when Christianity has to fend off the intolerance of non-Christians, here is an intolerant Christian doing the same thing to one of his brothers. That's hypocrisy if I ever saw it. Beyond that, Earl has openly challenged anybody who so desires to dispute his beliefs. All he asks is that any rebuttal be based on Scripture."

"That sounds fair enough. Thank you for the information. Now I'll see what the other side has to say." She turned off the mike and trotted down to the Church entrance, followed by her camera man and equipment handler. Electrical cables followed their path.

"The reporter's gone down to talk to Wilson, Earl," Joyce said. "Now they're setting up the camera in front of the entrance, which seems to be locked. The reporter is knocking now, and she's starting to pound her fists." She laughed. "There's no answer. Nobody inside has responded, and the reporter just turned around and shrugged her shoulders. They're leaving now."

Earl was temporarily elated by the running news from Joyce. Then he told her that he had to finish clearing his desk. "Thanks, Joyce. It's wonderful to know that others care. I'll be seeing you soon." He hung up and finished the job at hand.

Earl opened the door that evening, stooped down to shoulder a box, and stepped inside his home. "Well, that's that," he said disconsolately.

Joyce laughed. "I don't think so," she said with an I-know-something-that-you-don't sparkle in her voice. "Your blog has gone viral."

"What?" He dropped the box, amazed.

"You heard me. You're going to have thousands of responses, maybe more. You should have enough, as a matter of fact, to either reinforce your beliefs or to have them effectively refuted. Be prepared to address them."

"You know, it doesn't really matter which way it turns out. It's not about me. Great theologians will now address the issue and whatever happens next, we'll all probably have a better understanding of who God is."

Joyce was right. Already there were dozens of responses to his blog. He decided to hold off addressing them until tomorrow. After dinner he and Joyce relaxed on the couch watching TV. They were interrupted by the ringing of the phone. "Oh, oh," Joyce told him as he got up to answer it. "Now they're going to be pestering us on the phone too."

But it wasn't just anybody on the phone. It was Walter. "Earl, would you consider coming back to work Monday?" he asked after introducing himself with uncharacteristic politeness. "We've had TV and newspaper reporters on us like flies. They're congratulating us on having such an original thinker as a member of our staff. I, ah, I didn't tell them that you're no longer with us, Earl. What do you say?"

"Wait, please," he asked Walter. He put the phone down and went over to Joyce. "That's Walter on the phone. He wants to give me my job back."

"Oh, no," Joyce said indignantly. You're not going to let him get away with that, are you? After what he did to you?"

Earl smiled at his wife. "Yes, I think I will," he told her. "It's in my heart to forgive him."

"If you do that, you'll have to include Frank Wilson."

"Yes, I know."

She smiled at him. "That's my Christian," she said.

Also by Arthur Perkins:

Cathy: Encounters with the Holy Spirit

(the new sequel to *Buddy*)

We hope you enjoyed reading
Buddy: Encounters with the Holy Spirit
by Arthur Perkins.
For further reading including novels and non-fiction titles by
this author and others, please go to our online catalog at
http://www.signalmanpublishing.com

Signalman
Publishing